Bello:
hidden talent rediscovered

Bello is a digital-only imprint of Pan Macmillan,
established to breathe new life into previously published,
classic books.

At Bello we believe in the timeless power of the imagination,
of a good story, narrative and entertainment, and we want to
use digital technology to ensure that many more readers
can enjoy these books into the future.

We publish in ebook and print-on-demand formats
to bring these wonderful books to new audiences.

www.panmacmillan.co.uk/bello

Richmal Crompton

Richmal Crompton (1890–1969) is best known for her thirty-eight books featuring William Brown, which were published between 1922 and 1970. Born in Lancashire, Crompton won a scholarship to Royal Holloway in London, where she trained as a schoolteacher, graduating in 1914, before turning to writing full-time. Alongside the *William* novels, Crompton wrote forty-one novels for adults, as well as nine collections of short stories.

Richmal Crompton

CAROLINE

First published 1936 by Macmillan

This edition published 2015 by Bello
an imprint of Pan Macmillan
20 New Wharf Road, London N1 9RR
Basingstoke and Oxford
Associated companies throughout the world

www.panmacmillan.co.uk/bello

ISBN 978-1-5098-1006-2 EPUB
ISBN 978-1-5098-1004-8 HB
ISBN 978-1-5098-1005-5 PB

A CIP catalogue record for this book is available from the British Library.

Typeset by Ellipsis Digital Limited, Glasgow

Visit **www.panmacmillan.com** to read more about all our books
and to buy them. You will also find features, author interviews and
news of any author events, and you can sign up for e-newsletters
so that you're always first to hear about our new releases.

Chapter One

CHARLES CUNLIFFE drew himself up to his full height, pulled down his waistcoat, and studied his reflection in the dressing-table mirror. No one would think he was over sixty. "Fiftyish," people would say of him, and it was the early fifties they'd mean, not the later ones. Perhaps even "fortyish" ... No, "fortyish" was a little too optimistic. Better leave it at "fiftyish." ... He studied with particular gratification the rich chestnut tints of his scanty hair. This was the result of a special preparation, which, its makers claimed, did not dye the hair but merely restored the natural colour. Its conception of what the natural colour of Charles's hair had been was a flattering one.

His gaze—still with gratification—travelled slowly downward. He'd always been good-looking—regular features, fine eyes, perfect teeth. He opened his lips now and showed his teeth in a faint smile. Probably no one in the world except himself and his dentist knew that they were false. He hadn't been to a Bartenham dentist, of course. He'd been to the best man in London and had cloaked the process by the story of a visit to the Continent. Certainly Maggie didn't know, but that was little credit to his finesse, as Maggie never knew anything that wasn't pointed out to her. It was possible, of course, that old Nana knew (he'd long ago given up trying to hide anything from old Nana), but one could be sure that even if she did she wouldn't tell anyone. Nana never told anyone anything.

His gaze rested on his waist. The line was excellent. He had a good figure naturally, and he'd always taken care of it. So many middle-aged men let their figures run to seed. He'd been worried about his own a year or so ago, but the new belt (a bit complicated to get into but quite worth the trouble) had made a world of difference—that and his exercises. He felt a glow of virtue as he remembered the conscientiousness with which he rose early every morning to perform his exercises, conquering the temptation to enjoy the luxury of bed for quarter of an hour longer. One owed a duty to oneself and one's appearance, and he'd never been a man to shirk his duty. He took up the hand-glass and studied the reflection of his back. No good taking care of one's figure and going to a cheap tailor. The fellow he went to now was wonderful. Not a crease, not even the shadow of a crease. . . .

Again he drew himself up smartly. He'd always prided himself on his military bearing (the local beggars knew that they could get sixpence out of him any time by addressing him as "Colonel"), and he quite frequently thought of himself as a retired army man, though actually he had worked in an insurance firm before his retirement.

He glanced at his watch. Caroline had asked them to be there by four, and it was nearly half-past three now. He'd better go and see if Maggie was ready. She probably wouldn't be. She'd probably have forgotten that she was going to Caroline's at all. He wondered if there had ever been anyone else in the whole world quite as scatter-brained as Maggie. His mind went back to their childhood, and he remembered how her vagueness used to infuriate their father. The old man had had a ferocious temper and would fly into violent rages on the least provocation. Poor Maggie had always been so frightened and bewildered by his rages that she never knew what they were about and was as likely as not to repeat her offence the next minute with devastating results. Charles sometimes thought that it was the fact of having passed her childhood in a constant state of nervous terror that had made her just a little foolish now. Only a very little foolish, and even "foolish" was too hard a word. Some people called her "simple," but Charles disliked that word even more. She was extremely sensible in most ways, and always so gentle and well-meaning that no one could help liking her. Charles himself was devoted to her. He could soothe her better than anyone when she was frightened or upset, and on the days

2

when she was like a happy little girl he felt an almost paternal tenderness for her, though he was two years her junior. But, of course, she wasn't any use at housekeeping, and it was a good thing they'd got old Nana for that. She was a wonderful old woman. Eighty, if she was a day, but as straight as a ramrod and still able to put the fear of God into an idle housemaid or a disobliging tradesman. She'd been grim and unbending to them when they were children, but she'd shielded them from their father's tyranny as best she could, and they'd always been fond of her, despite her dourness. . . . He glanced at the portrait of the old man that hung over his mantelpiece—the square jaw with its fringe of whiskers, the thin tight mouth, the stern deep-set eyes—and the ghost of the old terror came back to him across the years.

He himself had been his father's favourite, but that had not saved him from savage punishment for the most trivial misdemeanours. It was against Gordon, however, that the old man's ill-humour had been most consistently directed, perhaps because he was, in a way, not unlike the old man, and it was inevitable that their temperaments should clash. Oh, well, they were dead now, both his father and Gordon. Poor old Gordon hadn't had too easy a time. His first wife had deserted him after five years of marriage, leaving him with two children, Caroline and Marcia, to bring up; and his second wife, after bearing Robert and, five years later, Susan, had died, six years after that, at Fay's birth, leaving him with the five of them on his hands. He only survived her by one year, and when he died it turned out that he had speculated foolishly, mortgaged his life assurance to cover his losses, and that his assets would do little more than pay his debts. Charles had experienced some hasty qualms at that time, seeing himself responsible for the orphans, but the nineteen-year-old Caroline, who had just won a scholarship in Modern Languages at Girton, had quickly shown the stuff she was made of. She had resigned her scholarship and set to work at once to earn money for the young family. She had canvassed the local schools for coaching and obtained a contract from a publisher, to whom a friend had given her an introduction, for some French translations. Her success in both fields was assured from the first, for she was clever, charming, and tremendously hard-working. She had sent Robert to a public school and paid all his expenses till he was fully qualified as an accountant. Susan she had sent to the local High School and then to Girton, and Fay was still at school. They were lucky to have a sister like Caroline, thought Charles for the hundredth time (Charles himself felt a secret gratitude to her for relieving him of that nightmare of responsibility), and they knew it. He would say that for them. They realised what they owed to her and were grateful. More than grateful. They adored her. Had done ever since they were children. Once when Susan was a little girl she had been discovered sobbing desolately because she was sure she would go to hell when she died for loving Caroline more than God. . . . She couldn't help doing, she said. She always had done and she always would.

Susan had been appointed modern languages mistress to a local school after leaving college, but she had given up the post on her marriage about three months ago. Charles suspected that Caroline was not too pleased by the marriage. She had been ambitious for Susan and had wanted her to have a career. She had, of course, always looked on the three of them as her children. She often said that she felt like a grandmother now that Robert had youngsters. Oddly enough, she got on better with Gordon's second family than with her own sister Marcia. The two had never had much in common, and, now that Marcia had married and gone to live in London, they saw little of each other. Idly his mind went to her mother, Philippa—the woman who had run away from Gordon after five years' of marriage. None of them had seen her or heard from her since she went away, though the news had reached them that she had married again several years after leaving Gordon, but not the man for whom she had left him, and that she now lived in the South of France. Charles wrinkled his brows as he tried to remember her. He knew that he had thought her beautiful, but he couldn't recall a single feature. Catching sight of his frown in the mirror, he hastily banished it and leant forward to examine his face carefully. He'd go up to that fellow again soon and have

4

another massage treatment. It certainly improved the texture of the skin and kept the lines down.

He took a clean handkerchief from his drawer, sprinkled it with eau-de-Cologne, and arranged it neatly in his breast-pocket. Then he walked slowly downstairs, his shoulders squared, humming lightly to himself.

Nana was in the hall. She wore a black dress, with white collar and cuffs and a long white apron. Her face was yellow and wrinkled, but her eyes seemed as keen as ever, her sunken mouth as firm. Her eyes flicked him over from head to foot in the way that always made him feel he might be sent back to wash his hands or brush his hair. He laughed and held out his hands for her inspection, palms up, then palms down, as they had had to do when they were children.

"Hands washed—nails cleaned," he said.

Her grim face lightened somewhat, but she did not smile.

"I hope Miss Maggie's not forgotten that we're going to tea to Miss Caroline," he went on.

"I reminded her," said Nana. "She went up to get ready at three."

He wandered into the drawing-room. It was as uncompromisingly Victorian as it had been in his father's day—whatnot, fire-screen, china-cabinet, "silver table," even a *tête-à-tête* sofa in faded pink brocade, trimmed plentifully with plush balls. There was a highly ornamental fern-stand in the window, holding six ferns, and on the draped mantelpiece an ormolu clock ticked sedately between two bronze equestrian groups. The wall was covered by water-colours of indifferent execution.

Maggie's desk stood near the fireplace. It was piled high with papers and bits of needlework. She would frequently burrow among the accumulation of odds and ends like a terrier after a rat, but she seldom found anything.

On the top of the desk stood a small gilt cage, containing a not very lifelike mechanical bird that hopped about and sang when it was wound up. This had been the "best toy" of Maggie's childhood (the solitary present of a rich but neglectful godmother) and had had for her always a strange and potent fascination. Her parents considered it too elaborate for ordinary use, but on Sunday evenings, when she had been officially "good" during the week (a very rare occurrence), it was brought out and wound up in her presence. Even then she was not allowed to touch it. It was still invested for her with the glamour of her childhood, and on Sunday evenings she would wind it up and watch it with a kind of fearful delight. She never wound it up on a weekday, and even the Sunday winding was accompanied by secret feelings of guilt. She called it Sweetie and treated it with awed respect, moving the cage out of the sun on hot days and putting it near the fire when it was cold.

There was a piece of paper under the desk. Charles stooped down to pick it up. It was the list Maggie had made out of the things she meant to do today. "Water ferns. Match silk. Order coals. Mend gloves."

Each morning Maggie made out a list of things that she meant to do that day, but she never did any of them because she invariably lost the list.

He replaced the list on the desk, almost knocking over as he did so a little paper screw of sugared almonds. Maggie loved sugared almonds and generally bought some on Saturdays. Though she had now plenty of money, some influence from her repressed childhood prevented her ever spending more than a penny or twopence on them, and she never bought them on any other day than Saturday. He went to the window and stood looking out over the garden. At one side could be seen the square patch, outlined with shells, that was Maggie's garden. It was the same one she had had as a child, and she still tended it, buying penny packets of seed in the spring, and sowing them thickly over every inch, allowing no one to thin them out because she said it seemed so unkind. She generally sowed Virginian stock and nasturtiums because she had sowed them as a child and they "did well" there. After sowing them she would come out every morning before breakfast to examine the ground minutely, and her excitement at the appearance of the first green shoots never abated. It always seemed a miracle to her, and she could never get used to it.

He heard a bedroom door opening and went out into the hall.

Maggie was coming downstairs, hurrying, as she always hurried, wherever she was going, whatever she was doing, for even when she was merely going up to bed at night she gave the impression of being on her way from one piece of vitally important work to another, between which not a moment must be lost.

Her hat was a little on one side, and her face wore its usual harassed peering expression. Her manner was, as always, eager and deprecating. She was very small and seemed to be trying to shrink into herself all the time, so that she appeared to be even smaller than she was.

"Am I all right, Nana?" she said anxiously.

Nana straightened her hat.

"One necklace will be enough, I think, Miss Maggie," she said.

Maggie looked down in dismay at the three necklaces she was wearing—one of amber, one of pearls, and one of red and green beads that she had bought at Woolworth's.

"Oh dear!" she said, deeply distressed. "Which shall I keep on?"

It was clear that the responsibility of choosing which necklace to keep on was a distressing one, and that in another minute she would be in what Nana called a "state."

"Keep on the amber," said Nana, gently withdrawing the others; "and have you got a clean handkerchief?"

"Yes," said Maggie, all her happiness restored by the knowledge that she had a clean handkerchief.

Nana's gaze went to the gloves that Maggie was now drawing on.

"Not those gloves," she said. "There's a button off. Whatever would Miss Caroline think of you going in gloves with a button off?"

The dismay returned to Maggie's face as she gazed down at the gloves.

"But I mended it," she faltered. "I know I did. I must have done. I remember distinctly putting it down on my list."

"I got another pair out for you," said Nana. "Didn't you see it? ... Harriet!" A housemaid came out of the kitchen. "Go up to

Miss Maggie's bedroom and get the clean pair of gloves that's on the chest of drawers. One minute, Miss Maggie."

She began to tuck the straying ends of wispy grey hair into the "bun," moving several hairpins to secure them. They all knew that this attention was useless. Maggie's hair would never stay tidy for more than five minutes. It was straight and fine and thin and seemed to consist solely of short ends that detached themselves with quiet persistence from any structure in which they were incorporated.

But Maggie was still looking worried.

"Nana, I ought to have rung someone up about something this morning. What was it? . . . Oh dear, whatever *was* it?"

"It's all right, Miss Maggie," said Nana. "It was the coals. I've seen to it."

Nana was in the habit of giving Maggie little household tasks to see to in order to keep her busy, because Maggie liked to be busy, but she was always ready to see to them herself if Maggie forgot or lost the paper she had written them down on, as generally happened.

Harriet came in with the gloves, and Maggie drew them on, then began to fumble with the buttons. In the end Nana took one hand to button and Charles the other, and Maggie stood between them, laughing her happy, breathless, little-girl laugh, as if she sensed something of the protective tenderness they both felt for her.

"Oh dear! Aren't I *stupid?*" she said.

"Now you're ready," said Nana. "Off you go! And be sure you're back by six, then you'll have time for a little rest before dinner."

She stood at the door till they were out of sight, just as she used to stand in their childhood when they went out to tea. She probably still saw them as a little boy and girl in their best clothes, thought Charles. He knew that she still frequently referred to them as "the children."

Maggie was chattering happily, excitedly, about nothing in particular. She generally kept up a stream of disconnected observations, and didn't mind whether anyone was listening to her or not. He knew that she loved walking through the streets with him like this. She always enjoyed doing things and going to places.

She liked her life to be a perpetual bustle. When she had nothing else to do she took up one of her odds and ends of needlework that lay about on her desk and worked at it feverishly. It was as if she were building up endless little defences against she didn't quite know what. She was terrified of an unoccupied moment and didn't seem to care how useless were the things she found to fill her time. She must have known quite well that not even the Poor could wear the socks she knitted, that not even the Heathen could accommodate their shapes to the shapes of the garments she fashioned from unbleached calico, but she continued to make both socks and garments, working in frantic haste, as though it were essential that they should be finished as quickly as possible. Sometimes Charles thought that this was the result of her having been chivied relentlessly from task to task throughout her harassed childhood. Their father had seen to it that Satan should find no idle hands in his household, at any rate. . . . She had been wound up in those far-off days and couldn't run down.

He wondered what would happen to her when Nana died. She did nothing without consulting the old woman—never even went to bed till Nana had put her head in at the drawing-room door and said, "Time you went to bed, Miss Maggie," adding generally, "And I wouldn't stay up much longer either if I was you, Mr. Charles."

Well, he'd just have to find someone else to look after her. And if he died . . .? He didn't like to think of Maggie's being left to strangers. She was so nervous and timid. She needed such perpetual reassurance. Strangers wouldn't understand. But there would be Caroline to look after her then, of course. Caroline would shoulder Maggie with the rest of her burdens. She had a strong sense of duty and would never let Maggie be looked after by strangers while she was alive. He wished that Maggie weren't so frightened of Caroline. He couldn't understand it. No one could be kinder than Caroline was—she went out of her way to be kind to Maggie—but Maggie was always frightened of her. She wouldn't even go to tea there without him. Something about Caroline's brisk efficiency seemed to scare her, and she became silly and panic-stricken as she used to be with their father. Her eager gentle voice was going on and on by his side, like the burbling of a stream. "Such a lovely day.... The shops look so pretty, don't they?... Such lovely colours. ... *Isn't* that pink pretty? ... When I was a little girl I used to pray to have a pink dress, but I never did, of course, and it's too late now. It would be unsuitable. ..."

It was a perfect day in late September. The sun shone brightly, but there was a faint tang of autumn in the air that Charles found most exhilarating. It was all he could do to restrain his steps to Maggie's slow scurrying pace. He glanced at himself covertly in a shop window and felt a thrill of pride in the knowledge that this handsome, upright, military-looking man was himself. He hoped he'd meet someone he knew. He liked to stroll through the quiet, old-fashioned streets of Bartenham like this, greeting his friends and replying to their greetings, feeling part of it all, aware that he contributed in a small degree to the general amenity of the little town. Young Mrs. Ludlow was passing them. He took off his hat with a flourish. She smiled at him, a subtly flattering smile, the sort of smile that a woman gives to a man who admires her, whom she in her turn admires. ...

He'd had coffee with her in the town on Monday morning. He was going to tea with her next Tuesday. He enjoyed discreet (very discreet) flirtations with young married women—nice women in love with their husbands, who yet found a certain excitement in his attentions and thought him a "dear." It was years since he'd been really in love. Once or twice when he was younger he had seriously considered marriage, but on each occasion he had saved himself in time. He hadn't enough money to keep a wife in comfort, and married life without sufficient means was the devil. It might quite well be the devil even with sufficient means. And, of course, Maggie had always been the deciding factor in the situation. One could hardly expect any woman—even one's wife—to put up with Maggie, and nothing would ever induce him to send Maggie away from home. After all, he frequently told himself, there wasn't much in marriage once the glamour wore off, and it wore off pretty soon in most cases. Mentally he compared himself with his married contemporaries. They seemed a shabby careworn lot. They'd all let their figures go and looked years older than they were. No, sometimes he felt vaguely lonely and pathetic, but generally he was convinced that he had chosen the better part. He'd always liked women and been friendly with them, and, now that he was middle-aged ("fiftyish"), a pleasant avuncular quality had crept into the relationship. Avuncular—that brought him back to Caroline. He wondered if she'd ever marry. With her looks she could have married anyone if she hadn't sacrificed herself so completely to her stepbrother and stepsisters. How old would she be? She'd been eighteen at the time of Gordon's second wife's death. (A colourless little creature—what was her name?—Oh yes, he remembered now ... Nina.) That was eighteen years ago. Nina had died at Fay's birth, and Fay would be eighteen this year. She must be thirty-six. Getting on. For a woman, he added hastily. Getting on, for a woman, certainly. He'd heard a rumour that Richard Oakley was in love with her, but he didn't think that there was anything in it. Richard came to the house a good deal, of course, because he'd been Gordon's solicitor (though he'd known nothing of Gordon's, foolish speculations, unfortunately, till it was too late), and had always looked after her money affairs. He must be nearly fifty—quite young, for a man—and Caroline had always been old for her age. Still, he didn't think there was anything in it. ...

Maggie had stopped chattering, and a tense anxious look had come over her face. She was clutching at her scarf and coat collar and necklace, making ineffectual attempts to straighten them.

"Here we are," she whispered nervously.

Caroline's house, The Elms, stood before them—mellow, Georgian, ivy-covered, separated from the road by a small strip of garden. It had been Gordon's house, and Caroline had refused to sell it even when things had been most difficult.

Charles walked up to the green six-panelled door, followed by Maggie, and knocked firmly with the shining brass knocker.

Chapter Two

CAROLINE, tall, fair, and slender, came into the hall to greet them.

"How nice to see you!" she said. "Come in and sit down. You must be tired after your walk."

Her voice was low-pitched, curiously level and devoid of inflections. As she spoke, her cool blue eyes rested just for a second on the straying ends of Maggie's hair, and at once Maggie began to tuck them behind her ears with jerky nervous movements. Maggie had an ostrich-like faith in that action, seeming to think that, when she had performed it, the ends automatically vanished from sight, instead of hanging down behind her ears in an erratic sort of fringe.

As they entered the drawing-room, Richard Oakley rose from an armchair by the fireplace, and Susan uncurled herself languidly from the sofa. Susan had a round, soft, childish face, with velvety eyes and full cupid's-bow lips. She was generous and impulsive, charming at her best, but disposed to be moody. She didn't look a particularly happy bride, thought Charles, noticing the pout of her full lips and the smouldering lights in her dark eyes. Kenneth Melsham, her husband, was a nice enough chap, but as young and headstrong as Susan herself, and—well, after all, the Melshams weren't quite the same class as the Cunliffes. Old Melsham, in fact, who had started and built up the business—a large furnishing store in the middle of the town—had been quite uneducated. Kenneth wasn't uneducated, but he naturally lacked the background that is given by a cultured home. Charles had heard rumours that the business hadn't been doing too well lately, had, in fact, been going steadily downhill ever since Kenneth's father died, but that wouldn't be altogether Kenneth's fault even if it were true. Most of the old-established local shops were finding things difficult nowadays, with branches of the big combines opening on every side and cutting down prices till it was almost impossible to compete. Fox & Glazonby, from Tottenham Court Road, had just opened a branch at Ellington, only ten miles away, and Bartenham was beginning to go there to buy its furniture. He looked at Susan's beautiful moody face. Perhaps that was the trouble. No woman who'd had a taste—however short—of an independent income, as Susan had had when she was teaching, liked to have to stint and cheese-pare and "manage" on an erratic and generally inadequate allowance. She wouldn't have been an easy wife in any case, of course, and Kenneth hadn't Caroline's knack of banishing her demons of ill-temper by a smile or quiet word.

His glance passed on to Caroline. She was talking to Maggie, or rather listening to Maggie's nervous rambling monologue, and, as Charles watched, her eyes met Richard's in a smile of understanding, almost of intimacy. Charles's interest quickened. Perhaps there was something in the rumour, after all. Pleasant fellow, Richard. Quite handsome, too, in his way, though he looked older than he was. Good figure, but grey on the temples and beginning to go bald. Complacently Charles compared his appearance with his own. No one would ever think that there were about fifteen years between them.

Well, Caroline would make any man a perfect wife. His gaze travelled round the room, with its restful tints of blue and grey—grey carpet, blue and grey chintz curtains and chair-covers, cream-coloured walls, one or two really good water-colours. The surface of the furniture shone like glass. She was a wonderful housekeeper, doing in a few odd minutes each day what most women made their whole day's work. She coached pupils every morning and often worked at her French or Italian translations late into the night, but she held the reins of the household in her slender capable hands, ordering the meals, shopping, supervising everything. She was talking to Richard now (Maggie was making nervous overtures to Susan, who was ignoring them completely), and Charles's eyes dwelt on her admiringly. He admired her air of poised detachment and her good looks, though he could see what people meant when they said that they were "academic." There was something austere in the regular features, the level brows, the grave blue eyes, the fair hair parted in the centre and taken severely back into a knot at the nape of her neck. It was as if she scorned any attempt at embellishment. Even the slight natural wave of her hair seemed to be apologetic for its presence. There was something Quaker-like, too, in the plain blue dress, with its white collar and cuffs. Not that her appearance was in any way dowdy. That would have grieved Charles indescribably. On the contrary, she dressed well and chose her clothes with care, but there was always that suggestion of austerity about her.

Susan rose with an abrupt movement, interrupting Maggie in the middle of a somewhat confused account of the Vicar's last sermon.

"I'd better go now, Caroline," she said.

Caroline looked at her tenderly.

"Oh darling, must you? It's been such a short visit."

"I know," said Susan.

"Can't you stay to tea?"

"I'm afraid not. . . . Kenneth's being in for tea, and I said I'd be there."

"Ring him up. Or shall I?"

"No, Caroline. I wish I could, but——" She shrugged dispiritedly and ended, "Oh, well, it's no use having rows when one can avoid them. I'd better go."

Caroline's face hardened.

"Kenneth seems a little unreasonable," she said in her quiet level voice.

Susan shrugged again.

"I'd love to stay. You know I would. It's gone so hatefully quickly. It always does."

"Darling. . . ." Caroline slipped an arm affectionately round her waist. "When can you come again? . . . What about tomorrow? Come and have lunch with me. Fay's having it at school, so I shall be alone."

"I—may I ring you up? I'd love to. I will if I possibly can."

They went out together, Caroline's arm still round Susan, Susan leaning against her like a disconsolate child. When Caroline returned, her brow was drawn into a frown.

"What's the matter with Susan?" said Charles. "She's a bit depressed, isn't she?"

"I'm afraid that her marriage isn't turning out very well," said Caroline, closing the door behind her.

"Why?" said Richard. "He seems a decent chap."

"So nice-looking," put in Maggie. "I like his curly hair."

"I suppose he's been spoilt," said Caroline. "Only sons so often are, and"—she shrugged—"he's been brought up in quite a different atmosphere from Susan, of course."

"Don't be a snob, Caroline," said Richard.

She laughed.

"It's not that. It's——" She grew serious again. "I was afraid from the beginning that it wouldn't be a success. I hoped and prayed that it would be. I still hope and pray that it will be. If only Kenneth——" She stopped, and added, "Susan was getting on so nicely at St. Monica's."

"You're a fussy old mother hen," said Richard.

"They say that Melsham's isn't doing any too well," put in Charles.

Again that slight hardening came into Caroline's face.

"If it isn't, it's Kenneth's fault. He had everything in his favour. His father made the business one of the best in Bartenham."

"Times are changing, you know, Caroline," said Richard.

She smiled at him, her sudden sweet disarming smile.

"I'm tired of hearing that given as an excuse for everything," she said. "Anyway, let's forget Melsham's and talk about something more cheerful. What do you think of those new houses they're building out at Merrows, Uncle Charles? Richard says that they're exactly like the ones he used to build with his bricks when he was a little boy."

"Yes," agreed Richard. "Whenever I go down that road and see them, I expect to hear someone saying, 'Put those bricks away now, Richard. It's nearly bedtime.' "

Caroline steered the conversation lightly from that to other local topics and then to politics. It was amazing, thought Charles, how she managed to keep abreast with current events everywhere. However busy she was, she always seemed to find time to read the papers and know what was going on. She had her own ideas about things, too. She didn't just repeat what she read or heard like a parrot. And she didn't make you feel stupid, either, as so many clever women did. Charles never felt that he'd talked better or been more interesting than after a visit to Caroline. . . . He was sorry when the telephone bell rang and Caroline had to go to answer it. She came back a few minutes later.

"It was Evelyn," she said. "She wanted a recipe I'd told her about. I gave it to poor little Effie, but she lost it, of course."

Evelyn Marston was another of Caroline's strokes of genius. Robert's wife, Effie, was a pretty empty-headed little piece of goods, who had no more idea of running a house than the man in the moon. She had muddled along anyhow—the house badly run, the children badly brought up—still a year ago, when Caroline had come to the rescue and discovered Evelyn Marston. Evelyn was officially a mother's help, but in reality she had taken over the management of the entire house, and the improvement she had made there in the short time since her arrival was amazing. The children, from being little savages, had become well-behaved and well-mannered; the house, from being a kind of perpetual chaos, had become almost as well conducted as Caroline's own. Evelyn was a charming, intelligent woman, a woman after Caroline's own heart, and the two were firm friends.

Caroline was still smiling reminiscently.

"Poor little Effie!" she said again.

The tenderness in her tone touched Charles deeply. Caroline's attitude to Effie, ever since Robert's marriage, was proof—if proof were needed—of her large-heartedness. Most women with as many calls on their time as Caroline would have felt themselves justified in washing their hands of a brother once he'd married. Not so

Caroline. She had taken infinite trouble helping Effie with her housekeeping and trying to secure for Robert something of the comfort he had known when he lived at home. Effie was a stupid, rather sulky little person, but Caroline had been as kind and as patient as if she had been one of her own beloved brood. No amount of patience or kindness, however, could put brains and method into Effie's pretty empty head, and the problem had seemed insolvable till the arrival of Evelyn last year. He hoped that Effie realised what she owed to Caroline. He was afraid that she was one of those selfish modern young people who take everything for granted. Certainly she never seemed particularly grateful, which made Caroline's unfailing patience all the more wonderful.

A maid brought in tea, and Caroline sat down at the low tea-table to pour it out.

"We won't wait for Fay," she said. "I don't expect her back till about five today. She's working very hard just now. She's got her Scholarship exam in November."

"I suppose she stands quite a good chance?" said Richard

An almost fanatical light shone in Caroline's blue eyes. (Fay's like her own child to her, thought Charles.)

"I believe so," she said quietly. "Certainly, unless the standard's much higher than it was when I got mine, she'll do it easily."

"As much to your credit as Fay's if she does," said Richard.

Caroline smiled.

"Oh, well. . . . I've coached her a good deal, of course, but she's worked like a little brick, and she's got an excellent brain."

"So pretty," put in Maggie vaguely, "and plays so nicely."

Caroline frowned slightly and ignored the remark.

"It'll do her good to go to college," said Richard. "She needs bringing out of herself. She doesn't make many friends at school, does she?"

"She makes quite as many as are good for her," said Caroline lightly. "I hate indiscriminate friendships—gangs of schoolgirls going about arm-in-arm, yelling 'old thing' and 'old bean' at each other. Fay has too much good sense and good taste for that sort of thing."

How indignantly she rose to the defence of her chick, thought Charles amusedly, though she'd hardly been attacked!

"I didn't mean that exactly——" Richard was beginning slowly, when Maggie put in:

"What's happened to the piano, Caroline? Surely it used to be in that corner by the window."

Caroline laughed rather shortly.

"Auntie darling, you ask that question every time you come. I keep telling you. I simply hate a room cluttered up with furniture, and when I got that tallboy the obvious thing seemed to be to move the piano out." Her eyes rested with pleasure on the mellow gleaming surface of the old walnut. "It's a lovely thing, isn't it? That corner's been crying out for it for years. Pianos are such ugly articles of furniture. I love this room without it."

"Fay played on it so nicely," said Maggie. "Where is it now?"

"It's stored," said Caroline. "There wasn't room for it in any other room."

She's irritated with Maggie for harping on the subject of the piano like that, thought Charles, watching her. It's silly of Maggie, of course. She can't remember things. She asked just the same questions the last time we were here. ... Funny how Caroline's eyes betrayed her exasperation rather than her voice or manner. They were almost grey when she was pleased, but they turned a clear cold blue when she was annoyed or irritated.

"I hadn't realised that you'd actually stored it," Richard was saying. "Surely Fay will miss it."

Caroline smiled at him. Her eyes were a soft grey again. Richard, of course, could never irritate her whatever he said.

"It was Fay's own suggestion," she said. "She knows that she can't afford to fritter away her energies just now. It was her own idea, too, to give up her music lessons last year. She felt that she hadn't time for anything but her scholarship work, and, of course, while the piano was there it was a constant temptation. She says that she can always take it up again later on."

"That's what one says of so many things when one's young,"

sighed Richard. "The tragedy is that one so seldom does take up anything again later on."

"Well, it won't matter if she doesn't," said Caroline. "I'm sorry I ever let her learn with Mr. Hyslop, but she begged to, and I find it so hard to refuse her anything."

"I know you do," smiled Richard, "and so does she! But why regret that in particular? He's supposed to be an excellent teacher."

Caroline shrugged.

"I suppose he is, but all his geese are swans. He put the most ridiculous ideas into Fay's head. The child has just ordinary average talent, and"—she smiled in tender amusement—"he really almost convinced her that she was a genius. She had a crazy idea at one time of taking up music professionally. I didn't oppose it, of course, but gradually she came to see herself how foolish it would be. And since then she's worked like a brick at her scholarship work."

"Still—it's a pity for her to give up her music altogether," said Richard.

"That, too, was her own choice," said Caroline. "I think she was right, but it was definitely her own choice. I tried not to influence her in any way at all."

Maggie's face wore the look of ludicrous dismay it always wore when she realised that she had irritated Caroline. Charles could see that she was nervously searching for something to say to propitiate her, but all she could think of was, "She looked so pretty when she played at the Prize-giving last year."

Caroline threw her a smile.

"*Dear* Auntie!" she said affectionately.

The maid came in to clear away the tea-things, and when she had gone Caroline's face grew serious.

"There's something I want to tell you all," she said. "I didn't want to tell you while Susan was here because she has enough to worry her just at present, and then I thought I'd better wait till after tea. . . . I heard from mother this morning."

There was a tense silence.

Caroline's mother. . . . Charles's eyes went to the portrait that hung over the mantelpiece, the pretty characterless face of Nina.

But Nina wasn't Caroline's mother. She was Robert's and Susan's and Fay's.

Caroline's mother was Philippa, who had run away from Gordon more than thirty years ago.

"You mean—Philippa?" he said at last.

"Yes."

"I didn't know. . . . Is it the first time you've heard since——?"

"Yes."

"Philippa?" said Maggie eagerly. "I remember Philippa. She was so kind. So kind and——" She stopped and her face clouded over. "Oh, but she was wicked. I remember now. She was wicked. She——"

"One moment, Auntie," said Caroline clearly. She turned to the others, and Maggie subsided with little nervous flutterings of dismay. "I've never heard from her since she left us till today." She went to her writing-desk and took out a letter. "This is the letter. Her—husband died last month, and she wants to come back to England."

She handed the letter to Charles, who read it in silence. It was short and business-like, merely announcing her husband's death and her intention of coming to live in England. "I should very much like to see you and Marcia again, of course. Perhaps you'll let me know how you feel about this." It was signed Philippa Meredith. He stared at it in silence. . . . It seemed to bring the past suddenly to life. . . . Philippa . . . He remembered her now. He used to think what a lucky dog Gordon was.

"Philippa," Maggie was saying, "Philippa. . . . But she *couldn't* come back. She was wicked. I don't understand."

Thin straying wisps of hair hung about her face, and she was plucking at her necklace and scarf with nervous fingers.

Richard was reading the letter.

"Well?" he said. "How are you going to answer it?"

"I have answered it," said Caroline. "I've asked her to come and make her home here."

"Here? With you?"

"Yes."

Caroline's eyes were bright, her cheeks softly flushed. She looked young and eager and gallant. Charles realised that there had been a suggestion of restrained excitement about her all afternoon.

"But she can't come *here*," said Maggie almost tearfully. "Not *here*. Not *Philippa*. You don't understand, Caroline. You don't remember. You were too young. It was so long ago. You were only a baby. She . . ." Her voice trailed off unsteadily.

She's getting upset, thought Charles. I'd better take her home to Nana.

"You've actually written?" Richard was saying.

"Yes. I posted it just before you came."

"Caroline, my dear, I wish you'd consulted us first."

She smiled again—not her usual grave smile, but an eager tremulous one that made her seem pathetically young despite her thirty-six years.

"I was afraid you'd advise me not to," she said, "and I wanted her to come. After all, whatever she's done, she's my mother."

"I know, but if you'd just suggested meeting first on neutral ground, as it were, to see how the land lay. . . . Then, if you judged that it would be a success, you could have asked her to make her home with you."

"Oh, Richard!" she laughed. "What a horribly cautious mind you've got!"

"It's such a risk, my dear."

"I know it's a risk, but I'm willing to take it. I want to take it."

"But, Charles," burst out Maggie, "tell them about Philippa. They ought to know. She can't come here. Gordon would never have allowed it. Never. He——"

"Listen, Auntie," began Caroline patiently.

"It's all right, Caroline," said Charles, rising. He knew that Caroline's explanation would only confuse Maggie the more. "She's a bit tired. It's rather exciting for her, coming out to tea, in any case. I'll take her home now."

"I'm not a bit tired, Charles. Not a bit."

"I know you aren't, dear. But Nana will be expecting you. I dare say she'll be wanting your help with something. We oughtn't to keep her waiting."

Maggie rose quickly, forgetting all about Philippa in her pleasure at the thought that Nana might be wanting her help with something.

On the way home, however, the look of bewilderment crept over her face once more.

"But, Charles," she said. "About Philippa. ... I don't understand. ..."

Charles smiled at her reassuringly. He was enjoying the pleasant summer evening, holding himself very erect, and thinking that he'd look in at the club when he'd taken Maggie home and have a rubber or two of bridge and assure himself once again how much younger than his contemporaries he both looked and felt. It was a pleasure he never tired of.

"Don't worry, Maggie," he said kindly. "Nana will explain it all to you."

Chapter Three

"Poor darling!" said Caroline, as she came back to the drawing-room after seeing Charles and Maggie off at the front door. "She gets so upset over things. . . . Perhaps I oughtn't to have told her about mother, but I don't see how I could have avoided it."

Richard Oakley, standing by the mantelpiece, absently knocked the ash from his cigarette into the fireplace.

"I'm worried about this, Caroline," he said.

She sank down into a chair and smiled up at him.

"Why should you be?"

"You know that whatever affects you affects me."

"I didn't mean that. I meant—what aspect of it in particular worries you?"

"I think you've undertaken this responsibility rashly and on impulse. You don't know what sort of complications it's going to bring into your life."

She looked as grave as he now.

"It wasn't rashly or on impulse, Richard. I've always known at the bottom of my heart that some time or other she'd want to come back, and that I'd have to let her. After all, she is my mother."

"She's your mother, but she hasn't the shadow of a claim on you. She didn't bring you up or make any sacrifice for you, and she deserted you at a time when you most needed her care. As far as having any claim on you goes, she put herself out of court when she left your father for another man."

"I'm not pretending that she has any claim on me exactly," said Caroline slowly. "I'm not even pretending that her coming mayn't, as you say, bring with it certain complications. But I feel that it's my duty to ask her here. I know it is. I've never questioned it once, since I got her letter. . . . Even the thought of Fay . . ."

"Yes, there's Fay to be considered."

"I know. I put Fay first. I always put Fay first. I wouldn't do anything in the world that I thought might harm Fay."

"And don't you think this might harm Fay?"

"No," she said proudly. "I know it won't. Fay's too—sound to be contaminated, if that's what you're thinking of. And she's loyal to the core. Whatever this means to me, I'm sure of Fay's support."

"Of course. And mine as well."

"I know. . . . I admit I did just wonder about Fay at first. I don't know what sort of life mother's lived since she went away. But I *know* she couldn't do Fay any harm. . . . You never saw her, did you, Richard?"

He shook his head.

"And I don't remember her at all. I've never even seen a photograph of her. Father destroyed them all when she went away. I've often thought of her, of course. Nina was always kind to me, but I used to long for my own mother when I was a child."

He looked down at her compassionately.

"Poor little Caroline!"

She drew herself up with a faint smile.

"No, please. I didn't mean to be pathetic. I'm not a bit pathetic."

"Yes, you are, whether you know it or not," he burst out. "You've carried the whole family on your shoulders ever since you were a child. You've given up your youth for them, you've given up all your own chances for them. You've worked yourself to death for a set of ungrateful brats."

"They aren't ungrateful," she put in hotly.

"Well, perhaps they're not, but that doesn't affect the case one way or the other. The point is that you've literally *slaved* for those three as long as any of us can remember, and it's time you stopped. This taking of burdens onto your shoulders is becoming an obsession. You were just winning through to a sort of freedom at last. . . . You've got Robert trained and set up in life and married, you've got Susan married and off your hands, Fay will be going to college next year. And, just when you should be seeing a little peace ahead, you must needs take on this. Honestly, I feel fed up about it, Caroline."

"Oh, Richard!"

"Yes, I know what you mean," he said savagely. "It's sheer selfishness. I hoped that once Fay had gone to college I could manage somehow or other to persuade you to marry me. I'd meant to ask you again this afternoon."

She made a little deprecating gesture.

"Richard dear, don't start that all over again. We've gone over it so often."

"I know you couldn't marry me while you'd got Susan and Fay on your hands. Then it was Fay alone. You wouldn't ever consider it till Fay had gone to college."

"Richard, you said you understood. She had to come first. I couldn't have done justice to her if I'd been your wife, too. I promised father when he died that I'd look after her."

"I know, my dear, and you've kept your promise magnificently, but—Caroline, after all, why should your mother's coming make any difference? We could get married before she came. She could live with us. . . . Caroline . . ."

His voice pleaded earnestly, but something dreamy and far-away had come into her eyes. She looked at him as if she did not see him.

"I can't—promise anything yet, Richard. I don't know how badly my mother may need me. She's probably had a terrible time. Life isn't easy for women like that, you know. I want her to find peace here. I want to—help her. It sounds silly and priggish and sentimental, I know, but that's what I feel about it."

He smiled wryly.

"What can I do to make you feel like that to me, Caroline? Shall I try going off the rails altogether, or would it do if I broke an arm or a leg?"

"Richard, please don't make fun of it."

"Does Marcia know about your mother's coming?"

Caroline's face hardened slightly.

"I don't suppose so. She's abroad just now, you know."

He looked at her curiously.

"Why do you dislike Marcia, Caroline?"

She opened her eyes wide.

"I don't dislike Marcia. I'm very fond of Marcia. She wasn't quite—loyal to me when she lived here, but I've never borne her any malice for that."

He rose and threw his cigarette end into the fireplace.

"Well, I must go now, I suppose." He looked at her in silence for some moments. "I'm still hoping that you'll change your mind about your mother, Caroline, for your own sake as much as mine."

"I've posted the letter."

"You can post another."

She shook her head, tightening her lips.

"No, I can't."

"Well, goodbye, my dear. I'm a very faithful man, don't you think? A sort of male Penelope."

She laughed.

"You're ridiculous . . . and terribly nice. Goodbye, Richard."

She returned to the drawing-room when he had gone and stood gazing unseeingly in front of her. Her eyes were still bright and there was a heightened colour in her cheeks. Now that she was alone, the excitement that had smouldered in her heart ever since she received her mother's letter this morning seemed to blaze out exultantly. The secret dream that she had treasured from the earliest days of her adolescence had suddenly come to life. When she thought of her mother in those days, she had always thought of her as tortured by a bitter remorse and a ceaseless longing for the children she had deserted. She imagined that the memory of them had poisoned all her pleasure and had yet been a sweetening influence in the life of degradation that, she took for granted, had been her lot since leaving them. She had always been convinced that her mother would come back in the end to ask her forgiveness for the wrong she had done her. And she would grant that forgiveness freely, would even go further and hold out hands of love and pity to rescue her from the sordidness into which she had inevitably sunk.

She had been about thirteen when first she pictured their meeting, but the picture had not altered in any essential detail since then. Her mother—a wretched, broken-down woman—looked at her for a moment in silence, then covered her face with her hands and fell sobbing upon her shoulders, while Caroline held her closely, murmuring words of comfort and reassurance. Sometimes, instead of being broken-down and wretched, the woman had been hard and brazen, but always the end had been the same. She had fallen sobbing into her arms. The more mature and critical part of her had come to realise that the picture was somewhat melodramatic, but she could never bring herself to alter it. It had grown with her from childhood to womanhood. The news of her mother's marriage had made no difference to her general idea of her. Such women frequently did marry, but they were too hardened to change their ways. And she had not married the man for whom she left her husband. That in itself condemned her.

She took up the letter and looked at it dreamily.

"Mother darling ... don't cry like that. ... It's all right. ... You've come home. ... I'll look after you now ... always."

So real was the scene that she seemed actually to hear herself say the words, and as she did so the familiar glow of self-sacrifice pervaded her whole being.

She loved Richard and had looked forward to being able to marry him when Fay had gone to college, but she was accustomed by now to giving up her personal happiness for the sake of others. She'd given up her career for the sake of the children, she'd consistently denied herself luxuries and at times even necessities in order that they might have everything they needed. No sacrifice, not even the sacrifice of Richard's love, would ever be as great, it seemed to her, as the giving up of her scholarship at her father's death, for she had been a born student, hard-working and full of an eager zest for knowledge. The last remnants of her youth had died then and had never come to life again. Yet even then a certain fanatical joy had been mingled with the anguish. She had felt that, wherever her father was, he knew about it and was proud of her.

There had always been a strong bond of affection between herself and her father. Marcia was wilful and difficult, his second wife's children meant little to him. Caroline had always been his favourite child, the only one of his children, indeed, whom he really loved. His rigidity unbent with her, his harshness softened. He was always ready to listen to her, to grant her wishes if he possibly could. When little more than a child, she had on more than one occasion intervened between him and Nina, shielding Nina from his too great exactions.

"Do talk to your father about it, Caroline," Nina would say in her sweet complaining little voice. "He won't listen to a word I say."

His fondness for her did not make him relax his standards in her case, but rather tighten them. As the eldest she had grave responsibilities. Hers must be the stern duty of setting a good example to the others in every detail of her conduct. Duty must come first, self-love must be severely eradicated. He watched her with anxious care, and, aware of this, she made almost superhuman efforts to justify his hopes of her. She gave her favourite toys to the others, spent her pocket-money on treats for them, settled their little disputes with unchildlike wisdom, calmed their tempers with unfailing patience, performed all her tasks with conscientious exactitude. Her reward was to be called "father's good girl," his "right hand," to be told that he "didn't know what he'd do without her." There was nothing of the hypocrite about her. She was pathetically earnest and humble, striving with desperate eagerness to conquer her faults and to be worthy of her father's trust and love. She had inherited from him a strong sense of duty, and his training had magnified it into an obsession. Looking back, she did not seem to herself ever to have been a child. That anxious brooding desire to do her duty, that terror of failing in it, which never left her by day or night, had made her old before she reached her teens. The longing to please her father had persisted even after his death. When she felt most dispirited and exhausted by the task she had set herself, she often seemed to see his slow rare smile, to hear his deep voice, praising and encouraging her ("That's my good girl"), and she would take up her work again with renewed cheerfulness and vigour. There were other compensations, of course. There was the love and gratitude of the children themselves, which had never failed her.

She looked at the signature of her mother's letter. Philippa Meredith. . . . Neither name nor handwriting awoke any chords of memory. Her father had never mentioned her, had been, she knew, deeply incensed and wounded by her desertion. But, still, this, she was sure, was what he would have wished her to do—to offer a refuge in which the woman he had once loved could end her days in peace. As she thought of her answer to the letter she seemed to feel again the glow of love and happiness that his approval had always given her.

She heard the opening of the front door, the sound of Fay's attaché-case being flung down on the hall table, then the door burst open, and Fay appeared, holding her school hat in her hand.

Fay was tall and fair and slender, like Caroline, but there the resemblance stopped. Her features were not classical, her expression not austere. Her face was perhaps too small in proportion to her height, but it was an exquisite little face, the features delicately chiselled, so expressive that every passing mood seemed to show on it like reflections chasing each other over water.

She was breathless as if from running, and her cheeks were flushed.

"I've run all the way from the cross-roads," she said. "Am I terribly late?"

"No, darling," said Caroline, smiling at her affectionately. "I mean, I knew you'd be late today. You've not had tea, have you?"

"No. I'll go up and wash."

"All right. I'll order tea for you. Don't be long."

"Rather not!"

Caroline's face wore an expression of brooding tenderness as she listened to the sound of the light footsteps taking the stairs two at a time. She'd always hated the thought of Fay's growing out of the particular stage at which she was, but each stage, as she reached it, seemed more adorable than the last. At eighteen she was a fascinating compendium of all the stages she'd been through, with the addition of a delicious womanly gravity that peeped out occasionally through her childishness. She was clumsy, yet with an appealing childish grace; shy and sensitive with bursts of sudden confidence; tomboyish at one moment, at the next withdrawn and dignified; sometimes wistful and diffident, sometimes eager to come to grips with life. She passed from one mood to another so quickly that even Caroline, with all her understanding of her, found it difficult to follow. Yet in them all she was sound and sweet and loving, starkly honest and true. The thing Caroline wanted most of all in life was to keep from Fay everything that might harm her, and for the first time a slight doubt came to her mind as to whether her decision had, after all, been wise. She would never forgive herself if her mother's presence clouded the child's happiness in any way or sullied her shining innocence.

When Fay came down she had changed from her school uniform to a pale green jumper suit.

"You must be tired and hungry, pet," said Caroline. "Come and have your tea."

Fay looked at the armchair by which the low tea-table was set.

"Do you mind if I have it on the other side, Caroline?" she said, and moved it carefully over to the opposite side of the hearth.

Caroline laughed amusedly.

"What a funny child you are! Why?"

"I like this side better."

"One would almost imagine you didn't like looking at my lovely tallboy. Don't you like it?"

"Of course I do. It's—oh, I like this side better, that's all."

Her face had looked pinched for a moment, but it crinkled up in childish delight as her eyes rested on the tea-tray.

"Oh, how lovely! Orange cake!"

"It's the remains of the party, but I got it because it was your favourite."

"How sweet of you! How did the party go off?"

"Very well."

"I suppose poor old Aunt Maggie was all flustered with coming out to tea, and Uncle Charles had to keep soothing her down. People make fun of him for dyeing his hair and wearing stays, but he's an awful pet to Aunt Maggie. Most people would get terribly irritated with her. . . . I thought perhaps Susan or Richard might be here still."

"Susan didn't stay long. She'd promised Kenneth to be back for tea."

"I think Ken's a dear, don't you? He met us when we were coming back from the sports field the other day and stood us all ices."

"You shouldn't take things from Kenneth, Fay."

"Why not?"

"He's not very well off, for one thing."

"Yes, but somehow it would have been horrid to refuse. It would have hurt his feelings. They were only threepenny ones."

"You shouldn't have accepted them, all the same. More tea, sweetheart?"

"Thanks. But why should you wait on me like this?"

"Because I love to. What sort of a day have you had?"

"Quite all right."

"Did you have your French prose back?"

"Yes."

"What did you get for it?"

"Beta plus. I'd make some silly mistakes. You said I had when you looked over it, didn't you?"

"Yes. You'd managed all the stiff parts beautifully and come down over the elementary bits."

"I'm always doing that."

"It's carelessness, darling."

"I know."

"Did she go over the unseen—the one you did on Wednesday?"

"No. She hadn't time. She said she would tomorrow. She'll probably forget."

Caroline went to her bookshelves, took down a book, and came back to the fireplace, turning over the leaves.

"It was this one, wasn't it? . . . Let's just run over it. I remember the places you went wrong."

"Thanks."

Fay spoke listlessly. Now that the excitement of homecoming was over, she looked tired and depressed. She wished that Caroline wouldn't always go over the day's work at tea-time. One simply never got away from it. She hated it, anyway. She hadn't been keen on it before, but, since she'd had to give up music, she'd loathed it. And Caroline wouldn't leave it alone. . . . A hot rush of compunction swept over her. It was hateful of her to feel like that about Caroline, who did so much for her and worked so hard for her and loved her so tenderly. What would she have done without Caroline? What would she do now without Caroline? She'd made up her mind to go through with the thing, to try her very best to win the scholarship because Caroline wanted her to, and she spoilt it all by doing it grudgingly and unwillingly, by even resenting the help that Caroline gave so unstintingly, however tired she was.

"You see, darling, you missed the point of the subjunctive there . . . and, of course, you got that piece all wrong, but there are some rather unusual words in it. Have you looked them out and made a list of them?"

"Yes."

"It's an involved sentence, too. I'd split it up more in the translation."

"Yes."

"It's a shame to worry you at tea-time, baby."

"Oh *no*," said Fay, smitten again with a sharp pang of remorse. "It's *sweet* of you, Caroline. I *am* grateful. You know I am."

"Of course you are, bless you! But we'll put it away now. We can go over it again later in the evening. And you can help me correct some of my St. Monica's papers."

Fay's heart sank again. She hated helping Caroline to correct her St. Monica's papers. She hated it chiefly because the "help" was only a pretence. It was just as much trouble for Caroline to go over her corrections as it would be to correct the papers herself in the first instance. But Caroline thought that it was good practice for Fay to correct other people's mistakes. It was really a sort of test paper for Fay herself. It wasn't fair. . . . Again the familiar compunction swept over her. What a *beast* she was to feel like that when Caroline was doing all she could for her!

"I'd love to," she said, and added, "Have you had a nice day?"

"Quite, thanks. I was at St. Monica's all the morning, you know. . . . They really have got a phenomenal set of idiots in the Upper Sixth this year. They make the most ridiculous mistakes." Fay bent down her head and dug her teeth into her lips. She couldn't *bear* it if Caroline were going to tell her some of the ridiculous mistakes they made and ask her to correct them. But she didn't. She went on, smiling. "I've got a piece of news for you that I think you'll like, dearest."

Fay's face lightened. She looked like an eager child.

"What is it?"

"You know they're doing *Midsummer-Night's Dream* next month at St. Monica's?"

"Yes."

"Well, Miss Frankson asked if you might play the piano in the intervals, and I said you could, if it didn't need any practice. You see, I've promised that you shall go to the play, anyway, and as you're there you may just as well——"

Fay's slender form had gone tense.

"No, Caroline," she said. "No . . . no."

"Darling, what's the matter?"

"I can't play . . . I *can't* . . ." said Fay breathlessly.

She couldn't even bear to think of it . . . playing for about five minutes . . . stopping and beginning again at a signal from behind the footlights. It would be like showing a starving man food and then taking it away from him.

She would never all her life forget the night when Caroline had come into her bedroom and had sat on her bed and talked to her so kindly and earnestly, showing her that those hours she spent at the piano were a futile waste of time, that her love of music was a self-indulgence that must be conquered at all costs because it interfered with her real duty. In a state of emotional exaltation Fay had offered to give it up altogether, and Caroline had kissed her solemnly and said, "Darling, you've made the right choice, as I knew you would. You'll never regret it."

But Fay hadn't known that it would be as hard as it was turning out to be, hadn't known what an emptiness it would leave behind, and that even the sight of the corner in the drawing-room where the piano used to stand would send a wave of panic and despair into her soul whenever she looked at it. And it didn't get any better as time went on. . . . It got worse.

Caroline was smiling at her tenderly. What a good little thing she was! Always so breathlessly eager to do what was right, to keep her promises in the spirit as well as the letter.

"But, darling, it would be all right just to play in the intervals. I shouldn't mind that at all. I——"

"Oh *no*, Caroline."

"Very well, dearest. Don't get excited over it. By the way, I had a long talk with Miss Frankson. She's very much interested in you. She said that she wished I'd sent you to St. Monica's instead of the High School. She said she'd have loved to have you."

"How nice of her!" said Fay dutifully.

"We were talking about your career. She says that Miss Parker will be retiring the year you get your degree, and that she's going to give Miss Sawyer Miss Parker's post, and she practically promised to give you Miss Sawyer's. It would be a splendid beginning for you, darling. You could go on living at home, and we could work together. . . ."

Fay tried hard to feel as she ought to feel—grateful, excited, eager. Of course it would be lovely to live at home and work with Caroline, whom she adored, who was so good to her. Of course she'd like teaching. Caroline always assured her that she would. If only her heart didn't sink down like this whenever she thought of it. . . .

"Dearest," Caroline was saying, "you don't know what it means to me to feel that you're going to—take on from where I left off, as it were. To do the things I meant to do. I remember that when I gave up my scholarship and chance of a career—you were only a baby then, of course—I thought: Perhaps Fay will do it instead—go to college and make a career for herself. And when I'd thought that I didn't mind half so much."

A wave of unbearable emotion swept over Fay's spirit.

"Oh, Caroline," she said, "you've been so sweet to me."

"Rubbish!" said Caroline briskly. "Have some more tea? You've eaten nothing. . . ."

"I have. . . . Anyway, I'm not terribly hungry."

She had been hungry at first, and the sight of the cosy tea-table had been lovely, but somehow she wasn't hungry any more. She didn't know whether it was that hateful French unseen (she'd racked her brains over it for so long that the sight of it again had made her feel almost sick), or the thought of playing in the intervals of *Midsummer-Night's Dream* at St. Monica's, or whether it was—just nothing at all, but she didn't even want to eat any of the orange cake that Caroline had bought specially for her. How angelic Caroline was! She was always doing things like that—buying one little presents, remembering the things one liked.

The maid came in to take away the tea things.

"I suppose I'd better start my home-work," said Fay, but still lay back in her chair, inert. She felt unusually tired. She'd got that hateful German test-paper to do tonight. She wished she loved languages as the other girls who were working for the scholarship did. It was the school subject she found easiest, but she didn't love it. She didn't love anything except music. To cheer herself, she looked forward into the future, and tried to imagine that she'd actually won the scholarship . . . but somehow even that failed to cheer her. She'd go to college, get her degree, and—teach at St. Monica's or some other school. . . . Her depression grew heavier and heavier till it became a sort of panic. She couldn't bear it—years and years and years of it . . . a whole lifetime of it. She tried to imagine herself rallying her courage and telling Caroline that she didn't want to go to college, didn't want to teach . . . but she couldn't. She couldn't hurt Caroline as much as that—Caroline who had given up all her life to her, who was so proud of her, who looked to her to carry on from where she herself had left off. She set her lips grimly. No, she'd go through with it, because she couldn't in decency do anything else.

"Not *just* this minute," Caroline was saying. "Let's have a little talk first. . . ."

She moved her chair to make room for Fay to sit on the hearthrug at her feet, as she loved to do. She ought to tell the child about her mother. She must do it very carefully.

Fay rested her head against Caroline's knees. She wanted to put off the moment of starting her home-work, but she felt that she couldn't bear one of Caroline's "little talks" just now.

"Sybil's got the sweetest kitten," she said, in order to start the conversation, at any rate, on a light note. "She's called it Smoke."

Caroline's figure stiffened almost imperceptibly.

"Sybil?"

"Sybil Dickson. I called at her house with her on the way home."

There was a short silence, then Caroline said:

"But, darling, I thought you'd come straight home from school."

"I wasn't there more than five minutes. I had to call anyway, because she'd got the copy of Heine. Fraulein had lent it to her and told her to hand it on to me afterwards."

"I see. . . ."

A faint resentment stirred beneath the listlessness and depression of Fay's spirit. Why did Caroline always make her feel that she'd done something wrong whenever she went home with any of the other girls or even waited for them after classes or games?

"I came home as quickly as I could after I'd got the book," she said.

"Darling, of *course* it's all right," said Caroline. "I had my party, so I was kept quite busy and occupied. It's only when I'm by myself and have had a lonely afternoon that I begin to expect you the minute I know the four o'clock bell's gone, and every second seems hours. I'm rather silly about my baby, aren't I?"

Once more that wave of loving compunction swept over Fay.

"Oh, *Caroline*!"

She *couldn't* ask her about Friday after that. But she must. . . .

"Caroline," she began and stopped.

It wasn't going to be easy. But why shouldn't it be, she asked herself impatiently. Why should she have this terrible feeling of guilt whenever she asked permission to go to tea with any of her school-fellows?

"Yes?"

"Sybil's having her birthday party on Friday. She wants me to go to it. She's asking all the Upper Sixth. May I?"

"Friday?"

"Yes."

"Oh, darling," Caroline gave a deprecating little laugh. "I'd just planned something for you myself for Friday. I thought I'd call for you at school and we'd take the train to Little Houghton and have tea there and see over the Manor. It's a wonderful old house and it's open to visitors on Fridays. I was going to spring it on you as a surprise, but you must go to Sybil's party now instead, of course, dear. You'd much rather go there, I'm sure."

"No, I wouldn't, Caroline."

"Of course you would, darling. It's only natural that you should. A lot of jolly young people instead of a dull old sister like me."

"*Don't*, Caroline! I wouldn't go to Sybil's party for anything, now I know there's a chance of going out with you. I'd much rather be with you. You know I would."

Her heart was full of fervent love for Caroline, but beneath it nagged the thought that it was strange how Caroline always seemed to have fixed some engagement for days when her friends asked her to tea. She hated herself for the thought, but she couldn't quite get rid of it.

"You ought to go to Sybil's, darling."

"No, I won't. I'd hate it, anyway. I don't want to go. I only want to be with you."

It was strange, too, how Caroline made you say things like that, thought Fay. You didn't really want to say them because they weren't quite true, and you tried hard not to, but you couldn't help it. Caroline wanted you to say them and expected you to say them, and her will was so strong that you couldn't hold out against it. It was only lately that she'd begun to feel like this about Caroline, and it worried her terribly.

Caroline was looking down at her with a tender smile.

"Well, then, we'll go off on Friday, shall we?" she said. "We'll forget that there are such things as exams in the world and just enjoy ourselves. It will be lovely, won't it?"

She *had* been meaning to take Fay out on Friday, she assured herself. She'd meant to take her out soon, anyway, and Friday was the most convenient day. . . . Fay didn't really care for girls of her own age—she'd often said so—and they did her no good. It was a kindness to give her an excuse for not going to Sybil's party. It would be a silly, noisy, schoolgirlish sort of affair that Fay would hate. And—she loved taking Fay out. She was such a perfect companion, intelligent, responsive, quick to see what one meant, to follow one's mood, with quaint original ideas of her own which she expounded with a delicious touch of shyness.

It thrilled Caroline to think that she had moulded this alert sensitive mind, that she knew its every turn of thought, that it belonged to her utterly, utterly. . . .

Fay sat motionless, her head turned away. She'd have to tell Sybil that she couldn't go to her party, after all. She'd hate doing it. It had happened so often before, and Sybil would think that she didn't want to go to it. They all thought her stand-offish and conceited because she joined in with so few of their activities, and hurried home the minute school was over. She'd been looking forward to Sybil's party terribly, not only because she liked Sybil, but—she ought to tell Caroline about that, too. She wanted to tell her, but somehow she couldn't. She'd tell her tomorrow. She didn't know why she felt so ashamed of it. She hadn't felt ashamed of it till she tried to tell Caroline and found that she couldn't. And yet there wasn't really anything to be ashamed of. It was just that, as she was setting out from Sybil's, Sybil's brother was setting out, too, to go to the pillar-box at the end of the road—and they had walked as far as the pillar-box together. That was all it was. Only—he'd been kind and friendly and had joked about the history mistress, who'd been to tea at Sybil's the day before, and had made her laugh, and afterwards, as she walked home by herself, she'd felt happy and excited and as if life were rather jolly after all. She'd still felt like that when she reached home, but she didn't feel like that any longer. Life wasn't really jolly at all, and. . . . She ought to tell Caroline about it. It was wrong not to. Caroline had often made her promise to tell her everything—every little thing that happened to her—and had promised faithfully on her side that she'd never be cross with her, even if she'd done something wrong, as long as she told her. It wasn't anything wrong, and it ought to be quite easy to tell her. ("Billy walked with me as far as the pillar-box. He had a letter to post. Sybil's brother, you know.") Caroline wouldn't be cross with her, but her eyes would go rather blue and it would all be spoilt. Caroline would think it cheap and silly (though she wouldn't actually say so), and it would *become* cheap and silly as soon as she'd told Caroline about it. . . . That was why she didn't want to tell her. Not tonight, at any rate. She didn't want it to be spoilt tonight. She'd tell her tomorrow. She *must* tell her tomorrow. She'd feel wicked until she had told her. Caroline wouldn't mind at all if she said that she didn't like Billy and hadn't wanted him to walk to the pillar-box with her, but that somehow would be the final disloyalty, worse than all the other hateful little disloyalties that surged continually beneath her love for Caroline, making her feel sometimes sick with shame.

"Fay, darling," Caroline was saying, "I've got something to tell you. . . ."

Fay looked up. A wild unreasonable hope had flashed into her mind that Caroline was going to say she could take up her music again and drop her scholarship work.

"You know about my mother, don't you?"

"Yes."

It always seemed strange to her that she and Caroline had different mothers. She didn't remember her own mother at all, of course.

"Well, I heard from her this morning. She's coming to England. I've asked her to come and live with us."

"You mean, here?"

"Yes."

Fay considered. ... Caroline's mother. ... Almost her own grandmother. Fay saw her—a little old lady in a shawl, leaning on a stick, creeping about the house, sitting in an armchair by the fire, knitting. It would be rather a nuisance in a way, but she probably wouldn't make much difference. Old people didn't. Molly Master's grandmother lived with them. She was very deaf and spent most of her time dozing in armchairs. And she kept thinking that Molly was one of her own daughters. ... It was rather funny, but, of course, one mustn't laugh at it. Caroline's mother would probably be like that. She'd run away from her husband with another man, which was a very wicked thing to do, but it was so many years ago that it didn't matter much now. Like the things in history that were wicked, but no one minded because it was all so long ago. She couldn't be wicked still, of course. Old people were never wicked. They repented and turned good as soon as they got old.

"I don't think that her coming need affect you at all," Caroline was saying. "I'll give her a bed-sitting-room upstairs, and, of course, we shall love to have her down here if ever she likes to come. But I think that what she'll want is just peace and rest and quiet. You know about her, don't you, darling?"

"Yes," said Fay, feeling rather uncomfortable, as she always did when Caroline's voice took on that deep solemn note.

"I don't want you to judge her. I don't judge her myself. I'm sure that she's been amply punished for anything she did wrong. We must just try to make her happy and comfortable for the rest of her life."

"Yes," said Fay, deciding that the old woman was going to be a dreadful nuisance, but that one must just put up with it.

Caroline was drawing her fingers gently through Fay's curls.

"Your hair was just this colour when you were a baby," she said dreamily. "I used to be so afraid it would grow darker, but it never has done. ..."

Again that quick response of loving gratitude stirred tumultuously at Fay's heart. Throughout her childhood she had found comfort in Caroline's arms for every little hurt and unhappiness. Ever since she could remember Caroline's tenderness had surrounded her on every side. It still surrounded her as much as it had done in the days when she had cried herself to sleep if for any reason Caroline was not there to give her goodnight kiss, when her worst nightmare was to look for Caroline and not to find her. It still surrounded her, but often now it seemed to hem her in, to suffocate her. The stark disloyalty of that thought made her catch her breath with horror. Suppose Caroline ever discovered how unworthy she was of all she had done for her, how resentful and grudging and ungrateful. . . .

Even the happiness she had felt after walking to the pillar-box with Billy seemed just another proof of her wickedness.

A rush of mingled emotions swept over her. She gave a little choking gasp, then turned and buried her face on Caroline's knee, sobbing uncontrollably. Caroline leant down and put her arms about her tenderly.

"Sweetheart . . . why are you crying?"

"I don't know," sobbed Fay.

She was crying because she was unhappy and tired, because she loved Caroline so terribly and yet was so hatefully disloyal to her. . . .

Chapter Four

CAROLINE walked slowly up the narrow path to the small newly-painted front door. She hated the poky jerry-built houses of the little "garden estate," and felt indignant whenever she thought of Susan's having to live in one. The spurious artisticness that was the delight of the estate agent's heart (he described it as "old-world atmosphere") only damned them the more in Caroline's eyes. The green-painted shutters served no ostensible purpose, the diamond-paned windows let in insufficient light, the pretentious little porches were quite out of keeping with the style of the rest of the architecture. They were inhabited chiefly by a fleeting population of people who were attracted by the green shutters, diamond panes, porches, and the smallness of the deposit required to secure immediate occupation, and who discovered too late that the "rest as rent" did not leave sufficient margin in their budget for solvency.

Susan had at first been delighted with the little house and had refused even to listen to Caroline's criticisms. But then Susan had been mad in those days, her reason and common sense swept away in the whirlwind of her love for Kenneth. Caroline had done her best to save her. She had certainly nothing to reproach herself with on that score. She had pointed out to her what such a marriage would mean. She had reasoned with her and pleaded with her, but Susan, intoxicated with happiness, had only laughed and said, "Oh Caroline, what nonsense you talk! You don't even begin to understand."

Poor little Susan! She was learning her mistake at last, and Caroline was deeply thankful that she was at hand to help. Susan had thought that she could do without her but she couldn't. She needed her now more than she had ever needed her in her life before. Caroline's face softened at the thought. It gave her a warm happy feeling to know that her "children" still needed her, still turned to her in all their troubles. Robert . . . Susan . . . Fay. Robert's marriage would have been a failure but for her, she was standing by Susan now to steer her course into calmer waters, while Fay was almost as dependent on her as when she'd been a baby. If only one could prevent those one loved from making such tragic mistakes! If only she could have prevented Robert from marrying Effie, Susan from marrying Kenneth!

She glanced at the neglected little garden, and her lips tightened. Surely Kenneth might keep that tidy at any rate. Even if he had to live in this appalling place he might at least keep a remnant of self-respect.

Susan opened the door. She wore a flowered cretonne overall and looked flushed and excited.

"Come in, darling," she said. "I've cooked a lovely lunch for you all by myself. I'm really growing into the world's best cook. Ken said so last night. Let me hang up your coat. He said he'd never tasted such delicious stew in his life. We co-operate so well that we're thinking of going out as cook and housemaid if all else fails. I do the cooking and he sets the table and washes up and does the grates. . . . Take your hat off, darling, and make yourself at home. . . . That's right. . . . Now come along in. . . ."

Caroline followed her into the little dining-room. It was furnished in fumed oak—pull-out dining-table, chairs, sideboard, bureau, and bookshelves. The fireplace consisted of a gas stove set in a blue-tiled surround with a white-painted shelf above it on which were a clock and a china bird. The walls were distempered in cream colour. At the windows hung curtains of flowered cretonne of the same pattern as Susan's overall. One or two coloured woodcuts hung on the wall. The whole contents of the room could not have cost more than a few pounds, and it was probably the counterpart of hundreds of other dining-rooms throughout the "estate," but, for all that, it struck a pleasant, cheerful, welcoming note. The table was laid for lunch, with embroidered mats on the bare wood and a bowl of roses in the centre.

"How do you like the bureau in the window?" said Susan.

"Wasn't it there before?"

"Oh Caroline! After much heart-searching Ken and I decide to move it there and you don't even know it wasn't there before!"

Caroline laughed.

"I'm sorry, but one can hardly see the wood for the trees in this room. Everything's so close to you that you can't focus it."

"Oh, you and your spacious Georgian rooms!" teased Susan. "I've no patience with the airs you put on. I believe you're jealous. I'm just going to dish up, darling. I won't be a minute."

She went into the kitchen and soon returned with a dish of chops and mashed potatoes.

"A very simple meal but quite good chops and cooked to a turn. . . . You know, it's a great honour for you to have lunch in here. I generally have it in the kitchen myself."

"Oh Susan!"

"Don't look so horrified. I love the kitchen, especially since I put up those blue-and-white check curtains, and I've got a table-cloth to match, and the Windsor chair's in there, and it gets all the morning sun."

"This room certainly doesn't get much. Nor does the lounge, does it?"

"The lounge gets the afternoon sun."

"Or rather what the window lets in."

"Yes, you have to sit well in the window to get it, I admit, but that makes one appreciate it all the more."

"Darling, you don't know how I admire you for making the best of things like this."

"Oh Caroline, you adorable idiot!" Susan was still smiling, but something of her glow had faded. "I suppose it does seem horribly pokey and cheap to you."

"Of *course* it doesn't, darling," said Caroline hastily. "I think it's all lovely. Simply lovely."

Dear old Caroline, thought Susan affectionately. She's overdoing

44

it now. She looked round the little room and saw it suddenly as Caroline must be seeing it. It had seemed so perfect before Caroline came, but now it didn't seem perfect any longer. It seemed cheap and shoddy and makeshift. Her happiness turned slowly to a vague discontent.

"How's Kenneth going on?" said Caroline.

The glow returned to Susan's face.

"He's an angel, he really is, Caroline. He gets up early and lights the fire and brings me a cup of tea every morning. He's so sweet to me."

"But darling, the other day you said——"

"I know," interrupted Susan, flushing. "We'd just had a row. It was my fault really. We made it up as soon as I got home."

Caroline shrugged faintly and was silent.

Susan collected the plates and dishes on a tray.

"Now I've got a really lovely soufflé for you, darling. You never thought I'd turn out such a good cook, did you? I won't be a minute."

"Can't I help?"

"Of course not."

She returned a few moment's later with a banana soufflé and a jug of cream.

"How do you like the dish?" she said as she set down the soufflé. "I got it at Woolworth's."

"Susan, darling, can't Kenneth really afford to buy you *any* decent things?"

"I adore shopping at Woolworth's," said Susan lightly, and added after a slight pause, "When's your mother coming, Caroline?"

"I haven't heard yet. I expect she has a fair amount of settling up to do before she can get away."

"I think it's perfectly marvellous of you to have her."

"My dear, it's only my duty."

"You want a spoon for the cream, don't you? Aren't I an idiot? I never can learn to set a table properly." She went to the kitchen and returned with the spoon. "You don't mind having lunch with me in an overall, do you, darling?"

Caroline smiled wryly.

"I won't pretend I enjoy watching you being gradually transformed into a household drudge," she said half whimsically, half seriously. "After all, I gave up a good many years of my life so that you should have a better fate than that."

"Oh, darling. . . ."

"I'm not complaining. Anything I did for you, for all of you, I did because I loved doing it, but—*can't* Kenneth afford even to keep a general servant?"

"I have Mrs. Pollit three mornings a week, you know, and she's an awfully good worker. She gets through all the rough work. She went only just before you came this morning. Honestly, I quite like housework, Caroline."

"Well, my dear, it's your own business, of course. I don't want to interfere."

"Don't talk about interfering, Caroline. I couldn't bear it if you didn't always say just what you thought. Ken says that he hopes things will be better next year and then we can spend a bit more on the house."

Caroline said nothing, and there was a short silence.

"How's Fay?" asked Susan at last.

"Quite well. . . . She's working very hard, of course."

"Ken saw her in the town the other day and thought she looked rather tired."

"How ridiculous! She doesn't look tired at all. She has quite enough relaxation. She's having Sybil to tea this afternoon."

"Sybil Dickson?"

"Yes. Sybil asked her to her birthday party last week, and she couldn't go as we'd planned to go over to Little Houghton that day, so Fay asked her to tea today to make up for it. She didn't really want to have her. She said only last night that she wished she weren't coming."

"She's a funny kid, isn't she? How do you like the soufflé?"

"It's delicious."

"You'll admit that I'm a good cook?"

"Y-yes."

46

"Why so doubtful?"

"Any fool can cook, dearest, and, as I said before, I consider it rather a waste of your talents."

"Ken doesn't," smiled Susan. "I made him an omelette last night, and he said that even his mother had never made a better one."

"I've always heard that the way to a man's heart is through his stomach," said Caroline dryly. "It's evidently true. Now I suppose you've got to wash up, darling. Let me help you. I think if I had to get meals ready and clear away and wash up I'd come to loathe the business of eating so much that I'd die of starvation."

"Oh no, you wouldn't," laughed Susan, "and I'm not going to wash up, anyway. You can just help me clear away. We'll leave everything on the kitchen table. . . . Thanks so much. . . . Now do come upstairs and look at the bedroom. I've got the bed-spreads at last, and I've finished staining the surround. It really does look rather nice."

"I wonder you haven't broken your neck a dozen times over these stairs," said Caroline, as she followed Susan up the steep narrow staircase.

"Oh, I know them so well I could come down them in my sleep."

She threw open the bedroom door.

"There! Don't they look nice? They just match the curtains."

Caroline looked at the twin beds placed side by side, covered by the new spreads of deep-blue silk, and as she looked a sudden hatred of Kenneth seemed to catch her by the throat, choking her. . . . leaving her breathless.

"Yes, they're charming," she said, speaking, with an effort, in her usual level voice.

Susan was opening the wardrobe.

"I've had one of those expanding rods put up, so that I can get nearly all my things in here now."

"That's splendid," said Caroline. She held out the sleeves of a coat that hung in the wardrobe. "You do need a new coat, though, my dear."

"Oh, I don't think so," said Susan. "I told Ken I shouldn't need any new clothes this summer."

"What on earth has it got to do with Kenneth? You have a dress allowance, haven't you? You surely don't allow Kenneth to dictate to you what clothes you need."

"Well—he is going to give me a dress allowance as soon as he possibly can, but, honestly, Caroline, he's going through an awfully bad patch just now. Melsham's is doing terribly badly. You'd be surprised how little is left when he's paid out the wages on Saturday. And he's got to help his mother, too. He's worried to death sometimes."

Caroline's mouth had taken on a hard tight line. Her eyes were very blue.

"My dear, he's married you, and he must keep you properly. You must insist on it. He shouldn't have married you if he couldn't provide for you."

"He *is* awfully hard up, Caroline."

"Nonsense! Men always talk like that. He doesn't stint himself, I've no doubt. He still belongs to the badminton club, doesn't he?"

"Yes . . . he needs the exercise."

"And he got a new wireless this year."

"His old one was absolutely useless. He got it before things were so bad."

"He can have anything he needs himself, of course. It's only you who have to go without things. Oh Susan, I've seen it happen so often. It's fatal for you to give in to it."

"The coat's all right, Caroline. It was a very good one. It looks almost new."

"It looks dreadfully shabby."

"All right . . . I'll talk to Kenneth about it tonight."

They went slowly downstairs. Susan's shoulders drooped dispiritedly. Perhaps Caroline was right. Perhaps Ken really had more money than he made out. Some men did keep their wives short of money on principle. And, of course, it was rather a pokey little place, though she was so fond of it, and having no maid did mean a lot of work.

"I'll get the coffee, Caroline. Go into the lounge. I won't be a minute."

She went into the kitchen and soon came back with two cups of coffee. Caroline drank hers in silence.

"Darling," she said at last, "I want to talk to you. We must get this straight."

She spoke in the grave tender voice that always seemed to make Susan a little girl again. Responding to it almost automatically, she sank down onto the hearthrug and rested her head on Caroline's knee. She remembered how she used to sit like that in the evenings in her childhood, while Caroline read aloud. Sometimes Robert would be there, sitting on the arm of Caroline's chair, and sometimes Fay would be there, on Caroline's knee, but Robert was five years older than Susan, and Fay six years younger, and there had never been very much comradeship between the three, though each had been devoted to Caroline.

"Susan," Caroline was saying, "I do want you to think very seriously about this. It's all right now, perhaps, for you to have all the work of the house on your hands, though I don't really think that it's right even now. But just think of its going on day after day, week after week, year after year, till you're nothing but a household drudge. That's what does happen, you know. I've seen it over and over again. A man's apt to think that if you've once done it you might as well go on doing it. It isn't fair to yourself or to him to put up with it."

"But, Caroline, if he *hasn't* the money. . . ."

"I'm sure he has the money. There's a mean streak in him. I've noticed it from the beginning. If he hasn't, then it's up to him to make it. Melsham's was a good business when his father was alive, and it can only be Kenneth's slackness that's let it down. Honestly, Susan darling, it isn't any real kindness to him to put up with things as you're doing. It's sweet of you, but it's wrong. You ought to *insist* on adequate help in the house and a proper personal allowance. I see nothing but unhappiness before you if you don't. I think I've earned the right to have a little say in your life, haven't I? And this isn't the sort of life I dreamed of for you. I've got an idea, darling. It came into my mind when we were upstairs. I think it may be the solution of the whole problem."

49

"What is it, Caroline?"

"If Kenneth really hasn't the money to keep you properly, why shouldn't you take a post?"

"But, Caroline——"

"Listen, darling. I couldn't get you to St. Monica's again, because their staff's full now, though I hope to get Fay your old post there when she's graduated. But I know that Miss Bruce wants an extra modern language mistress at Merton Park School. I met her the other day, and she was asking me if I knew of anyone. If you got that post you'd be able to have a really good maid to run the house, and you could give yourself to the work you've been trained for. You could have lunch at the school, and Kenneth could have it in the town, and then you'd both come home to a properly cooked meal in the evening. You could, of course, give it up as soon as Kenneth's making enough to keep you properly."

"Y-yes," said Susan doubtfully.

"Don't make up your mind all at once," said Caroline. "Think it over and talk it over with Kenneth. Or rather tell him that, if he can't get a proper maid or maids and give you a proper allowance, you must take a post yourself. Darling, I think you'd be much happier teaching than cleaning and scrubbing and cooking like this. After all, you're an educated woman, not a charwoman. Now don't worry any more, my pet. I'm sure that everything will come right if only you'll be firm with Kenneth." She glanced at the clock. "And now I must fly. I promised Evelyn to call there, and I must be back home in time to have tea with Fay and Sybil."

"Oh, but, Caroline, do stay a little longer. You——"

There was the sound of quick footsteps on the garden path, then the door burst open and Kenneth entered. He was tall and thin and boyish-looking, with unruly hair and clean-cut features. There was something ingenuous and honest about the grey eyes and wide mouth, something, too, suggestive of impulsiveness and the quick temper that matched Susan's own.

The eagerness fell from his face when he caught sight of Caroline, and he pulled himself up in his impetuous entrance.

"Hello!" he said. "I didn't——" He stopped.

"Didn't expect to find me here?" supplied Caroline quietly. "Surely Susan told you I was coming."

"Yes, but I had an idea that you'd have gone." He grinned at her in an awkward deprecating fashion rather like a dog that wants to be on friendly terms but is unsure of its reception. "I'm very glad to find you haven't, of course."

"I didn't know you'd be coming home this afternoon, Ken," said Susan.

He turned to her and his face lit up.

"Darling, things were so slack that I felt I must rush home and see you just for five minutes. I can only kiss you and tell you I love you and then rush back. I haven't seen you since breakfast, and I felt I had to see you again or die."

"Things probably *will be* slack, Kenneth," said Caroline in her level voice, "if this is the way you attend to business."

"I've been working frightfully hard lately, haven't I, Susie?" Kenneth justified himself. "I've had to get rid of another clerk, and I'm doing half the office work myself."

Caroline was standing by the window.

"If you are in the habit of taking afternoons off like this," she said, "you might put an occasional one in on the garden."

He made an obvious effort to control himself.

"I'm not in the habit of taking afternoons off," he said shortly. "I've been getting back too late at night to do anything to the garden." He looked at Susan and smiled suddenly. "Darling, I do adore you in that dress."

Caroline turned from the window.

"I've just been telling Susan that she needs a new coat," she said.

He looked at her with a boyish scowl, wary, on his guard.

"She said she could manage quite well with the one she has."

"She can't possibly."

"But, Caroline——" began Susan.

"It's all right, dear," interrupted Caroline. "Don't worry. I'll buy you one."

Kenneth's face flamed.

"Thanks very much, Caroline," he said, "but I can provide for my wife myself."

Caroline shrugged.

"That's apparently just what you can't do," she said.

He squared his shoulders aggressively.

"What exactly do you mean by that?"

"What I say. If you can't earn enough to keep Susan in decent comfort, she can easily go back to her own work. I've just been suggesting to her that she should do that. She could easily get a post in the neighbourhood, and then she could engage a trained maid and run the house properly."

His face darkened.

"Oh, so that's your idea, is it?" he said. "Well, I've had enough of your damned interference——"

Susan was suddenly as angry as he.

"How dare you speak to Caroline like that!" she flamed.

Throughout the interview Caroline had been cool and detached, showing no sign of emotion whatsoever.

"It's all right, Susan," she said quietly. "I'll go now."

"You *shan't* go," said Susan hysterically. "I *won't* have you driven away like this after all you've done for me."

Kenneth laid his hand imploringly on her arm, but she shook it off.

"Go away, I hate you."

His anger rose again at the rebuff.

"All right," he said, "I'll go." He threw a narrowed glance at Caroline. "There certainly doesn't seem to be room in this house for both of us."

With that he flung himself out, slamming the front door violently behind him.

Susan stared after him for a few moments in silence and then dropped sobbing into a chair.

"Oh Caroline . . . I'm so ashamed."

Caroline went over to her and placed an arm tenderly about her shoulders.

"It's all right, darling. Of course I don't mind. He didn't know what he was saying. You mustn't blame him."

"I do blame him. I hate him. I never want to see him again."

"Now, look here, Susan, you've had a hard time lately, and today has been the finishing touch. You must have a rest from it all. Come home with me for a few days. Just leave a note for Kenneth."

Susan raised tearful eyes.

"Oh Caroline," she gasped, "I couldn't."

"Why not?"

"Ken . . . he'd be furious." Caroline smiled.

"I bear him no malice at all, dear, as you know, but don't you think he deserves a little punishment?"

Susan shook her head again.

"I couldn't, Caroline."

"Just as you like, darling," said Caroline lightly. "It was selfish of me, of course. I was thinking how I'd love to have you to myself for a few days. It would be like old times. And I could look after you and spoil you. You must be tired with all this housework."

"I'd love to come, Caroline, but—oh, I mustn't."

Caroline rose.

"I'd better go now, dear."

"Must you really?"

"Yes, darling. Evelyn will be expecting me. . . ."

"I can't bear to let you go."

"Darling . . . come with me."

"Don't tempt me. I should hate myself if I did."

"You mustn't, then. But, Susan——"

"Yes."

"I don't bear the shadow of a grudge against Kenneth. You know that. But—he was very rude to both of us. . . . I shouldn't forgive him too easily if I were you. He ought to be made to realise how badly he's behaved."

"Yes, Caroline," said Susan miserably.

"And—don't worry, sweetheart. Meet me tomorrow in the town, and we'll have coffee and buy the coat——"

"You mustn't do that, Caroline."

"I'm going to, so it's no use arguing. And I shall be free all tomorrow because they're having a rehearsal for *Midsummer-Night's Dream* at St. Monica's, so we can have all the day together. And now I must go. Come and help me put on my hat."

Before Caroline went she held Susan closely to her and kissed her.

"Darling," she said, "you know you've got me behind you whatever happens, don't you?"

Susan clung to her tightly.

"I don't know what I'd do without you," she said.

Chapter Five

CAROLINE walked away from the little house with a heavy heart.

This marriage of Susan's was turning out disastrously, as indeed she had foreseen it would. She had felt an instinctive dislike of Kenneth from her first meeting with him, and (again she assured herself on that point) she had done her very best to prevent the marriage. There was, of course, a strain of weakness in Susan. She needed someone at hand to support her, to stiffen her resolution, to help her form and keep her decisions. Alone, she'd have let Kenneth ride roughshod over her.

Again Caroline was conscious of a deep thankfulness at the thought that she was there to comfort and reassure, to see that Susan's life was not completely spoilt by the marriage. Everything considered, it really would be best for her to take a teaching post again. She'd be independent of Kenneth then, have outside friends and interests, not be completely absorbed by household drudgery, as she was now in danger of becoming.

Kenneth's attitude to the plan was ridiculous. If he persisted in it, they must just ignore him. It might, of course, be necessary for Susan to come and live at home again. Her heart lightened at the thought. It would be lovely. . . . The three of them together as they had been before Susan married.

She slackened her pace as she neared Robert's house. It was a solid Victorian house on the outskirts of the town. Caroline looked with approval at the fresh net curtains that hung at the windows and the gleaming whiteness of the old-fashioned front doorsteps. Odd how a house could proclaim from afar, not by any particular feature, but by some elusive intangible suggestion, whether it was well or badly kept. This house had fairly shrieked neglect and incompetence when Effie was in charge of it. Nothing in it had ever been actually dirty. It had just been—Effie. She certainly hadn't neglected the house in order to go out and enjoy herself. She'd struggled along with it in her muddling ineffectual way—her fluffy hair tumbling about her face, her shoes down at heel, her apron torn and stained, cooking uneatable dishes, dropping brushes and dusters wherever she went (Robert generally found one or both in his chair when he sat down in the evening), always tidying and cleaning, yet somehow leaving everything as chaotic as it was before she started. She couldn't keep maids, she couldn't cook a decent meal or "turn out" a room properly, she couldn't manage the children. ... She'd made Robert acutely uncomfortable and had received all Caroline's offers of help with insolence and defiance. Poor Effie! She'd been little more than a child when Robert married her—a silly, pretty, spoilt child of seventeen. There again Caroline had foreseen trouble from the beginning. It wasn't only her inefficient housekeeping. It was the fact that there was no possibility of intellectual comradeship between them. Robert, though somewhat slow and heavy, was an intellectual man, and Effie had the mentality of a child of twelve. She had seemed sunny-tempered and good-humoured before marriage, but even that had not lasted long. She had soon turned sulky and resentful, blaming Caroline, illogically enough, for Robert's disappointment in her. It was about a year ago that Caroline had suggested to Robert that he should engage a mother's help to run the house properly. Effie had made one of her usual scenes over the proposition. It turned out that her chief objection was to Caroline's interviewing the applicants and engaging a suitable one, and Caroline had good-humouredly offered to stand aside and let Effie do it herself, but Robert had insisted on Caroline's doing it, and in the end Effie had sulkily given way.

It had been a kind providence that sent Evelyn Marston to them. Caroline had taken to her from the first. She was a well-bred cultured woman, with an excellent practical knowledge of housekeeping and an amazing fund of tact. She had lived abroad for many years, and Caroline had been afraid that she would find

Bartenham too dull, but she had settled down at once and got on so well with them all that it was difficult to realise she had only been there a year.

Effie had grown much quieter and more self-contained since her arrival, which was certainly an improvement; the children had become well-behaved and well-disciplined; while Robert found in her the intellectual companionship he needed. The problems of the entire household, indeed, seemed to have been solved.

Caroline knocked at the door, smiled pleasantly at the maid who opened it, gave a glance of commendation at the clean tidy hall, and entered the drawing-room. Evelyn sat at the window, a basket of household mending by her side.

She was a good-looking woman, dark, full-figured, her features just a little too pronounced. She was not very tall, but her upright carriage and assured manner made her seem taller than she was. She dressed well, in plain tailor-made clothes, and her dark hair was always immaculately waved and dressed.

Caroline's expression changed to one of disapproval as her eyes rested on Effie, who was curled up in an armchair, reading a novel. Her fair hair was untidy, she wore a shapeless tweed skirt and jumper, and there was a long wide ladder all the way up one stocking. The novel, Caroline knew without looking at it, was of the "trashy" kind.

Bubbles, a fat little girl of two, sat on the floor, playing with bricks.

Evelyn put down her mending and came across the room to greet Caroline.

"This is lovely," she said, kissing her. "I was so afraid that Susan would keep you by force."

"She tried to," smiled Caroline, "but I said I'd promised you faithfully to come on here before tea. And I've got to fly back immediately afterwards, because Fay's having a friend in."

"We must make the most of every minute of you, then," said Evelyn. "Let me take your coat."

Caroline slipped off her coat. Evelyn's welcome had given her again the warm happy feeling of being loved and needed that alone made life seem worth living to her. She went over to Effie and patted her shoulder affectionately.

"How are you, darling?" she said.

Effie raised her face from her book.

"Quite well, thanks, Caroline," she said and returned to her reading.

What a pity she was so unresponsive and ungracious, thought Caroline with a sigh. Everyone round her was doing all they could for her, and yet she didn't appear to feel a spark of gratitude. She was losing her looks, too. That sulky expression was drawing lines on her face that hadn't been there a year ago. Caroline shrugged and dropped on her knees beside Bubbles.

"Hello, sweet!" she said. "What are you doing?"

"Arny," Bubbles greeted her and laughed. Caroline built up a little tower of bricks, and Bubbles knocked them down, chuckling at Caroline's look of assumed surprise and dismay. Caroline had a way with children and always got on well with them.

Effie continued to read without raising her eyes again or speaking.

Evelyn came back and smiled at Caroline and Bubbles indulgently.

"Naughty auntie!" she said. "She's spoiling Bubbles—isn't she?—playing with her before tea. We don't let even Mummy do that, do we? But we'll let Auntie do it this once."

Caroline rose from her knees. Bubbles was an adorable little person—lovely to play with and cuddle—but Evelyn was quite right. She said that it was very important that a child should learn to play by itself and not expect to be entertained by other people, and, except for half an hour after tea, before she went to bed, Bubbles had to play by herself. She was a placid little thing and generally seemed happy enough with her bricks or Noah's ark.

"I must get you nice and clean for tea now, my pet," said Evelyn. She went across to Effie's chair and sat on the arm of it, putting a hand on her shoulder. "And what about this baby? Is she going to get nice and clean for tea, too? I thought she'd have changed earlier when she knew Caroline was coming." Leaning forward, she traced the course of the ladder up the slender leg with her finger. "Shocking!" she said. "Caroline will think I don't look after you at all, and I do really, don't I, darling? I'm always scolding you. . . ." She leant her head affectionately against Effie's hair and smiled at Caroline. "This is my youngest and naughtiest baby," she said.

Effie smiled rather constrainedly and went from the room. After a few moments Evelyn followed with Bubbles, and Caroline, left alone, took up a weekly review that lay on the table by the window.

It was opened at a crossword puzzle, which was finished except for two words. Some of the blanks were filled up in Robert's handwriting, some in Evelyn's. They were both fond of crossword puzzles and anagrams of the more abstruse kind. Last week they had been doing a German one, and Evelyn had rung her up several times for help.

While Caroline was puzzling over it, Effie entered. She had washed and tidied her hair and changed the offending stockings.

Caroline read out one of the clues to her from the paper.

"What on earth can it be?" she said pleasantly.

"I don't know," said Effie. "I can't do crossword puzzles."

She took her novel and curled up in the armchair again, as if Caroline were not there. Caroline conquered her feeling of irritation. One must try to be patient.

"What are you reading, dear?" she said.

Effie did not answer. Caroline's eyes grew grave. How ill-bred and badly-mannered the girl was! Poor Robert! It was the old story. He had yielded to a momentary infatuation, to find himself fettered for life to an uncongenial companion. It was what, she was afraid, was happening to Susan. She must at all costs prevent its happening to Fay. Not that she really thought there was much likelihood of its happening to Fay. Fay was too fine, too fastidious, for that sort of thing. And Fay was too fond of her. She could not imagine the child's ever wanting to leave her. She looked into the future and saw herself growing old, her old age sweetened by Fay's companionship, Fay's devotion. . . .

There came the sounds of the other two children returning from school, scampering upstairs to get ready for tea, then Evelyn's voice was heard, saying sharply, "Come here at *once*, Carrie."

Effie did not raise her head from her book, but her whole slender body went rigid. She sat there, tense, alert, listening. . . .

The next sound, however, was the tea-bell, and Effie uncoiled herself languidly from her chair and followed Caroline into the dining-room. Evelyn was at the head of the table behind the tea-tray, with Bubbles, in her high chair, by her side. Effie took her place at the foot of the table. Bobby, aged six, and Carrie, aged four, entered, their faces shining, their hair well brushed, kissed Caroline dutifully, then took their places at the table. Evelyn looked at them approvingly.

"It's all right," she said. "You can have jam today. You were in by half-past."

They were supposed to come straight home from school without loitering, and had to have dry bread instead of bread and jam if they were not in the house by half-past four. They set to work eagerly upon the thick well-spread slices. Evelyn poured out Bubbles' milk into a mug and held it to her lips. Bubbles objected, trying to take the mug into her own small fat hands.

"Bubbles hold it," she demanded.

"Very well," conceded Evelyn, "but remember, if you spill a *drop*, you'll be severely punished."

Sometimes Caroline wondered if Evelyn were a little too strict with the children, but when she thought of them as they had been before she took them in hand—noisy, insolent, disobedient—her doubts vanished. Effie had made several scenes with Evelyn about her treatment of them when first she came, but Robert had always supported Evelyn, and now Effie never interposed, except occasionally in the case of Bubbles.

Bubbles drank her milk slowly and carefully, then put down her mug with a little smile of triumph at Evelyn.

"Good girl," said Evelyn. She turned to Caroline. "When is your mother coming?"

"I've not heard yet," said Caroline. "I expect she'll come as soon as she's settled things up. I'm going to make the spare bedroom over the garden into a bed-sitting-room for her. I expect she'll want to be very quiet."

Effie looked at Caroline curiously.

"Do you remember what she's like at all?" she said.

"No, dear," said Caroline with a warning glance at the children.

"Effie's made such a pretty jumper for Carrie," said Evelyn. "You must show it to Caroline afterwards, darling."

Effie shrugged and said nothing more. Evelyn told Caroline about a new biography that she and Robert had been reading. As she talked she kept a keen eye on the children. They were not allowed to speak at meals, and, as any lapse in manners or deportment meant instant dismissal from the table and an end to the meal, they were at pains to behave well. Caroline often thought of meals at Effie's in the old days—the chattering and laughter and really appalling table manners.

Finally Bubbles folded her dimpled hands and said grace, and they all went back to the other room.

Caroline felt now at liberty to play bricks with Bubbles on the hearthrug. Bobby and Carrie sat at the table, looking at a children's annual. Effie took up her novel again.

"Mummy," said Bobby suddenly, "may I play with my train?"

"Yes, Bobby," said Effie.

"I think not, darling," put in Evelyn gently. "There really isn't room in here. You'll only be breaking or upsetting something."

"There's room if we move the table," said Bobby.

"I don't want the table moved. It's silly to disarrange the whole room just before bedtime like this. You must wait till your half holiday."

"It isn't *fair*," burst out Bobby.

"Bobby!" said Evelyn warningly.

Red with anger, Bobby returned to his book.

"Caroline, darling," said Evelyn, "do help us choose some material for the new spare room curtains. We've got a whole bookful of patterns, but we can't make up our minds." She went to her bureau and, taking out the book of patterns, began to turn over the pages. "We rather liked this, didn't we, Effie?"

Effie did not answer.

"Isn't it a little dark?" said Caroline, leaving Bubbles to play by herself and going over to Evelyn's bureau.

"Yes, perhaps it is," agreed Evelyn. "We weren't quite sure about it. We didn't want to decide in any case, of course, till we'd asked you. Just look them through and see if there's any you think would be better."

Caroline turned over the leaves of the pattern-book one by one, holding each to the light. It always pleased and flattered her to be consulted by Evelyn over household affairs like this, and Evelyn never failed to consult her. She seldom, indeed, made any decision affecting the household without first asking Caroline's advice.

"Mummy," said Carrie, "may I crayon?"

"Ask Auntie Evelyn," said Effie, without looking up from her book.

"May I, Auntie Evelyn?"

"Yes, darling, if you get a piece of newspaper to do it on. You mustn't put crayons on the table."

"This one's pretty, Evelyn," said Caroline.

"Yes, but would it go with the rest of the room?"

"I think so."

Effie put her book down and picked up Bubbles from the hearthrug.

"I'll have Bubbles upstairs till bedtime, Evelyn," she said.

"All right, darling," said Evelyn and flashed a quick smile at Caroline.

Effie was devoted to Bubbles, but one of her silly little affectations was to ignore her when Evelyn was present. Often, however, she would take her up to her own bedroom after tea for her official playtime.

"I think you're right, Caroline," went on Evelyn. "It's really much prettier than the other, and it would tone quite nicely with the wallpaper. I think I'll decide on that. Oh, there's something else I wanted to ask you. What *do* you use for the parquet at The Elms? It looks better than any others I ever see anywhere. We can never get ours to shine like that."

Caroline glowed and expanded as she gave Evelyn particulars of the polish she used, and then told her of several books to add to her library list.

"You may not like them, of course," she said.

"If you do, I'm certain to," said Evelyn. "I've never yet not liked a book you've told me to read, and I seem to hit on such rubbish when left to my own devices. I'm sure Robert will like them too. He enjoyed all those on the last list you gave us. You really are a wonderful person, Caroline. I've never known anyone else who could tell one the best floor polish *and* the best books. I simply don't know what any of us would do without you. Robert's always saying that."

"Rubbish!" said Caroline, but she flushed with pleasure. What a dear Evelyn was! How beautifully she ran the house and looked after the children! How nice to think that this home of Robert's had at last won through to peace and security!

From upstairs came the sounds of pattering feet and peals of laughter—Effie's and Bubbles'. Effie's was a rather foolish high-pitched little laugh. It used to irritate Caroline in the early days of the marriage, but one seldom heard it now except when she was alone with Bubbles like this.

Bobbie was advising Carrie about her crayoning.

"Cows must be brown, Carrie," he was saying. "You can't have a green cow." As Carrie rather reluctantly took up the brown crayon, he added, "You'd be frightened if a big cow like that ran after you, wouldn't you?"

"No, I wouldn't," said Carrie stoutly. "I'd knock it down and *twead* on it."

Caroline laughed, then rose from her seat.

"I must go, darling," she said to Evelyn.

"Can't you stay till Robert comes? He'll be so disappointed not to see you."

"I'm afraid I can't. Fay's having a friend to tea, you know."

"Oh yes . . . I remember . . . but why not let her have her alone?" Caroline smiled.

"She'd be heart-broken if I weren't there. She didn't want to

63

have her at all. She's an unsociable little thing, you know. I think she'd be perfectly happy to see no one but me from day's end to day's end."

"Very sensible of her," commented Evelyn. "I could even endure it myself."

Caroline smiled and said "Flatterer!" but she didn't really think that Evelyn was flattering her. Evelyn really was fond of her. She gave her constant proof of her affection. It was nice to be welcomed and made much of in this house, instead of being exposed to Effie's ungraciousness and insolence as she had been in the old days. Robert's loyalty had, of course, never faltered, and more than once he had made Effie apologise to her, but her visits had been uncomfortable, paid solely in obedience to that sense of duty that had always upheld her even in the most exacting tasks. It was all so different now. Even if unhappiness threatened Susan's home, she had cause for nothing but thankfulness here.

She kissed the children, sent a message of love to Effie, who was still playing with Bubbles upstairs, and hurried away, glancing at her watch every now and then, thinking how disappointed Fay would be if she were not back in time for tea.

Chapter Six

As Fay tidied her hair before the mirror she tried hard not to think how lovely it would be if Caroline didn't get back from Robert's in time for tea; but, however hard she tried, she couldn't quite shut out the picture of a pleasant *tête-à-tête* tea with Sybil, at which they could chatter and laugh and be as silly as they liked, and another picture of the same meal with Caroline there—Caroline, grave and aloof, very kind to Sybil, but, as Fay would know, criticising her silently all the time, steering the conversation away from foolish trivialities, smiling disapprovingly at Sybil's jokes. . . . She shook her head with an impatient little gesture, as if to shake the thought out of it. Caroline was perfect, so perfect that it made one despair of ever being worthy of her. But—she set her lips—she must try, try her very very hardest. She must fight down these disloyal thoughts as soon as they arose. And it wasn't only disloyal thoughts. It was actual deceit. Billy Dickson had come to watch the hockey match on Saturday and had talked to her and Sybil in the interval, and afterwards the three of them had walked back together as far as the Dicksons' house, and—she hadn't told Caroline about it. She'd tried to, but somehow her courage had failed her at the last moment. She hadn't even told her about Billy's walking with her to the pillar-box the other week. She'd kept putting it off all the next day, and, of course, after the next day it was too late. If she'd told her then, Caroline would have turned that grave penetrating look on her and said, "But, darling, why didn't you tell me about it at the time?" and she'd feel so guilty that—oh, she *couldn't*. Even now she felt guilty though she didn't quite know why. Then she thought of Billy, of his jolly friendly grin, of the kindness that underlay his cheerful banter, and the feeling of guilt died away. He and Sybil seemed to make life simple and pleasant, not, as Caroline made it, so heavy with responsibilities that sometimes one could hardly bear it. "You see, darling," Caroline would say, "I love you so much that I can't bear to see you being slack over the tiniest little thing. I'm always telling you how important little things are, aren't I? Every little thing you do goes to form a habit and it's your habits that make your character. And it isn't only yourself. You can never know how what you do and say may influence someone else for good or for bad. In every personal encounter I believe that we leave something of good or bad behind with the other person. . . ."

That was all right for Caroline, who was so perfect that she never need worry about it; but it worried Fay dreadfully. She had an uncomfortable feeling of not doing her duty if ever she wasn't feeling earnest and responsible and trying to form a good character. She knew that she was terribly unsuccessful, and that whatever character she was forming certainly wasn't a good one, and that she was far too unimportant to have any influence over other people at all, but that if she hadn't been it would have been for bad.

The pleasure she took in Sybil's and Billy's light-heartedness was, of course, yet another proof of her general unworthiness, because, as Caroline often said, one shouldn't fritter away one's energy on inessential things, and, though the jokes that Sybil and Billy made and the pranks their high spirits led them into were innocent enough, they certainly weren't in any way essential.

When Fay went to tea there last week they had all laughed heartily over an old-fashioned sentimental novel that Billy had discovered in a secondhand bookshop. Billy had lent it to a friend, but he and Sybil knew whole pages by heart and repeated them dramatically to Fay.

"You must read it," said Billy. "It's priceless. The chap who's got it now is bringing it back tonight. I'll post it on to you, shall I?"

"Oh *no*," Fay had said quickly, and then had coloured at their look of mild surprise.

She couldn't explain that Caroline saw everything that came by post as a matter of course and opened all her letters, if she were not on the spot to open them herself. She seemed to see Caroline taking the book out of its wrappings, frowning slightly as she looked at its title, and saying "What's this, dear?" And Caroline, of course, wouldn't think it funny. Caroline disapproved of "making fun of serious things," and, as most things seemed to be serious in her eyes, there wasn't much left to make fun of.

Billy had seemed to sense something of her fear.

"All right," he had said reassuringly. "I'll give it to Sybil to bring to school for you."

"Thank you," she said.

She still spoke rather doubtfully. Even if he did that Caroline would be sure to see it. Caroline went through all her drawers and cupboards regularly to make sure that they were tidy. She liked Fay's things to be kept exactly as they had been kept when she was a little girl and would comment adversely on any alteration or innovation made by Fay. It wasn't that she was inquisitive or suspicious. It was just that it never occurred to her that Fay wanted any privacy.

Fay often thought with envy of the little bureau that Sybil had in her bedroom, in which she could lock up anything she didn't want people to see. Last Christmas she had almost asked Caroline if she might have one too, but she had realised in time how deeply the suggestion would have hurt her. She knew that Caroline only felt like that because she loved her so, and life without Caroline's love would be unthinkable, unbearable, and therefore it was ridiculous to complain when it seemed irksome. One couldn't have things both ways. . . .

She leant out of the window to see if Sybil were coming yet. She'd said that she couldn't be here till half-past five, because she had a test-paper to do and must be at school till five. It seemed rather silly to ask her on a day when she would only be able to stay such a short time, but Caroline had said that that day was most convenient for her.

There was no sign of Sybil, so she turned from the window and began to move restlessly about the room, putting away the navy blue skirt and white blouse she had just taken off. Sybil had never been to tea before, and it was terribly important that Caroline should like her. If Caroline didn't, of course, it would be the end of the friendship. Caroline wouldn't let her invite her again, and she couldn't go on being friendly with someone she couldn't ask to the house. Last night she'd said to Caroline that she wished Sybil weren't coming to tea today. The memory of that made her feel deeply ashamed. Somehow she hadn't been able to help saying it, so acutely aware had she been of Caroline's unspoken longing for her to say it.

She hoped that Susan and Evelyn had been nice to Caroline, so that she'd be in a good temper. Effie wouldn't have been nice to her, of course—she never was—but no one took any notice of Effie. Fay had rather liked Effie once, but then Effie had begun to say horrible untrue things about Caroline, and after that, of course, she had avoided her.

Again she pictured Sybil and Caroline and herself having tea, and again her heart sank. If only . . . She wished she could give Sybil a hint, but, of course, she couldn't without being terribly disloyal to Caroline. Only—it would be all right if Sybil made rather a fuss of Caroline, asked her advice about something, seemed to admire her. It was hateful to think that, but it had happened so often. There was Freda Torrent, a fat stupid girl in the Upper Fifth, who'd been a private pupil of Caroline's and had a "crush" on her. She brought her flowers, and discussed spiritual difficulties with her, and asked her advice, and confided her troubles in her, and kept gazing at her sentimentally and saying, "Oh Miss Cunliffe!"

Caroline was always suggesting that Fay should ask her to tea, but Fay disliked her so much that she never did. Caroline, of course, was kind-hearted and conscientious and felt that she ought to influence Freda for good. . . .

Oh well, it was no use worrying about it. She'd go down and see that everything was ready. They'd decided to have a high tea with eggs, as it would be so late. She had to pass the spare room door to reach the stairs, and on an impulse she opened it and went in. She knew that Caroline had already begun to get it ready for her mother. Yes, the spotted muslin curtains hung at the windows. An easy-chair, brought up from the morning-room, stood by the fireplace, and next to it a small table that Caroline had bought in the town yesterday. There was a footstool by the chair. How kind and thoughtful Caroline was! Already the place looked cosy and homelike. Caroline's mother was very lucky to have a daughter like Caroline. She, Fay, must try to be kind to her, too. She'd read to her, and go out for walks with her, walking very slowly and guiding her carefully over the crossings. She'd probably be nervous in traffic. Old people always were. She hoped she wouldn't be *terribly* deaf—so deaf that one would have to learn the deaf alphabet in order to talk to her. On the whole, Fay rather wished she weren't coming.

She heard the sound of the opening of the front door and went slowly downstairs. Caroline was just entering the hall.

"Hello, darling!" she said. "I'm back in good time, after all. Were you getting worried? Has Sybil come?"

"Not yet."

Caroline put her arm through Fay's affectionately and drew her towards the stairs.

"Come and talk to me while I take my things off. How did you get on with the German essay?"

A sudden unexpected fury seized Fay. She couldn't understand it. She'd never felt it before. It took her entirely by surprise. The touch of Caroline's hand on her arm, the sound of Caroline's voice asking about the German essay, made her want to scream, to fling her arm off, to run away—right away—and never come back. . . . She controlled herself with an effort and went upstairs with Caroline, telling her in a rather unsteady voice what the German mistress had said about the essay. . . .

She was glad when the ringing of the front-door bell announced Sybil's arrival. She went downstairs to open the door. Sybil was laughing and breathless.

"Am I late?" she panted. "I've run like the devil. We had the foulest test-paper you ever saw. I don't suppose I shall get a mark. . . ."

"Come along in and take your things off," said Fay, glad that Caroline was still upstairs and couldn't have heard "like the devil."

"Old Monks will be livid," went on Sybil, still laughing as she came into the hall. "She put 'execrable' on my last report, so I don't know what she'll find to put on the next. Isn't 'execrable' a heavenly word? I wouldn't have missed having it for anything. I'd never come across it before and I keep trying to say it to myself, but I can never get more than half-way through. . . . Where shall I put my things? I'm an awful sight. Do you mind? I came straight from school. We had gym this morning, and I've not had a minute to change."

Sybil was short and plump, with a round rosy face, mischievous brown eyes, and brown curly hair. She wore her gym tunic with white blouse and school tie. Caroline was coming downstairs now. Sybil stepped forward and held out her hand.

"How do you do, Miss Cunliffe?" she said. "I hope I'm not too terribly late."

"Of course not, dear," said Caroline graciously. "Come straight in. Tea's all ready."

They went into the dining-room, and Caroline took her place behind the tea-tray.

That strange feeling of sudden fury had left Fay rather shaken. She still couldn't understand it. It was as incomprehensible as the sudden desire to cry that sometimes came to her nowadays for no reason at all.

"I had my tea at Robert's," said Caroline as she took up the teapot, "so I can give my whole energies to seeing that you both have a good tea. Take an egg, Sybil. You've got to have two, you know. What was your paper like?"

Fay wished that Caroline either hadn't come home to tea or had asked Sybil to tea on a day when she could have had it with them. She looked just like a mistress in charge, sitting up straight behind the tea-tray and eating nothing. But it took more than that to overawe Sybil. Sybil had disposed of her test-paper in a few cheerful sentences. "Didn't know a thing. Not a darn thing. The only date I know is the battle of Waterloo, and they didn't ask it. I think history's awful rot, anyway, don't you? I don't care two hoots who conquered what or where or why, and I don't see why anyone else should."

Caroline smiled rather constrainedly, and Sybil continued to chatter light-heartedly as she ate her way through an extremely hearty tea. She made fun of the mathematical mistress, who was a great friend of Caroline's. She said that she didn't care a damn whether she passed the exam, or not. She described some of the pranks played by herself and her brothers and sisters on each other. She mimicked an aunt, who was "so pi, my dear, you'd hardly believe. Literally *lives* in church." And she ignored Caroline, addressing all her remarks to Fay. That, of course, as Fay knew, was the crowning sin. If she'd made a fuss of Caroline it would have been all right. It wasn't that Caroline was conceited. She was the least conceited person in the world. It was that—oh, it was difficult to explain even to oneself. It all came back to the fact that she loved Fay so much that she couldn't bear to feel shut out even from a school friendship. It had to include her, too, or else somehow or other it had to come to an end. And a school friendship that included Caroline—Caroline going for walks with them, Caroline having tea with them, Caroline reading with them—wasn't a friendship at all. Fay had experienced several of them, and none had lasted long. It all came back to the fact of Caroline's love surrounding her on all sides, guarding, protecting her, hemming her in, choking her, like some soft, warm, clinging mist.

The tea-party certainly wasn't being a success. Caroline sat silent at the head of the table, her grave eyes fixed on Sybil . . . weighing her in the balance, finding her wanting. Fay made a desperate effort to save the situation, talking in a quick nervous voice, appealing to Caroline, trying to draw her into the conversation, but it was useless. She couldn't make Sybil see how terribly Caroline mattered.

To Sybil Caroline didn't matter at all. She was just someone's rather dull grown-up sister. She had grown-up sisters of her own who ignored her and whom she in her turn ignored. She didn't understand about Caroline, probably wondered what on earth she was doing there at all.

"Billy said he thought you played a top-hole game in the match on Saturday," Sybil was saying, "though he told you that himself, didn't he?"

Fay threw a quick glance at Caroline, but Caroline's eyes remained fixed on the volatile little guest, who was merrily and unconsciously damning herself with almost every word she uttered.

Billy . . . yes, that was really why Fay couldn't bear the thought of losing this friendship. Beneath his hilarity was the hint of a tenderness that was new to her, a tenderness that wasn't exacting like Caroline's, that didn't want to possess one entirely, that wanted one to go on belonging to oneself. She had an odd sense of relief when she was with him, as if everything was all right and she needn't worry about anything. But . . . it was all over now. Caroline didn't like Sybil, and that meant that it was the end. It was no use struggling against it. Caroline was too strong.

"Oh, I've brought that book we were telling you about," went on Sybil. "You'll simply howl over it."

Fay coloured and glanced again at Caroline, but Caroline didn't look at her.

When they got up from tea Sybil said, "You've never shown me your bedroom, Fay. Come on."

Fay felt guilty and ill-at-ease as she took Sybil upstairs. When she'd been to tea at Sybil's, the two of them had gone up to Sybil's bedroom afterwards and stayed there, gossiping and examining all Sybil's belongings, and, of course, Sybil didn't realise that it was different here.

Sybil looked round Fay's room with approval.

"What a jolly little place!" she said. "Let's stay here. Your sister won't want us messing about downstairs, will she? Let's be cosy." She drew up the armchair to the fireplace, pushed Fay into it, and, sitting down on the hearthrug, switched on the electric fire. "Isn't it jolly?"

"Perhaps we ought to go down," said Fay unhappily.

"Why on earth?" protested Sybil. "It's so nice up here. I'm quite certain your sister won't want us."

That wasn't the point. The point was that they ought to want Fay's sister, but—somehow Fay couldn't explain that, couldn't explain the unpardonable offence that their staying upstairs by themselves would be in Caroline's eyes. So she took the line of least resistance, leaning back in the chair, listening to Sybil's chatter, aware of Caroline in every nerve, listening intently for every sound from downstairs. Caroline wouldn't be angry, of course. She never was angry. She'd be "hurt," which was so much worse.

At the sound of Caroline's footsteps on the stairs her heart began to beat unevenly. The door opened, and Caroline stood on the threshold.

"Whatever are you children doing up here?" she said. "I couldn't think what had happened to you."

She was smiling, but her eyes were very blue.

"We thought you wouldn't want us downstairs," said Fay. Her eyes shifted guiltily from Caroline's as she spoke.

"Nonsense!" smiled Caroline. She went over to the electric fire and switched it off. "You monkeys! Wasting electricity like this when there's a fire in the drawing-room!"

"I'm sorry," said Fay, flushing.

"Come along," went on Caroline cheerfully. "Let's all go down to the drawing-room and have a chat, though——" She glanced at her watch and left the sentence unfinished.

Sybil leapt to her feet.

"I must go, mustn't I? It's terribly late."

They followed Caroline downstairs. Sybil put on her hat and coat in the hall, said goodbye to Caroline, and went down to the gate, accompanied by Fay.

"Thanks so much, old thing," she said. "It's been great. You must come along and see us soon. Billy wants to teach you Mah Jongg. ... He can't play for nuts himself, but that's a detail, of course."

A wave of thankfulness swept over Fay. It hadn't been so terrible, then, that Sybil would never want to have anything more to do with her. The thankfulness was followed by a sudden sinking of her heart. It didn't, after all, depend on Sybil. It depended on Caroline. . . .

Caroline greeted her cheerfully on her return to the house and began to tell her about the new curtains at Robert's, and how Carrie had said, "I'd knock it down and *twead* on it." If her eyes hadn't still been very blue, and if she hadn't avoided any mention of Sybil, Fay might have thought that the afternoon had been quite a success. Throughout dinner Caroline continued to talk pleasantly of trivial matters, though Fay was well aware of the invisible breach between them that Sybil's visit had caused. It wasn't only that Sybil had ignored Caroline and talked foolishly and irresponsibly, "making fun of serious things" and using a good deal of what Caroline called "undesirable slang." It was that she had seemed to consider Fay and herself united in a freemasonry of youth from which Caroline was excluded. That would not be mentioned, of course, but that, Fay dimly realised, was the cardinal sin.

"You're looking very tired, darling," said Caroline as they rose from the table. "I do wish you hadn't to start on your home-work now. You really ought to go straight to bed."

"I haven't much to do, Caroline."

"My dear, you have the French prose and unseen, haven't you? If you hadn't had Sybil to tea you could have got most of it done before dinner. You must please yourself, of course, but honestly, dear, I think it rather foolish to have people to tea when you're working for your scholarship."

"But, Caroline——" began Fay.

"Yes, I know, dear. I agreed to your having her because you couldn't go to her birthday party, but I think it was a great mistake. It's a kind of vicious circle, you see. Now you've asked her here, she'll ask you back again. It's such a complete waste of time all round. It isn't as if it did you any sort of good. I know you need recreation, but we can easily find something that's worth while *and* a change from your work."

Fay was silent.

It meant the end of her friendship with Sybil, she thought. And with Billy.

Caroline had taken her usual seat by the fire, drawing Fay gently down to the hearthrug at her feet. She sat there, very straight, not leaning back against Caroline's knee, her eyes fixed on the fire, her lips set, her cheeks flushed.

"Darling," Caroline began tenderly, "I don't think Sybil has a very good influence on you. You're not quite—*my* Fay when you're with her. . . . I don't mind her rudeness to me at all, of course——"

"She didn't mean to be rude to you, Caroline," put in Fay breathlessly.

"I dare say not, dear. Ill-bred people never realise that they're ill-bred. She hardly spoke to me at tea time, although I was her hostess, and—well, I thought that staying up there in your room after tea was in very bad taste. I don't blame you for that, dear, because I know that it was a thing you'd never have thought of doing yourself, and, of course, as she was your guest you had to do what she suggested."

Fay opened her lips to explain to Caroline that Sybil didn't understand, that people just did what they liked in her house, and no one minded what anyone else did. Then she shut them again. It wasn't any use trying to fight against Caroline. She was too strong.

"And, darling," went on Caroline, "what was it she said about her brother's having been at the hockey match?"

Fay's slender form went rigid.

"Oh yes. . . . He did. . . . It was last Saturday."

"You didn't mention it to me."

"Didn't I?"

"No. . . . What exactly happened?"

"Nothing. He just came to watch the match, and talked to us in the interval."

"Talked to whom?"

"Sybil and me."

"Did he stay to the end?"

"Yes. . . . We all went home together. As far as Sybil's, I mean."

"I see. . . . He didn't walk home with you, did he?"

"No—but,"—Fay hesitated for a moment, then went on jerkily—"Caroline . . . would it have mattered much if he had?"

Caroline laughed.

"Of course not, darling, but it would have been a little suggestive of Doris Pemberton, wouldn't it?"

Fay drew a deep breath. It was spoilt now. Spoilt for ever. Doris Pemberton, who paraded the streets of Bartenham with an innumerable succession of "boys"—flashily dressed, giggling, ogling every man she met . . . Doris, who had been the joke and scandal of the school till the head mistress had asked her parents to remove her last year on the grounds that she was doing so little work that it was useless for her to remain there . . . Doris, who stood for all that was cheap and tawdry and second-rate. She'd never be able to go anywhere with Billy now without thinking of that. . . . Oh well, it would have been spoilt anyway, so it didn't really matter. She rose wearily.

"I'd better do my home-work now, hadn't I?"

She fetched her case from the hall and, sitting down at Caroline's desk, where she generally worked after tea, began the piece of French translation that had been set for tomorrow. But she couldn't concentrate, could hardly see the words even. If only she could have played herself back to peace, as she used to when things went wrong before she gave up music. Tears welled suddenly into her eyes. She rose abruptly and, controlling herself sufficiently to say, "I've left a book upstairs, Caroline," went quickly from the room.

Upstairs she locked her bedroom door and flung herself on her bed. It was a physical relief to give way to the oppression that choked her, to sob in a luxurious abandonment of grief. She didn't know why she was crying. It would be terrible if Caroline came up and found her . . . asked what was the matter . . . tried to comfort her. She couldn't *bear* that. With a great effort she checked her sobs, rose from the bed, and examined her reflection carefully in the glass. No, Caroline wouldn't notice anything. Her eyes were red-rimmed, but they were often inflamed in the evening. If Caroline mentioned it, she'd say that they were smarting again, and Caroline would make some more boracic lotion for her.

Downstairs Caroline still sat back in her chair, gazing into the fire. She felt very tired and was surrendering to an unwonted access of self-pity. If only they didn't all seem to need her every minute of every day! It drained her vitality till she felt utterly exhausted. She was fairly happy about Robert's household now, but there was Susan entangled in a marriage that seemed to hold no possibility of happiness, and there was Fay, who required such constant help and guidance. Fay was weak, and her weakness laid her open to unworthy friendships, unworthy interests. She would never knowingly do wrong, but she lacked judgement, and was too easily influenced. Quite obviously these Dicksons weren't good for her. That danger, however, was over. Fay was really very sensible, quick always to perceive and acknowledge when she had been at fault. But—she felt so tired with the strain of it all, the heavy unremitting burden of responsibility. And—there would soon be another claim on her care and protection. Perhaps, after all, she'd been unwise in asking her mother to come here without first finding out more about her. . . . Then she braced herself to the task she had undertaken. She'd never shirked her duty yet, and she wasn't going to start now. . . . She'd carried so much on her shoulders all these years that a little more would make no difference. Robert . . . Susan . . . Fay. . . . Beneath the weariness and depression stirred the almost sensual thrill of gratification that the thought of their dependence on her always brought with it.

Chapter Seven

MAGGIE stood in the hall, fidgeting nervously, while Nana arranged her scarves and necklaces. She'd put on far too many scarves and necklaces, as she always did when she was frightened or flustered. It consoled her and gave her a feeling of protection, as though she were a knight going into battle, and the festoons of beads and silk her armour. Usually Nana was ruthless in removing the superfluous ones, but today, sensing something of her mistress's agitation, she left them all on, merely arranging them so that as many as possible should be concealed beneath her coat. Charles stood at the front door, looking up at the sky and wondering whether to take an umbrella. It looked fussy and elderly to carry an umbrella when it wasn't raining. On the other hand he had a new suit on and didn't want to get it wet. Perhaps it would be best to suggest Maggie's taking one, then if it rained he could hold it over her and keep the rain off himself at the same time. He hummed softly under his breath. He was feeling quite excited at the thought of meeting Philippa again. She'd been, he remembered, rather an exciting sort of person. She'd have lost her looks, of course. The kind of life she'd presumably led was generally considered ageing. Splendid of Caroline to give her a home. That girl was a brick.

"Have you got your handkerchief, Miss Maggie?" Nana was saying, and Maggie at once began a feverish search through all her pockets, sending the scarves and necklaces that Nana had so carefully arranged flying in all directions.

Perhaps it would be a graceful gesture to take her some flowers, thought Charles. He could easily buy some on the way. Charles always enjoyed making little presentations of flowers. He'd taken some chrysanthemums to Mrs. Lawrence this morning because he'd found out quite by chance that it was her birthday, and he'd given Mrs. Ludlow a buttonhole of violets when he had coffee with her in the town yesterday. Both had been prettily grateful—Mrs. Ludlow especially—and it had made him feel delightfully young and debonair. Everything had been going well with him lately. His morning's measurement had shown nearly a quarter of an inch decrease in his waist compared with the same day last year (he kept records carefully in a little note-book), and Mrs. Lawrence had giggled and said, "Don't talk such nonsense," when he referred to himself as an "old man."

"There! You're quite tidy now," Nana was saying soothingly. She had discovered the handkerchief in Maggie's handbag and had tucked the superfluous scarves and necklaces neatly away again.

"Hadn't you better take an umbrella, dear?" said Charles solicitously. "It looks as if it might rain."

"Do you think so?" said Maggie, all her agitation returning at the thought that it might rain.

"I'm certain to leave it somewhere. I always do. What do you think, Nana?"

"Better take one, Miss Maggie," said Nana, "then it will do for both of you if it comes on to rain."

She glanced at Charles as she spoke, and he tried not to look like a small boy detected in an act of deceit.

"And come back by six," went on Nana firmly. "You know you'll be overtired if you don't."

They set off together down the road.

"How long is it since she went away, Charles?"

"Who, dear?" said Charles, rousing himself from vague daydreams of waist measurements and flower presentations.

"You know . . ." said Maggie nervously.

"Oh yes. . . . Thirty years," said Charles and felt somewhat depressed at the thought because it made him seem so old.

"I'm very worried about it, Charles," went on Maggie tremulously.

"Why?" said Charles.

"It doesn't seem right by Gordon. I'm sure he wouldn't have

allowed it if he'd been alive, and I'm sure it would have made Father very angry indeed."

"Y-yes," agreed Charles, "but, after all, it's a long time ago, you know. Half the people in Bartenham weren't here when she ran away. And, anyway, people soon forget."

"It wasn't her running away, Charles," protested Maggie. "I often used to want to run away myself, but I daren't, because I knew that wherever I went Father would find me and bring me back and be *terribly* angry. . . . It was running away with a *man*."

Miss Maguire, the Vicar's daughter, was passing them. Charles took off his hat and gave her a pleasant but strictly impersonal smile. He was rather scared of unmarried women, especially those who were "getting on" and might be supposed to have matrimonial designs on him for want of anyone younger. He'd once been asked his intentions by a Victorian parent, and he'd never quite got over the shock.

"I shouldn't worry about it, Maggie, if I were you," he said gently. "After all, it's Caroline's business, and if she feels it's the right thing to do . . ."

"Oh, of *course*," said Maggie hastily. "Please don't think I'm criticising Caroline, Charles." She looked quite terrified at the idea that anyone might think she was criticising Caroline. "I wouldn't do that for a moment. Not for a moment. Caroline knows best, of course."

He glanced down at her and wished that he knew how to put her tidy with a few deft touches as Nana did. She had looked quite tidy when they set out, but now the necklaces had all escaped their moorings, her hair was coming down, and her hat was on one side. He was afraid that the very sight of her would irritate Caroline, who was always so scrupulously neat. And probably she'd ask her about the piano again, and that would irritate Caroline, too. She never irritated him, however stupid she was or however often she asked the same question. He saw her, not as an exasperating old woman, but as a frightened little girl in a holland pinafore with very thin legs and black woollen stockings that were always coming down and at which she kept making nervous little dabs to pull them up. No one else, of course, could be expected to see her like that.

He stood for a moment at the front door and drew himself up to his full height before ringing the bell. He had reluctantly decided against the flowers. It would be a little difficult, he thought, to take flowers to Philippa and not to Caroline, who was his hostess. And two bunches of flowers would look silly.

The maid showed them into the drawing-room, where Richard Oakley stood by the fireplace.

He turned round as they entered.

"Oh, there you are!" he said. "Caroline asked me to make her apologies. She'll be down in a moment. She's just gone up to Mrs. Meredith."

"When did she arrive?" said Charles rather nervously.

"Not till this afternoon. Caroline was expecting her last night."

"I know."

"There was some sort of a breakdown on the Paris line, it appears. Caroline persuaded her to go upstairs and rest till tea-time."

"You've not seen her, then?" said Charles, studying himself furtively in the mirror and pulling down his waistcoat.

"No. ..." Richard was moving restlessly about the room, obviously ill-at-ease and worried. "I only hope this isn't going to be too much for Caroline."

"I can't feel it's right," put in Maggie tearfully. "Gordon was always so particular. Nearly as particular as Father. But, of course," she added hastily, "Caroline knows best."

"Here they are," whispered Richard.

The door opened and Philippa entered, followed by Caroline. Charles looked at her. He'd forgotten how tall she was and how well she carried herself. He'd forgotten, too, how lovely she was. Her age, which she made no attempt to hide, detracted nothing from her loveliness. Her hair, though now silver, had the soft natural wave of her girlhood. The crow's-feet round her deep-set eyes seemed only to emphasise their beauty. The lines from nose to mouth couldn't hide the perfect curves of the lips. Her pale skin was smooth and unwrinkled. Her beauty, he remembered, had always consisted less in actual features than in the moulding of her face. The outline of cheek and jaw was still exquisite.

She came across the room to Charles and Maggie with outstretched arms.

"How nice to see you again!" she said.

She kissed Maggie tenderly, reassuringly. Charles remembered that she had always understood about the frightened little girl in the holland pinafore with the untidy stockings, though, of course, she'd never seen her.

Maggie heaved a long quivering sigh. Quite suddenly it was all right. One needn't worry any more about Gordon and Father and Philippa running away. It was all right. She didn't know why, but she knew it was all right. Philippa was shaking hands with Charles now.

"Why, Charles, you've hardly changed at all," she was saying.

Charles blushed with pleasure.

"I've put on a bit of weight, I'm afraid," he said.

"Oh, we've all done that," laughed Philippa, "and secretly we think it rather becoming."

"This is Mr. Oakley," said Caroline. "I don't think you've met him before. He wasn't in Bartenham when you lived here."

Philippa greeted Richard with her pleasant unaffected smile. Charles watched her covertly. Beautiful. A finished woman of the world. And you felt that for all her charm and beauty she was capable and courageous. She'd be the mistress of any situation in which she found herself. She made Caroline seem suddenly rather immature—immature, angular, and a little spinsterish. Poor Caroline! She'd struggled along so wonderfully, looking after the whole family. It would be nice for her to be looked after in her turn. And Philippa, he was sure, would look after her. He had doubted the wisdom of this invitation of Caroline's, but now one glance at Philippa told him that it would be magnificently justified. Maggie was sitting next to her, listening to her, quite happy and at her ease, not frightened at all. It was a great relief to him that Maggie wasn't frightened.

"Is Bartenham just the same?" Philippa was saying. "Do tell me all about it. Is the funny little High Street modernised and widened? I hope it isn't."

Caroline watched her gravely. So often in her dream she had welcomed home the broken-down wreck of womanhood or the flashy hardened demimondaine, that she could have played her part with either automatically. But the reality—this poised and charming woman of the world—disconcerted her. Somehow she'd never even considered the possibility of her being still beautiful. And her clothes! Caroline's lips hardened into a tight line as she looked at them. They must have cost a small fortune. While she'd been straining every nerve, working day and night to bring up the children, this woman must have been living in luxury, spending probably as much on a single dress as would have kept them all for weeks. But, of course, Caroline had to admit to herself, she couldn't have known that they were in need. No one had written to her. Her father had been well off when she left him. She translated the obscure resentment that this woman's appearance roused in her into terms of righteous disapproval. Personal extravagance was unpardonable at a time when there was so much real want in the world. Then—she had expected her to show a little embarrassment, a little contrition, at their meeting, but she hadn't done. She had been completely assured.

"Caroline, it's sweet of you to ask me here," she had said, but not brokenly, ashamedly, as Caroline had always pictured her saying it. It was Caroline who, illogically, had felt embarrassed, Caroline, with all her loving forgiveness left, as it were on her hands. She watched her now with narrowed blue eyes. There was something brazen in the way she was asking questions about Bartenham. One would have imagined that the very thought of her old associations with the town would have filled her with shame. But, of course, a woman who had led the life she had led would naturally be hardened. She must be patient, very very patient. She had undertaken the task, and she mustn't flinch from it just because it was turning out to be more distasteful than she had realised it would be.

They were all laughing at something Philippa had just said, and again a wave of anger surged over Caroline. She had meant this little gathering to be a solemn pledge of family forgiveness. She hadn't meant it to form a sort of court round Philippa, laughing at her jokes, encouraging her frivolous reminiscences. And they seemed to have forgotten her, Caroline, completely. Even Richard seemed to have forgotten her.

"He used to wear a straw hat all the year, winter and summer," Philippa was saying, "and an enormous muffler that went about three times round his neck and hung down to his ankles."

"Yes, I remember, Philippa," said Maggie eagerly. "His aunt had made it for Christmas. She'd ordered too much wool by mistake, and she said it was a pity to waste it, because it wouldn't really have come in for anything else."

"And is Mr. Cookson still at the Parish Church?" said Philippa.

"Rather!" smiled Richard.

"He used to be so, terribly absent-minded. I remember his mother once telling me that in the night he'd strike a match to look at his watch, then throw his watch into the fireplace and put the match under his pillow."

Caroline's cool grave voice cut across their laughter.

"He's a very hard-working man and does a lot of good in the town."

There was a sudden silence, and the frightened look came back into Maggie's eyes.

"Yes, of course, Caroline," she said nervously.

"We'll have tea now, shall we?" said Caroline. "Will you ring the bell, please, Richard?

"What's happened about that business of Boughton's, Richard?" she went on, referring to a local lawsuit of which Philippa could know nothing. "Is it going to be settled soon?"

Philippa relaxed in her chair and looked about the room. So she was back again. After thirty years. What scenes had taken place in this room between her and Gordon! She remembered sitting in that chair by the window and thinking that her heart was broken, that there was nothing left to live for. It must have been partly her fault, of course, though at the time it had seemed wholly his. A light-hearted inexperienced girl, she had fallen in love with his looks, and he with hers. It had been a short engagement, and during it there had been no serious clashes between them. They were both shy, deeply in love with each other, excessively polite to each other. It had been rather like a courtly minuet. Then came the marriage, and after that they had settled down to the serious business of life. The glamour with which her love had invested him soon vanished, and she found him narrow, intolerant, and domineering. He allowed her no will of her own. She was to obey him implicitly in everything on pain of his grave displeasure. Looking back in after-years she could find it in her heart to pity him as well as herself. He was obsessed by an unremitting sense of duty, weighed down by an ever-present burden of moral responsibility. He ruthlessly suppressed the softer side of his character, distrusting enjoyment of any sort, even the most innocent. Life must be consistently grim and earnest. He had tried to mould her to his pattern, crushing her youth as he had crushed his own. She was too proud and independent to submit, and there were constant scenes between them, scenes in which she wept and upbraided him, while he remained stern, aloof, controlled.

When the children came—first Caroline, then Marcia—it was inevitable that she should disapprove of his treatment of them. He was not unkind, but he repressed them continually, checking their natural impulses, crushing their childish exuberance, trying to instil into them almost from babyhood his own exaggerated sense of duty and responsibility.

Caroline, naturally serious and docile, had responded readily enough, but Marcia was headstrong and high-spirited, passionately resentful of discipline. The struggle between husband and wife intensified as the children grew older. Philippa deliberately encouraged in them the light-heartedness that their father wished to repress. She protected them from his displeasure, hid their misdemeanours from him, accused him of wanting to turn them into little prigs and hypocrites. The children were growing up in an atmosphere of open dissension. It gradually became clear to Philippa that her championship of them was doing more harm than good. And yet she could not stand by without protest and watch Gordon force them into the mould of his own character. He had already succeeded with Caroline. She was not a prig exactly—there was something too sweet and sound at the core of her for that—but she was earnest and conscientious, imbued with an anxious desire to do her duty and fulfil her responsibilities that was as ludicrous as it was pathetic in a child of four. Already she was looking at Philippa with disapproving eyes. She was Gordon's child, as Marcia was Philippa's. Something of the bitterness of the parents' struggle was entering into the children's relationship with each other. Even Marcia, thought Philippa, would be better without her. She was happy-natured, living entirely in the present, forgetting her punishments as soon as they were over, accepting life as it came, gaily and heedlessly. Better for both that they should be brought up entirely by Gordon than that their childhood should be made the battlefield on which their parents' bitterness fought itself out. It was just as she was coming to this conclusion that she met Freddy Warrington. Freddy was the opposite of Gordon. He was gloriously irresponsible. He could and did make a joke of everything that came his way. He had charm, wit, good looks, and no sense of duty at all. He fell in love with Philippa and Philippa fell in love—not so much with the man himself as with the contrast he presented to Gordon. It was such a relief to be able to laugh over foolish little jokes without being checked by a stern glance and a frown, to feel that she could say whatever came into her head without first wondering whether it was, according to Gordon's golden rule of conversation, "kind and true and necessary." She promised to run away with him on an impulse and kept her promise without giving herself time to think it over. She would still have gone with him, even if she had given herself time to think it over. Life with Gordon had become impossible. The whole house was being poisoned by their antagonism.

She lived with Freddy for two years and then they separated. Freddy wanted to marry her when Gordon divorced her, but she had discovered by then that the very irresponsibility that had delighted her so much at first had its drawbacks. Freddy was always ready to take the way of least resistance, and the way of least resistance not infrequently led him into quagmires from which he could only extricate himself by actual dishonesty. Yet he was as well meaning in his way as Gordon had been in his. Philippa felt that she had tried both kinds of men and found them equally unsatisfactory.

Several years after she and Freddy had separated she met Rodney Meredith—a quiet middle-aged man who had been crippled in a motor accident and suffered almost constant pain. Something about him appealed to her thwarted maternal instinct, and, when he very tentatively and diffidently proposed marriage to her, she accepted him. Their married life—spent mostly in moving from place to place on the Continent in search of some alleviation of his pain—was not unhappy. He was pathetically grateful to her for her care of him, and they had many interests in common. She had mourned sincerely at his death.

Then had come Caroline's invitation—like a voice from another world. It was the thought of Caroline that had made her accept it—the memory of the grave sweet little girl who had been so anxious to live up to Gordon's high ideals, so overwhelmed already by a sense of duty and responsibility. Would anything at all have been left of that disarming childish sweetness, or would it have been completely destroyed by Gordon's training? And then there were Gordon's other children. She felt curious about them, too. Nina . . . she remembered her well—a pretty, colourless, timid girl. She had borne Gordon three children and died at the birth of the third. Philippa always felt a pang of pity when she thought of her. Gordon had only lived a year longer, and the youngest child had been brought up by Caroline. She'd often wondered what sort of a job Caroline had made of the youngest child. And what sort of a job life and Caroline herself had made of Caroline. She was still wondering now that she had met her.

The prig was there, of course, the prig whom Gordon had set to guard her every word and action but—the sweet simple little girl was there too. Philippa had been glad to recognise that little girl. She'd been terribly afraid lest the prig should have killed her.

And—there was something else that Philippa couldn't quite understand, something of which Caroline herself was probably unaware, something dark and secret and turbulent. It was as if all those natural impulses that Gordon had repressed had been driven inward, had festered and turned sour. She was beautiful in a cold passionless way, which she enhanced, probably deliberately, by the excessive plainness of her dress and the almost puritanical austerity of the smooth parted hair. The man—Richard Oakley—was obviously in love with her. She accepted his devotion gravely, detachedly, but she didn't return it, though perhaps she thought she did. And Charles. . . . He'd turned from a self-conscious rather pompous young man into a ridiculous old dandy, but his devotion to Maggie was as touching as ever. He'd always been kind to her, protecting her from Gordon's stern criticism, reassuring her, consoling her. Poor Maggie! She'd been frightened out of her wits by the old man in her childhood and had never quite found her way back into them.

"You've been living in Vienna, haven't you, Mrs. Meredith?" said Richard.

Philippa roused herself to take part in the conversation again.

"Yes, for the past year. A doctor there had discovered some new treatment that we thought might do my husband good."

"I went there once before the War," said Charles, "but I suppose it's all different now."

"Not so very, I believe," said Philippa. "The people are as charming as ever, and there's still the opera. And the country round is delightful."

They began to talk about Vienna and the Dolomites, then Richard told her that he was going to Madeira for a holiday, and it turned out that Philippa had spent several months there, and they all began to talk about Madeira, Richard growing quite excited and making himself really ridiculous, thought Caroline, sitting back in her chair and watching them with eyes that were growing bluer and bluer. She might not have been in the room for all the notice anyone was taking of her.

"I generally find," she said, smiling, "that the people who have most to say about the marvellous scenery abroad know little or nothing of English scenery. I suppose one does feel rather more important when one praises the Dolomites than when one praises—say, the English Lakes or the Scottish Highlands."

Again there was a constrained silence. Maggie's necklaces jingled nervously. Maggie could always tell when Caroline was annoyed, however kindly she spoke.

"Fay must play to us when she comes home," she said with a vague idea of propitiating her by praising Fay.

Charles coughed loudly and remarked that the days were drawing in. Philippa threw her daughter a look of quiet amusement. It was the second time since her arrival that she had deliberately snubbed her. Why had she invited her at all, she wondered. Perhaps the child herself didn't know. She was talking about a holiday that she had once spent at the Lakes with her father and the children.

"You could walk for miles without seeing a house, just the hills and valleys and rocks. I don't know how old the farmhouse was where we stayed, but it looked as much a natural part of the scenery as the rocks and lakes. It was rather thrilling to feel that everything as far as you could see must have looked just the same for hundreds and hundreds of years."

"I know," said Richard. "It is thrilling."

But she could tell that he wasn't really interested. Neither was Charles. They wanted to talk to Philippa again, to ask her about Vienna and Budapest and Berlin and all the other places where she'd stayed, to listen to her casual illuminating descriptions, her little flashes of wit. Everything that she, Caroline, said sounded suddenly heavy and pedantic. Wistfully and with a kind of fear, she remembered the last tea-party she'd had in this room, when there had been just Richard and Uncle Charles and Aunt Maggie. They'd listened to her with such obvious interest. And now it was all changed. There was a laboured politeness, a faint suspicion of boredom in their manner. Even in Richard's. The fear deepened. Again she faced the fact that she might have made a grave mistake in asking this woman to come here. She'd never forgive herself if her influence harmed any of those near and dear to her. She didn't like the way she'd made fun of Mr. Cookson or the way she paraded her knowledge of foreign places. Both were in very bad taste.

Chapter Eight

THEN Fay came in—eager and tremulous, like a leaf blown by the wind.

"This is Aunt Philippa, dear," said Caroline. She had decided on Aunt as the most convenient form of address in the circumstances.

Fay looked at the new-comer, then burst out laughing.

"Oh!" she said. "And I'd thought of you as an old lady in a black dress."

They all laughed, except Caroline.

"I'm so sorry," apologised Philippa.

"Oh, but it's *lovely*," said Fay. "I'm so glad you aren't."

"I'm an old lady in a red dress instead," said Philippa with dancing eyes.

"You're not old," protested Fay, "and it's too lovely a colour to be called red."

What on earth was the matter with the child, thought Caroline irritably. She was generally so shy and quiet and well-behaved. This woman seemed to have the most extraordinary effect on everyone round her. . . .

"Your tea's laid in the dining-room, dear," she said quietly. "We had ours at four. . . . Then you might begin your home-work there straight away when you've had your tea. You've got rather a lot to do tonight, haven't you?"

"Yes," said Fay. Her glow had suddenly faded.

"Run along, then. We'll all excuse you from coming in again."

Philippa watched her go slowly from the room. How adorably young and fresh she was! There had been a dewy sparkle about her when she entered, but it had died away at Caroline's tone.

Caroline had deliberately extinguished it. But Caroline, too, could light it again by a word or a look. It was quite easy to see that. And she hadn't extinguished the glow, as Gordon or his father would have extinguished it, because they distrusted it as worldliness or frivolity. It was something far more subtle than that.

Richard was rising to take his leave.

"I'll see you out, Richard," said Caroline.

She went with him into the hall, then drew him into the little morning-room and closed the door.

"Richard," she said, "do you think I've made a great mistake?"

"How do you mean, Caroline?"

"In asking her to come. I'd no idea she'd be like this."

"Like what?"

She threw out her hands.

"Oh, *Richard* . . . Didn't you think there was something—brazen in the way she talked about Bartenham? As if—as if she hadn't left it in the way she did."

He looked slightly embarrassed.

"I don't know. . . . After all, it's a long time ago."

"Does that make any difference?"

"Well, I think it does. . . . Don't worry, Caroline. You're just a little tired. I could see you were, in the drawing-room."

"I'm not at all tired," said Caroline coldly.

"It was splendid of you to ask her here as you did, and I know you won't regret it. She'll be able to help you in lots of ways. And she's charming."

"Do you think so?"

"Don't you?"

She looked at him with clear blue eyes.

"I can see that some people would find her so, but somehow I didn't think you'd be one of them."

"Why ever not?"

She shrugged.

"Nothing. . . . Well, I must get back to the others. Goodbye."

"Goodbye."

She stood in the hall when he had gone, her heart beating unevenly.

She and Richard had never come so near to quarrelling before. It was all her mother's fault. There was about her some indefinable quality that made for disharmony. And more than disharmony. It had turned Fay into a silly giggling schoolgirl. It had made Richard, for the first time in her experience of him, seem imperceptive and—yes, almost coarse-grained. It—blurred things, threw them into wrong focus. Nothing had seemed right and natural since she entered the house. Always Caroline had faced the fact that her influence might be evil, but she hadn't realised how much charm and loveliness might be left from the wreck of her life to strengthen that influence. But—she set her lips—she wasn't going back on her word. She'd asked her to the house, and if she brought with her an evil influence she would fight it. She'd never yet withdrawn from any task she'd set herself. . . .

She returned to the drawing-room, her cheeks flushed, her head held high, her eyes very blue.

"And I remember a kitten you had called Topsy," Philippa was saying to Maggie. "Once it got so completely tangled up in your wools that it took all of us all evening to disentangle it."

"Oh yes, I remember," laughed Maggie, then she saw Caroline and looked rather guilty, gathering her scarves together with little nervous movements. "We ought to go now, Charles. It's after half-past five."

They took their leave, Charles making his most courtly bow over Philippa's hand.

Maggie walked down the road with a little springing step that told Charles she was happy.

"She's nice, Charles, isn't she?" she said.

"Yes," agreed Charles. "Very nice indeed."

"She *couldn't* ever have been wicked, could she?"

"Of course not," Charles reassured her.

Maggie gave a little ineffectual tug at a scarf that was too short on one side and too long on the other.

"I expect the whole thing was a misunderstanding," she said vaguely. "Things so often are."

"What a delightful child Fay is!" Philippa was saying.

"Yes, isn't she?" agreed Caroline. "She's a little weak and easily led, that's all." She took some sewing from a work-basket that stood on the table near her chair and began to work at it with quick unsteady movements. "She's studying very hard just now for her scholarship examination, so I don't suppose you'll see much of her."

"I don't expect to," smiled Philippa. "Girls of that age generally have so many friends and interests that no generation but their own exists for them."

There was a silence, then Philippa said:

"Caroline . . . tell me about things since I went away."

Caroline cut off a strand of silk before she answered.

"There's nothing to tell," she said at last, lightly.

Philippa smiled wryly. *She's putting me in my place. I've no right to pry into her private affairs. She's quite right, of course. I haven't.*

Caroline looked up from her work.

"Wouldn't you like to lie down on the sofa?" she said kindly, and added after a slight hesitation, "Mother."

"No, thank you," said Philippa. "I'm not at all tired. And don't call me 'Mother' if you'd rather not, Caroline. After all, it does seem a little unnatural. I'm afraid I wasn't much of a mother to you. Why not just call me Philippa?"

"Very well," agreed Caroline.

There was another silence, in which Philippa decided to make a fresh assault upon Caroline's defences.

"Caroline, I know hardly anything of what's happened here since I left, except what I've seen in the Births and Marriages and Deaths column of *The Times*. I know I've no right to ask it, but won't you fill in the gaps for me?"

Caroline laid down her needlework and looked at her for some moments without speaking.

"If you like," she said at last in a jerky abrupt voice. "I'd just won a scholarship to Newnham when father died, and I gave it up to stay and look after the children. Nina had died when Fay was born, so I don't really see how I could have left them in any case, but father had been keen on my going to College. It was impossible, of course, when he died."

"Couldn't you have found someone to look after them?"

"It wasn't only that. It was a case of money. Father's affairs were very—involved. He'd been changing his investments because so many of them weren't paying and he'd mortgaged his life insurance and there was practically nothing. I got work—coaching and translations—and ran the house and looked after the children as well."

Philippa had gone pale. "My dear ... why didn't you let me know? I should have loved to help."

"I didn't want any help," said Caroline. Her voice was cool and detached, her head bent over her needlework again.

To herself she was saying: Why do I feel like this to her? I meant to feel so different. I meant to look after her and help her, and—she doesn't want it. I felt so sorry for her, but I needn't have done. She's worldly and hard and shallow. And she's got that easy charm that worldly people have. I could feel it with Richard and Fay—even with Uncle Charles and Aunt Maggie. They meant nothing to her, but she had to charm them. She'd have no scruples in coming between them and—someone who was really fond of them. She'd have no scruples in undermining my influence with Fay. . . .

"Tell me about the others, Caroline. What about Marcia?"

"I don't see very much of her. She went to live in London when she was married. Her husband has work there."

"Did she help you when things were so difficult?"

"She offered to take Fay, but, of course, I couldn't let Fay go."

"And what about Robert and Susan?"

"Robert's been married for about seven years—he has three children—and Susan married three months ago." Caroline paused and added, "They're neither of them very happy marriages, I'm afraid."

Philippa laid her hand impulsively on Caroline's arm. "Caroline, it seems dreadful that you should have had all this to go through alone. I'm so sorry."

There was a deep tenderness in both voice and touch, and for a moment something in Caroline that was tired and rather lonely longed to yield to it, to accept its promise of comfort and comradeship. But she pulled herself together, building up hastily the breach that it had made in her defences.

"There's nothing for you to be sorry about," she said in her quiet level voice. "It was just my job and I did it. It didn't, after all, concern anyone but myself. . . . By the way, I've arranged to take you to see Robert and Susan tomorrow. They're both very anxious to meet you, of course. I didn't ask them here today because I thought that you'd probably be very tired and that Charles and Maggie and Richard would be enough. Richard's such an old friend of the family that he almost counts as a member of it. He's looked after our affairs for us ever since father died."

"I thought him charming."

Caroline ignored the comment.

"We'll go to Susan's to tea and then on to Robert's."

"I don't want to be a nuisance, my dear. You must just leave me to amuse myself. I'm quite good at doing that. . . . I want to start flat-hunting as soon as I've found my bearings."

Caroline's needle stopped for a few moments. Then she said, "You're welcome to make this your permanent home, you know. That was my idea when I asked you to come."

"It was sweet of you, Caroline. I shall never forget it. But I couldn't think of it. It will be lovely, anyway, to have a *pied-à-terre* till I get settled. I thought I'd take a small flat in town."

Caroline was conscious of mingled relief and disappointment. Those vague fears that had haunted her all afternoon would never be realised, then. If her mother were not going to live here she couldn't—change things, spoil things. She couldn't take Fay from her, blur her relations with Richard. . . . And yet that dream of restoring a broken woman to sanity and self-respect had been so dear to her that it was rather hard to give it up.

Caroline saw herself as essentially a giver, giving continually of help and strength and comfort to those around her—to Fay, Susan, Robert, to poor little Effie, even to Aunt Maggie. This picture of herself had always been a secret source of pleasure to her, and she had looked forward to her mother's joining the circle of those who loved and admired her. Still—even now she might be able to help her. She mustn't give up hope just because things were turning out more difficult than she had foreseen. She must just be patient. Patient—and on her guard against the alien standards that this woman brought with her. After all, it was cowardly to run away, to be afraid of evil, whatever form it took. One must go to meet it boldly, trusting that it had no real power against good.

"Fay's very pretty, isn't she?" her mother was saying. "I suppose that the house is generally full of young people. It's such a perfect age for friendship."

Caroline's voice was rather cold as she answered, "Fay makes very few friends of her own age. She doesn't care much for young people. She and I have always been great companions. ... I've almost given up trying to get her to make friends of her own age. After all, if she's happy ..."

"Of course," said Philippa.

She was looking at Caroline keenly, trying to disentangle the curious mixture of characteristics that her daughter had presented in the space of a few hours. She was thinking: She's pathetically well-meaning. She'd sacrifice herself without stint for others, if she thought it was her duty. She'd work herself to the bone for them. She has worked herself to the bone for them. She's starkly honest with everyone but herself. She's no sense of humour, of course. Gordon had no sense of humour. ...

Caroline glanced at the clock. "We have dinner at eight," she said. "That gives Fay time to finish her home-work and have a little relaxation before she goes to bed."

Philippa rose.

"I'll go and finish my unpacking, then."

She went into the hall. Fay was just coming out of the dining-room, and they went upstairs together. Fay smiled at her eagerly, shyly.

"I'm so glad you're you," she said. "It's lovely. I thought you'd be deaf and always losing your spectacles."

Philippa laughed. She felt an odd bond of kinship with this youngest daughter of Gordon's.

"Isn't my room charming?" she said, throwing open the door and drawing Fay into the room, where a large trunk stood open and half unpacked. "I'm afraid I'm terribly lazy. I haven't finished unpacking yet. I've got a present for you somewhere and one for Caroline. Come and help me burrow for them."

Fay went to the dressing-table, on which stood enamel toilet-jars and brushes with golden monograms.

"Oh, what lovely things!" she said. "What's this?"

"It's a scent-spray," said Philippa. "A new kind. You press it here."

She pressed it, sending a spray of scent onto Fay's neck.

Fay laughed delightedly.

"Fay!" called Caroline sharply from downstairs.

Fay went reluctantly downstairs to the drawing-room.

"Were you in Aunt Philippa's bedroom, dear?"

"Yes," answered Fay, feeling guilty for no other reason than that Caroline's eyes were very blue.

"Darling, you mustn't make a nuisance of yourself like that."

The colour crept into Fay's pale cheeks.

"But, Caroline, she asked me."

"She doesn't really want you, dear. She naturally feels that as she's a guest here she has to be nice to you, but I know she isn't fond of children, and you mustn't take advantage of her politeness. Don't go into her bedroom again even if she asks you, because I'm quite sure that she doesn't want to be bothered with a child of your age."

Fay went upstairs again, her face flaming, her heart beating quickly. She felt as if she had been badly snubbed—not by Caroline but by Philippa.

Chapter Nine

"THESE new estates are so depressing," said Caroline, as she and Philippa made their way down the rough uneven road that led to Susan's house.

"Oh, I don't think so," replied Philippa. "There's something rather gallant and plucky about them. They remind me of the youngest son of the fairy tales setting out into the world to seek his fortune. The beginnings of everything are exciting in a way. . . ."

"I don't think there's anything exactly exciting about this estate," said Caroline with her faint smile. "I'm afraid that most of its inmates are irresponsible and impecunious young people who don't pay their bills or fulfil any of their social obligations."

"Ah, the youngest son!" said Philippa. "He turns out all right in the end. There's generally a good fairy looking after him in the background."

Caroline frowned but said nothing. She disliked the note of flippancy that Philippa seemed to introduce into every conversation. Throwing her a sidelong glance, she was conscious again of an obscure resentment. It was altogether unseemly that one's mother should give the thought and care to her appearance that this woman obviously gave. Worldliness, that was it. Worldliness and vanity. Things she'd always detested, things she'd always fought against. It's simply a question of values, she said to herself. Hers are material, and mine are spiritual. We've nothing in common . . . nothing. We live in different worlds. . . . She became aware that she was wondering how one of those small hats, worn a little on the side of the head, would suit her (she never wore any other but a plain "sports" shape) and caught herself up quickly with a hot flush of shame.

She mustn't let herself become contaminated. She must cling to her own standards, keep her banners flying.

"Am I walking too fast for you?" she said solicitously.

Philippa shot her a glance of amusement.

"No, thank you, my dear. I'm a very good walker."

"But I mustn't let you overtire yourself," said Caroline. "I must take care of you now, you know."

Her equanimity was restored. Kind, protective, forbearing, indulgent to an old woman's foibles, that was what she must be. For Philippa *was* an old woman. Why, she might have been a grandmother now if she, Caroline, had married. . . . That thought gave her a vague sense of comfort. An old woman. One mustn't be hard on her ridiculous little weaknesses and vanities.

"Here's the house," said Caroline.

Philippa stopped and looked at it.

"How charming!" she said.

"Inconvenient and badly built, I'm afraid, is a more accurate description," said Caroline. "Susan's being very plucky about it, but—well, it's hardly the sort of home I'd hoped for her."

"Oh, but, Caroline, just for the two of them—while they're young and beginning life—it's perfect. It must be such fun! Why, it's the sort of place she can run entirely by herself—isn't it?—without the bother of maids and all the rest of it. I'd have given anything for it when I was newly married. I was terrified of the maids, and I felt so hopelessly bored all day with nothing to do."

"Susan would not be likely to be bored in any case," said Caroline in her steady level voice. "She has plenty of resources in herself."

The front door opened, and Susan stood on the threshold. Philippa looked at her. . . . She was deeply interested in this second family of Gordon's. There was nothing of Gordon in Fay, but Susan had his colouring—brown hair, brown eyes, and rosy cheeks. Her lips, however, were soft and full where Gordon's had been hard and narrow, and her eyes were dreamy and gentle, with smouldering lights of passion in their depths.

She greeted Philippa shyly, then laughed as Fay had done.

"I don't know why we were all prepared for someone terribly old."

"I *am* fairly old, you know," smiled Philippa.

"I suppose it's because we think of Caroline as our mother, and you're *her* mother, and somehow the conventional idea of a grandmother is someone in a shawl and a cap. I don't know why it should be. You never see either in real life."

"Well, if you'll excuse the shawl and cap," said Philippa, "I'd love you to look on me as a sort of grandmother."

"I'd adore to. I've always longed to have a grandmother."

"As a matter of fact," put in Caroline, "there's no relationship at all between you. ... Darling, will it clutter up your hall too much if we leave our coats on the hat-stand, or shall I take them upstairs?"

"It *is* meant for coats, you know," smiled Susan. "It has three real hooks *and* a peg."

"I know, but it does rather crowd up the hall when it's actually used."

"I think it's delightful," said Philippa. "Do show me the rest of it. I believe it's the sort of house I've always longed to live in."

"It's an ideal quite possible of realisation," said Caroline dryly. "There are plenty of them about."

"No, I'm too old," said Philippa. "It belongs to youth. Every married couple ought to start life in one. How I'd have loved it! You can literally *make* a home of it. I was presented with a mansion, a lot of Victorian furniture, and a couple of elderly Victorian servants, and I'd nothing to do all day but be bored by myself and bullied by the Victorian servants. Life would have been so different if I'd had a place like this. But when you reach my age the zest has gone out of life. It's the service flat age. Deadly and unenterprising, without any of the thrill of the unexpected. It's the unexpected that makes life worth living. Even a burst pipe or the baker forgetting to leave the loaf or a fall of soot down the dining-room chimney. They all help to give zest to life. ...."

Susan was laughing, and Caroline was watching them with eyes that were changing slowly from grey to blue. She felt ashamed of the trivial nonsense that this woman talked, and amazed that Susan could even pretend to be amused by it.

"Oh, we get plenty of that kind of zest here," Susan was saying. "The tradesmen are awful and the soot's always coming down, it doesn't matter how often you have the chimneys swept. . . . Do come into the lounge."

They entered the sunny little room where tea was laid on a low table in the window recess.

"What a fascinating room!" cried Philippa. "I love the bay window. It's so picturesque and means you get all the sun there is, doesn't it?"

"There isn't much," said Caroline. "And those picturesque bay windows are turned out by the thousand. None of them fit, do they, Susan?"

"Just at present they're all right," said Susan. "Ken's planed away the wood where they'd swollen."

"Yes, of course," said Caroline. "That's simple enough. The difficulty will be when they start shrinking again." She turned to Philippa. "These houses are so badly built that they need constant tinkering to keep them up at all."

"Ken doesn't mind," said Susan. "He rather fancies himself at tinkering." She turned to Philippa. "Would you like to see over the house?"

"I'd love to," said Philippa.

They went upstairs, and Caroline stood by the window, frowning and tapping her foot as she listened to the sound of their voices in the room above.

"I'll just go and make the tea," called Susan from the hall when they had come downstairs.

Philippa entered alone. "I think it's simply charming," she said.

"Yes," said Caroline. "Personally I should prefer a little less charm and a little more convenience, but it's a matter of taste, of course."

Susan entered with the teapot.

"Now do sit down," she said. "Will you sit here——" she smiled at Philippa. "What do I call you? I can't address you as 'Caroline's

Mother,' can I? 'Granny' sounds too old and 'Mrs. Meredith' too formal."

"Won't you call me just Philippa?"

"Philippa ... it's a lovely name. ... May I really?"

"You're looking very tired, Susan," put in Caroline. "What have you been doing with yourself?"

"Nothing," said Susan. "Just the usual chores. I did out the dining-room this morning."

"Why on earth couldn't Mrs. Pollit do that?"

"She doesn't come on Wednesdays."

"What days does she come?"

"Only on Mondays now to help with the washing. I can manage the rest of the work quite easily."

"It's ridiculous. I'll speak to Kenneth about it."

"No, don't, Caroline. It was my suggestion. He was so worried the other night. ..."

Caroline's lips were tight.

"I do wish you hadn't all this housework to do. It's too much for you." She turned to Philippa. "I don't enjoy watching Susan being gradually turned into a household drudge. Some men seem to think that that's all a woman's meant for. It's the early Victorian view, of course. Before Susan married Kenneth I thought that it was quite extinct."

Philippa said nothing. Susan flushed and murmured:

"Caroline, it's all right. I don't mind a bit."

She didn't mind a bit ... and yet all the pride and elation that she had felt as she showed Philippa over the house was fading, and the self-pity that Caroline always seemed able to instil into her was slowly taking possession of her spirit. After all, it *was* rather rough luck ... housework day after day after day. ... As Caroline often said, she might as well be a charwoman ... And Ken *did* seem to take it all as a matter of course. As Caroline said, he didn't seem to realise that she'd given up a promising career in order to marry him. Of course, she hadn't liked teaching as much as Caroline thought she had, but still ...

Caroline was telling Philippa about the "estate," pointing out the drawbacks of the little houses, describing how in one of them the rain had come through the roof during the first winter, and in another dry-rot had been discovered only a few months after its owner had bought it. "Susan's so plucky about it," Caroline went on. "She just makes a joke of it all. .... It's the best thing to do, of course. We'd hoped that it would be only a very temporary arrangement, but unfortunately poor Kenneth doesn't seem very successful as a business man."

Philippa's eyes, grave and penetrating, went from one to the other. She's jealous, she was thinking, jealous of the little home and of Susan's husband. She can't bear the child to be happy without her, so she's trying to spoil them both for her. Susan's rather weak and has been dominated by her all her life.

Caroline rose from her chair and began to collect the cups and saucers onto the tray.

"You don't mind if we clear away now, do you, Philippa?" she said.

"Can't I help?"

"No, it won't take us a minute."

She carried the tray into the kitchen, followed by Susan. In the kitchen she closed the door behind them.

"We needn't have brought the things out," said Susan. "I could easily have done it when you'd gone."

"I know. I wanted to speak to you, Susan."

Susan looked rather nervous.

"Ken's frightfully sorry about the way he spoke to you the other day, Caroline. He simply didn't realise what he was saying. He wants to apologise to you."

"That's quite all right," said Caroline. "I never thought of it again. I certainly don't want an apology from him. I was sorry about it for your sake, not my own."

"Caroline, you don't understand. He——"

"Darling, I don't want to discuss him. What I wanted to ask you was, have you thought seriously about what I suggested last week?"

"What was that?"

"About your taking up your teaching again."

"Oh . . . I did mention it, Caroline, but Ken simply *hates* the idea of it."

"I think that's rather natural. I mean, all men wouldn't feel like that, but Kenneth would. He resents anything in you that makes you superior to himself. He resents your education and the fact that you are as capable as he—more capable than he, I should say—of earning your living. I think that's why he likes to see you degraded to the station of a charwoman."

Susan looked away, her lips tight, her eyes suddenly full of tears.

"Caroline, you're *horrid* about Ken. You don't understand. . . ."

Caroline slipped an arm about her.

"Darling, I'm sorry," she said tenderly. "I don't want to be horrid. It's only that—you mean so much to me. . . . You know that, don't you? . . . Listen, darling. Did you talk it over with Kenneth?"

"Yes. He said he wouldn't allow it for a moment."

Caroline's face hardened.

"Allow? It's hardly a question of his 'allowing' it. . . . Just think, dear, how much nicer you could have things here if you had your salary as well as what Kenneth earns. There would be no more worry about money at all. You could have a trained maid and run the house really well. It would be much better for Kenneth, too. He'd be freed from this incessant worry. He could go ahead with his own business with a clear mind. You'd both be so much happier. It isn't as if it would mean your leaving home. You'd be back every afternoon before his business hours are over. He'd come home to find you here as usual and a well-cooked meal. You could 'feed the brute' so much better if you had more money, couldn't you, darling?"

Susan's brown eyes were still unhappy.

"But—Caroline, it isn't worth quarrelling with him over it."

Caroline smiled tenderly.

"Susan, darling, when you really love anyone you have to try to do the things that are for their good ultimately rather than the things that will please them at the time. You don't want to drag Kenneth down, do you?"

"Oh, *Caroline*!"

"It's all right, darling. I only meant that now you're just an added expense to him, whereas, if you took a post and earned a salary, you'd be a real help. And—Susan——"

"Yes?"

"You *do* want to have children, don't you?"

"Of course."

"Are you waiting till Kenneth's better off?"

"No . . . Kenneth doesn't want to wait. He says that people who wait get into a sort of childless rut and end by not wanting them at all."

Caroline smiled.

"My dear, isn't it your obvious duty, then? If you just take a post for a few months, think how much easier you'll make it both for Kenneth and yourself. You'll have a little nest-egg to start on. You won't be a drain on Kenneth. . . . Darling, it's selfish of you to refuse."

Susan turned away. She looked like a downcast child.

"Caroline, I *can't* start it again. I mean, with Kenneth. He was so hurt when I spoke about it."

"That was just his vanity, sweetheart. His vanity wants you to be the helpless, dependent, clinging sort of woman. But he'll respect you far more if you make a stand. He'll be grateful to you later, when he sees what a difference it's made to your lives."

Susan was silent. It was so dreadful to be torn like this between Kenneth and Caroline. She loved them both so terribly. . . . And she owed everything to Caroline. . . . Ever since she was a child and had first realised what sacrifices Caroline had made for her, she had felt this burning sense of gratitude, this passionate determination not to fail or disappoint her.

"There's no need to say anything more about it to Kenneth," Caroline was saying. "And I don't want you to do anything about it yourself. Only promise me that if I hear of an opening for you you'll consider it very seriously. As a matter of fact, I think that, if Kenneth were confronted with it as an accomplished fact, he wouldn't mind at all. He'd probably be rather glad. If it comes to that, you could take a post for weeks without his knowing anything about it. You'd be at home when he went to work after breakfast and when he came home at night." She smiled. "I'm not suggesting that you should do that, of course. I'm merely pointing out how little it would really affect Kenneth. Now don't worry about it, sweetheart. You know that all I want in the world is your happiness, don't you?"

"You're sweet to me, Caroline. You always are."

Caroline rose.

"Well, we mustn't neglect our guest any longer, must we?"

"She's nice, isn't she, Caroline?"

"Who?"

"Philippa."

"I really feel I hardly know her. She only arrived yesterday."

"I thought she was rather sweet about the little house. So terribly interested in it all."

"Did you?"

"Didn't you?"

"She was just a little bit—patronising, don't you think? Rather like the grand lady district-visiting."

Susan flushed.

"I hadn't thought of it like that. . . ."

"She's very well off, you know. I believe they had quite a palatial villa at Cannes. I thought she seemed rather offensively amused by all your little arrangements. . . . Perhaps I'm wrong, darling. You know what I am. Up in arms in your defence before you're even attacked."

"Oh, Caroline! You are a darling."

"Come along."

They returned to the lounge where Philippa sat looking out at the road.

"I'm so sorry we've left you so long," apologised Susan. "It was terribly rude of us."

"It wasn't, at all," smiled Philippa. "You can't please me more than by treating me as if I belonged to the family. . . . Besides, I've loved sitting here watching everything. I've seen the baker and the butcher and the chimney-sweep and the most fascinating baby and a little boy in a new coat—I could tell it was new by the way he kept looking down at it—and even a real, old-fashioned muffin man."

Caroline smiled.

"Oh yes, anyone who doesn't actually have to live here can get quite a lot of fun out of it. . . . What was your villa at Cannes like, Philippa? How many rooms were there?"

Susan listened in silence while Caroline drew from a somewhat reluctant Philippa a minute description of her villa at Cannes. As she listened a feeling of depression and discontent surged over her. She began to feel ashamed of the little house with its makeshifts and shoddiness. It wasn't fair that she should spend her life scrubbing and cooking and cleaning in a jerry-built place like this, while other people lived in magnificent villas in the South of France with gardens that stretched down to the sea. Perhaps Caroline was right. Perhaps it would be better to take up her work again. It was, as Caroline said, rather strange that Kenneth couldn't make a decent living out of the shop, though it had done so well in his father's time. Was her marriage, after all, a terrible mistake? No, it wasn't. She loved Ken, loved him as much as she had ever done. It was just that she felt tired and depressed.

She said goodbye somewhat distantly to Philippa when she and Caroline took their leave. She'd liked her at first, before she'd begun to suspect that her pleasantness was merely patronage. It was really the limit to come here to tea and sit talking about her own villa at Cannes all the time. Caroline was always right about people. She was never deceived by superficial charm.

"What's her husband like?" said Philippa as they walked away.

At the mention of Kenneth, Caroline's face hardened. Kenneth . . . the casual happy-go-lucky youth who had appeared suddenly from nowhere and taken Susan from her—Susan, for whom she'd worked and schemed and denied herself; Susan, who belonged to her. He'd taken her without compunction or apology, as though Caroline's claims did not exist, as though the long years of her servitude and sacrifice counted as nothing against the short month or so of his acquaintance, for, despite the fact that both Kenneth and Susan had lived in Bartenham all their lives, they had met for the first time a few months before their marriage. And then—he had dared to make a slave and a drudge of her. Well—she set her lips—Susan would soon be freed from him. She'd see to that.

"Kenneth?" she said in her quiet voice. "He's a very ordinary boy. I'm afraid that, on Susan's part, it was just a case of infatuation. There's really nothing about him that could possibly hold a girl like Susan. He can't even keep her properly."

"Is he very poor?"

"He shouldn't be. His father was quite well off. I suppose he isn't a good business man. Susan has all the work of the house to do, and it's too much for her."

"She doesn't look delicate."

"She's not been brought up to housework. She has her own career. If he can't keep her she can keep herself. There's no need at all for her to put up with it. I've been telling her so."

Philippa glanced at Caroline. Her cheeks were flushed and there was a hard light in her blue eyes. She seemed to be talking more to herself than to Philippa.

"I'm worried about her," she went on with a smile, "but I don't see why I should burden you with my worries. . . . Here we are at Robert's. There's nothing at Robert's to worry one, thank goodness."

Chapter Ten

EVELYN was coming downstairs as they entered the hall. Philippa looked at her in surprise. The term "mother's help" had suggested someone drab and harassed and downtrodden, not this handsome assured woman. Caroline introduced them, and Evelyn greeted the newcomer in a guarded, non-committal manner, then turned to Caroline and kissed her affectionately.

"Darling, how nice to see you! Effie will be down in a minute. We've just put the babies to bed, and she's not quite finished changing. Robert should be here any time now, too. Will you come up and take your things off?"

"No, thank you, dear," said Caroline. "We'll just leave them in the hall. We've come straight from Susan's, so you mustn't mind our being grubby and unchanged."

Evelyn helped her off with her coat, arranging the collar of her dress with little caressing touches.

"You look lovely, Caroline, but then you always do. You can wear any colour you like and always look lovely. I do envy you."

Philippa glanced at Caroline, expecting to see some signs of irritation at this flattery, but Caroline had flushed with pleasure.

"Nonsense!" she smiled. "I never think about clothes. I spend the minimum of time and money on them. You know I do."

"And the result's perfect," said Evelyn, throwing open the drawing-room door, "isn't it, Mrs. Meredith? Do come in and sit down. . . . People with real taste don't need to think about their clothes. I've always said that. They know just what suits them by a sort of instinct. And that's Caroline. Everything she does and says and wears is perfect."

"Oh, *Evelyn*!" laughed Caroline deprecatingly. "What on earth will Philippa think of the nonsense you talk?"

"She'll agree with me, of course. ... You know how splendid Caroline's been, don't you, Mrs. Meredith?"

"Yes," said Philippa, deciding quite finally that she disliked Evelyn.

"The children owe everything to her," went on Evelyn. "You should hear Robert on the subject. Effie and Kenneth know they've got to take second place, and they don't mind because they adore Caroline, like everyone else. They're all terribly jealous of each other, of course. That goes without saying. Fay's the worst of the lot, the little monkey!"

"What nonsense!" smiled Caroline.

"It isn't nonsense," said Evelyn. "Darling, don't sit on that uncomfortable chair. Come over to the sofa. I'm sure you're tired. You work for other people all day long and never think of yourself. Doesn't she, Mrs. Meredith?"

Caroline allowed herself to be drawn over to the sofa and to be settled down upon it with much patting of cushions and affectionate little touches. Philippa watched them thoughtfully. Evelyn's position in the family, of course, depended on Caroline, and she obviously spared no pains to safeguard it. It was rather clever of her to have discovered that Caroline, so shrewd and self-contained on the surface, had that particular weak spot in her armour.

"What do you think of Bartenham, Mrs. Meredith?" she asked. Her tone was still carefully noncommittal, as though she were waiting to take her cue from Caroline, to be cold or effusive according as Caroline gave the lead. She went on talking to Caroline without waiting for Philippa's answer. "Don't the curtains look nice, Caroline? I'm so grateful to you for choosing that colour."

Caroline was lying back on the sofa, looking almost sleek as she basked in the sunshine of Evelyn's flattery.

"Everything looks so nice now," she said. "When one thinks of the old days——"

Evelyn laughed.

"Oh, the old days!" She turned to Philippa. "Effie used to let the children rampage over the whole house. There was hardly a decent bit of furniture left. As soon as I came, I made a rule that——"

There came the sound of light footsteps on the stairs, and Effie entered. She looked pale and sulky, as usual, and, though she had just washed and changed, vaguely untidy. Her dress of grey lace, too matronly for her slight girlish figure, was put on anyhow. Her hair was brushed straight off her brow and done into a careless knot at the nape of her neck, from which several loose ends protruded.

She's pretty, thought Philippa, but she's forgotten how pretty she is, and she doesn't care about it any more. . . .

The other two greeted her affectionately. "Don't you love her in that dress, Caroline?" said Evelyn. "She let her old Evelyn help her choose it. We thought we'd get a real grown-up dress this time, not one of the little-girl frocks that she buys when her stupid old Evelyn isn't with her. . . . This is Mrs. Meredith, darling—Caroline's mother."

Effie threw Philippa a faintly hostile glance, then sat down in an armchair by the fireplace. Her pale sulky face wore an expression of brooding resentment—a passive resentment that had ceased trying to make itself felt. It was as if the magnetic personalities of the two other women had sapped her vitality, and she had given up the struggle to assert herself against them.

Suddenly there came the sound of the front door opening, and a stir seemed to pass through the room. Though Caroline and Evelyn went on talking and Effie continued to gaze listlessly in front of her, Philippa could tell that the three of them were on the alert for Robert's entrance. Philippa, on her side, felt intensely curious to see Gordon's son. She turned her head sharply as the door opened. Yes, there was something of Gordon in him, as there was in Susan. He was short and thick-set where Gordon had been tall and thin, but, like Susan, he had Gordon's warm colouring—dark hair, brown eyes, ruddy complexion. Like Susan, too, he lacked any suggestion of the repressive severity that had been Gordon's most marked characteristic. He smiled pleasantly and naturally at

Philippa as he greeted her, then sank down into his chair with a faint sigh of weariness.

"How have the children gone on?" he said, turning to his wife.

Before she could answer, Evelyn began an amusing description of the children's day, making him laugh by repeating several of Carrie's quaint sayings. Effie relapsed into silence, but her eyes kept returning to Robert, and there was a faint flush on her cheeks. Philippa thought: She's in love with him. It would be so much simpler, of course, if she weren't.

"I've nearly finished the crossword puzzle, Robert," Evelyn was saying. "Caroline helped me, of course."

"Not much, darling," murmured Caroline.

"The only one we haven't done is 17 down."

He read out the clue, and Effie, with an air of mingled timidity and defiance, made an obviously impossible suggestion. There was a constrained silence, then Robert said kindly, "I don't think so, dear."

"Did you see an evening paper, Robert?" said Evelyn. "I'm longing to know who got in at Freshport."

"The Conservative," said Robert. "I was rather surprised."

In the political discussion that followed Effie made several futile remarks that the others ignored. She made them in a small breathless voice, glancing resentfully at Philippa as if daring her to notice what a nonentity the two women had managed to make her in her husband's eyes. Philippa watched her with deepening interest. She was trying, ineffectually enough, to rival them on their own ground. That was a mistake, of course. She wasn't intellectual and shouldn't have even tried to be. She was, by nature, light-hearted and irresponsible. She had been, Philippa was sure, gaily, artlessly amusing before Caroline and Evelyn took her in hand. And Robert? He worked hard at the office, and when he came home all he wanted was peace. He wanted it so much that he was willing to buy it at almost any price. Evelyn had, by a miracle, as it seemed, given him a well-run home, well-behaved children, and a quiet unexacting wife. He was honestly fond of Effie, and he thought that she had improved very much since Evelyn came to live with them. In the old days she had been tempestuous, high-spirited, and excitable, incorrigibly careless and forgetful. She had spoilt the children and was always having scenes with Caroline. Looking back on those days, he felt devoutly thankful for the change that Evelyn had brought into their lives. He was touched, too, by her affectionate manner to Effie. She looked after her as if she were a beloved wayward child, never taking offence when Effie was rude to her, as, he had to admit, she often was.

Philippa was covertly studying him as he talked. Like Caroline, he had obviously inherited Gordon's lack of humour. There was no gleam of it in his face or voice. Susan had a shy, uncertain sense of humour. It hadn't been given much chance by Caroline, and even now it was easily quelled, but it was there. In Fay it was there unmistakably. It sparkled in her eyes and bubbled up in her clear delicious laughter. Even Caroline hadn't been able to quell it in Fay. . . .

The gong sounded, and they rose to go in to dinner. Evelyn went up to Effie, smiling affectionately.

"Here's my untidy baby coming all to pieces again," she said, fastening a hook and eye in the grey lace dress. Then she tucked several straying strands of hair into the bun at the back of her slender neck, while the others stood round waiting.

"I don't know what this house and everyone in it would do without you, Evelyn," said Caroline.

"I don't either," agreed Robert good-humouredly.

Effie jerked herself away from Evelyn's hands with an ungracious "thank you," and again threw that sullen defiant glance at Philippa. Well, you see how things are, it seemed to say, and I hate you for seeing. . . .

Dinner was a pleasant enough meal. The food was well cooked and well served. Evelyn could certainly get the best out of servants. She and Caroline discussed local people and happenings. Effie had relapsed into silence. Philippa, too, was silent. It occurred to her that Caroline was deliberately keeping the conversation in channels where she could not join it, and that Evelyn was following her lead. Robert was tired, wanting only to be interested and amused, and the two women laid themselves out to interest and amuse him.

Suddenly there came the sound of a child's cry from upstairs. Effie laid down her knife and fork.

"It's Carrie," she said.

"Now, Effie," remonstrated Evelyn gently. "You know what Carrie is. She's remembered that we've got visitors, so she's determined to put herself into the limelight somehow. If no one goes up she'll be asleep again in five minutes, and if once you do start going up it'll be a game you'll have to play every night. Be sensible, darling."

Effie's figure did not relax. Her eyes were fixed on the door.

"She has bad dreams," she said. "She might be really frightened."

"Even if she is, dear," said Evelyn, "she'll be asleep again far sooner if she's left alone than if someone goes up making a fuss of her."

The sounds from above continued. . . . Robert went on with his dinner, frowning slightly.

"Effie dear," admonished Caroline, "do as Evelyn says."

Effie turned her eyes slowly to Caroline. They were very bright, and her cheeks were flushed.

"Why should I?" she said breathlessly. "They're my children—aren't they:—not hers."

"Don't talk foolishly, Effie," said Caroline. "You know perfectly well how much better behaved the children have been since Evelyn took them in hand. You——"

Effie pushed her chair back from the table. "Better behaved!" she flashed. "She's making them into little prigs, if that's what you mean. There'll be nothing real about them by the time she's finished with them. They may have been naughty when I looked after them, but they were real, they were themselves. She just wants little machines that behave nicely. She doesn't care what they're like inside as long as they've got nice manners to do her credit."

"Effie, Effie!" expostulated Robert.

"And she does her best to make them despise me," went on Effie, her voice rising hysterically. "She has done ever since she came here. She hasn't managed it yet, but she will." She sprang to her feet and went to the door. "I'm going to Carrie. . . . I don't care what any of you say."

"Effie," said Caroline in her quiet level voice, "please remember that when Evelyn came here you promised not to interfere in her management of the children."

Effie turned at the door and faced them, her cheeks flaming.

"Interfere!" she echoed unsteadily. "That's a nice word for *you* to use. You've done nothing but interfere ever since I married Robert. You've never given me a chance. From the very beginning you've never given me a chance. It might have been all right if I'd flattered you as *she* does, but I didn't know . . . I didn't understand. . . . Perhaps I would have done if I'd known what was going to happen. I don't think I would, though. I think I hated you too much even then."

Her voice broke and she went out of the room abruptly. They heard her running upstairs.

"Poor little Effie!" said Evelyn tenderly. "She gets over-tired and simply doesn't know what she's saying."

"It's nice of you to look at it in that way, Evelyn," said Robert, "but she's no excuse at all for speaking to Caroline as she did. She ought to apologise."

"Of *course* she mustn't," said Caroline. She was smiling, but her eyes were very blue. "As Evelyn says, she's simply over-tired and didn't know what she was saying. It just shows us again how lucky we are to have Evelyn here to help her. She's far too highly strung to cope with things alone."

"But she's so much better than she used to be," said Evelyn. "We used to have these little scenes nearly every day, you remember. . . . It's nothing to worry about, Robert. She'll be all right when she's had a rest. She doesn't mean any of the things she says about Caroline, and, anyway, Caroline's such an angel that she'd never take offence." She smiled across at Philippa. "It's Mrs. Meredith to whom we ought to be apologising."

Philippa was silent for a moment. She had an idea that she was responsible for the outburst, that it was her presence that had made Effie realise afresh the humiliation of her position and give voice to the resentment in what Evelyn and Caroline passed over so lightly as a "little scene."

"Oh no," she said at last. "I hate to hear a child crying, too. And some dreams can be very terrifying when you're only four."

They heard footsteps in the room overhead and the sound of voices. The child's sobs gradually died away. Then came the opening and closing of a door . . . and the opening and closing of another door.

Effie had evidently gone to her own bedroom.

They went back into the drawing-room for coffee, and, when she had poured it out, Evelyn slipped from the room. She returned after a few minutes, smiling.

"I've looked in at both babies," she said. "Carrie's asleep, and Effie soon will be. One can't take her any more seriously than one would a child. I understand her——"

"You're wonderful with her, Evelyn," put in Caroline.

"I'm very fond of her," said Evelyn. "She's a dear little thing and we get on together splendidly. As I said, an outburst like tonight's means nothing but that her nerves are overstrained. She'll be her own dear little self tomorrow. . . ."

Later she asked Caroline to go into the nursery with her to inspect a new rug that she had bought. Philippa and Robert, left alone together, kept up a desultory conversation. Robert, in his slow somewhat laboured fashion, told her of the changes that had taken place in Bartenham since the War. He seemed extraordinarily set for his age, inelastic in mind and body, intellectual without being intelligent. Yet there was something very likeable about him, a suggestion of simplicity and kindliness and stark unflinching honesty. He wasn't astute. He took things at their face value, without looking beneath the surface. He must have been like wax in Caroline's hands from the beginning. His loyalty to her was almost a religion. She had been both mother and father to him. She had sacrificed her youth and her career for him. He had never in his life seen her angry or ill-tempered. She had always been calm, controlled, unfailingly sweet and selfless. He looked on her as belonging to a world apart, perfect, inimitable. Effie, of course, had, had no chance against her. From the beginning, probably, Caroline had been able to distort her every word and action in Robert's eyes. Gradually, almost unconsciously, he had accepted her view—a view never put into words but urged subtly, irresistibly, by tone of voice and expression—that his marriage had been a mistake. He still loved Effie, but he had let them tacitly persuade him that she was a child, to be humoured and put up with, never to be taken seriously.

In the nursery Caroline inspected the rug rather absently. Suddenly she said, "What do you think of my mother, Evelyn?"

Evelyn had been watching Caroline all evening in order to have the right answer to that question when it came. She felt that she was making no mistake when she replied.

"Darling, I don't really feel I know her well enough to say."

Caroline was apparently satisfied.

"She's had an unhappy life, of course."

"Unhappy?" said Evelyn. "Anyone less kind than you would say that she'd made other people's lives unhappy. Your heart's too big, you know, Caroline. Will you never think of yourself?"

As Caroline and Philippa walked home that night, Caroline said lightly:

"Well, now you've met all the family. I expect you find us terribly boring. A very ordinary, humdrum set—not the sort of people that things happen to."

Philippa was silent for a moment. She was thinking of Susan's brooding tragic face, of Effie's passionate outburst. Then she said as lightly:

"I don't think you can say that of anyone."

Chapter Eleven

CAROLINE sat by the fire in the drawing-room, her eyes fixed absently on the flames. Richard had arrived home from Madeira last night, and she was expecting him to tea today. She had taken unusual pains with her appearance, arranging her fair hair more loosely about her ears and putting on a new dress of black georgette with a soft fall of lace at the breast and full chiffon sleeves. Philippa had now been with her a month, and Caroline was taking stock of the situation. It had not been a happy month. Philippa's influence—she admitted it reluctantly—had not been for good. There was nothing that one could actually lay one's finger on, but there was unmistakably a blurring, however faint, of those standards that Caroline had set herself so resolutely to maintain. Something of flippancy crept into nearly every discussion in which she took part. It was as if her spirit could not breathe the air in which Caroline's habitually lived. Worldliness ... it informed her every word and movement. It lay about her like a faint but noxious miasma. And it was affecting Fay, Fay who was so young and impressionable, so sensitive to every new suggestion, Fay whose standards were, of course, not yet sufficiently formed to enable her to resist this subtle encroachment of evil. Caroline had always disliked the giggling type of schoolgirl, irresponsible, disrespectful, interested in the trivialities of dress and personal appearance, and it was hard to see Fay, under the influence of her own mother, developing these qualities. At the sound of Fay's soft giggle coming from Philippa's bedroom, an actual physical pain would shoot through Caroline's heart.

Philippa encouraged Fay to mimic her school mistresses (Fay

was a good mimic, but Caroline, sensing the danger that lay in it, had always discouraged the accomplishment) and to arrange her hair in a different and more becoming way. She had even brought back a new dress for her from one of her shopping expeditions in London. The new dress had been particularly galling to Caroline. It was so plain in design that she could not reasonably object to it as unsuitable for Fay, and yet it had an air of sophistication that was actually, Caroline considered, more unsuitable than any amount of frills and furbelows would have been.

The old Fay, of course, was still there, and at a grave glance from Caroline would reappear at once—serious, responsible, earnest. She still listened docilely enough to those helpful little talks by which Caroline had always tried to mould her character and instil into her something of her own high aims.

"It's not that laughing and joking is wrong, dear. Why, you and I often have quite good jokes together, don't we? It's that—well, we're not put into the world just for fun, and once one begins making fun of things—even little unimportant things—one never knows where it will end. It tends to make one forget the real seriousness of life. So you see, darling, I do so want you to try hard to conquer the part of you—well, the part of you that isn't *my* Fay. . . ."

Fay would become serious, anxious, repentant, as she listened, but she seemed now to try to avoid the talks instead of, as once, looking forward to them. Philippa's influence, Caroline was sure, was coming between them, subtly poisoning their relationship. Only yesterday Caroline had heard Fay laughing in Philippa's bedroom, and when she came out had said:

"What were you laughing at in Aunt Philippa's room, dear?"

The new sulky look had come into Fay's face as she replied:

"Nothing, Caroline. Just a joke that Aunt Philippa made."

"What was it?"

"It wasn't *anything*. I mean, it would sound so silly repeated."

"What was it, dear?"

Flushing and looking still sulkier, Fay repeated a joke that seemed to Caroline utterly futile. She listened gravely, then said:

"And what did you find in that to laugh at?"

Fay, crimson-faced with shame or anger—Caroline had not been sure which—flung away from her into her own bedroom without answering.

A scene like that between them would have been impossible before Philippa came to the house. Caroline did her best to keep Philippa and Fay apart, of course, but she herself was away from the house a good deal, and it was clear that despite her precautions they were seeing a good deal of each other. More than once she had considered asking Philippa to go, but she could not help looking on herself as a personification of the forces of good and Philippa as the personification of the forces of evil, and to ask Philippa to go would be to own herself beaten, to betray the high standard that she had set herself, that she had never yet failed.

And it wasn't only Philippa and Fay. She was worried about Susan too. She had actually obtained from the headmistress of Merton Park School the promise of a post on the staff for Susan, and Susan, instead of accepting it with gratitude, was vacillating, putting off her decision, making excuses. When Caroline argued and reasoned with her, she would mutter that "Kenneth didn't like it," once bursting out with an "Oh, *do* leave me alone, Caroline." She had apologised immediately, but even so, refused to give a definite decision.

"Susan darling, she can't wait for ever. She'll have to appoint someone soon."

"Let her appoint someone else, then," said Susan as if with relief. "I don't want to worry Ken about it any more. He simply hates the idea."

Effie, too, was causing her anxiety. She had thought that Effie had at last reconciled herself to leaving everything in Evelyn's hands, but there had been several of the old scenes between them lately. Carrie had become somewhat difficult to manage, and Evelyn had rightly been very firm with her, but Effie had wanted to give in to the child and let her have her own way, talking a lot of nonsense about her "nerves," as if a child of four could possibly suffer from nerves. Evelyn had appealed to Caroline and in the end they had both appealed to Robert, and Robert had told Effie quite firmly that she must not interfere with Evelyn's management of the children. Once more Effie had sulkily acquiesced, but relations between them were strained, and there was an air of tension in the house. It was bad for the children and made things extremely awkward for Evelyn. Evelyn, of course, was the redeeming feature in the situation, loyal, dependable, clear-sighted. Only yesterday she had told Caroline that she had disliked Philippa since her first meeting with her.

Fay ... Susan ... Effie. ... Caroline felt more depressed than she ever remembered feeling before. She faced the fact that the poison was working in her own soul, too, blurring her serenity, undermining that faith in herself and her ideals that had never before failed her. Again she stiffened her resolution. This visit of Philippa's was sent as a test. It must not find her wanting. She must purge her mind of its dislike of Philippa and rekindle that old desire to help her and influence her for good. She must cling to the knowledge that good is stronger than evil.

She glanced at the clock. Richard would be here any minute now. Richard. She'd never missed him before when he'd been away, but this time she'd missed him acutely. Her thoughts returned to their last interview, at which he had asked her to marry him, and for the first time something within her weakened at the memory.

He loved her and—she realised it now as she had never realised it before—she loved him. Surely it wouldn't be cowardice to rest from the struggle in the comfort of Richard's love. He would probably ask her to marry him again today. She wouldn't actually make up her mind to say "yes," but—she felt very differently from what she had felt that day four weeks ago when he had last asked her. She had felt so strong then. Now she felt tired, dispirited, as if the burden she had taken upon her were more than she could bear.

Hearing the front door-bell, she threw a quick glance at her reflection in the mirror, drawing her hair a little farther down over her forehead, wishing for a moment (before she dismissed the thought as unworthy of her) that the lines of her cheek and jaw were as lovely as Philippa's, resenting Philippa's loveliness with a bitterness that was easily translated into righteous disapproval.

Richard was entering the room, his hands outstretched.

"How good to see you again," he said, "and how well you look!"

The warm reassuring kindliness of him seemed to enter her heart, soothing all its secret turmoil. She looked at him with a new sense of possessiveness. Philippa could spoil nearly everything else, but she couldn't spoil this. This was hers inalienably. There was approval in the smile with which she greeted him. His sunburn—acquired during his holiday—emphasised the blue of his eyes and the slight greying of his temples. She realised for the first time how good-looking he was. She had always before taken him and everything about him for granted. His devotion had seemed so integral a part of her life that she had not valued it. Now the whisperings of disloyalty in her kingdom made loyalty something to be valued, and his became doubly precious.

"Tell me all about your holiday," she smiled. "We've quite missed you."

His answering smile was quizzical and tender as he said:

"I wish I could believe that."

He sat down on the other side of the fireplace and began to tell her about his holiday, describing several incidents that had amused him. She laughed, not because she found them amusing, but because it was so good to feel herself again enclosed in the comfortable walls of his devotion. All her depression and weariness dropped from her. She was restored to her pedestal, surrounded by devout worshippers, for Richard's attitude made her doubts of Fay and Susan seem ridiculous. She had a pleasant sense of almost domestic intimacy as she poured out his tea, putting into his cup the right amount of sugar and milk. Their conversation was trivial enough, but beneath it she was conscious of a deep bond of understanding. Richard knew her as she was, loved her for what she was. Neither Philippa nor anyone else could blur his vision of her. A silence fell on them when the tea things had been removed, and in the silence all her tenseness seemed to relax. She longed to step down from her pedestal and be gathered into his arms. If he asked her again to marry him, she would say "yes."

He broke the silence.

"Your mother's not at home?"

"No. She's gone up to town for the day. She was going to her dressmaker and milliner and to have her hair waved." She smiled indulgently. "Really, Richard, isn't it *absurd* for a woman of her age to spend so much time and trouble over her appearance?"

"Oh, I don't know," he replied. "She's so beautiful that it somehow seems quite natural that she should."

Her smile faded.

"Do you think her beautiful?"

"Of course . . . don't you?"

She shrugged. Her face had hardened. She stood upon her pedestal looking down at him with cold blue eyes.

He continued, unaware that he had said anything to offend her:

"And extremely attractive. I've been feeling so glad for your sake that she's come here."

"Why glad for my sake?"

"For all our sakes," he corrected himself. "She's belonged to a larger life than any of us here have known. She'll jerk us out of our ruts."

She looked at him in silence for some moments, then said:

"I'm sorry you think me narrow, Richard."

He glanced at her in surprise.

"Narrow?"

"Of course, we can't *all* have lived the life my mother has lived. I think it just as well that we haven't, though I gather that you don't agree with me."

She spoke lightly enough and smiled as she spoke, but she was trembling with anger.

He looked uncomfortable.

"My dear," he said, "you know quite well that I didn't mean that."

"What else could you have meant?"

"All that happened such a long time ago."

"She's the same woman now as she was then."

"Caroline, it isn't like you to be so ungenerous."

She caught her breath sharply. For a moment she couldn't believe her ears. So a goddess might have felt whose worshipper had suddenly arisen from his knees and slapped her in the face. Ungenerous! She whose generosity and unselfishness were famous through the town. Why, she was literally a byword for unselfishness. Ungenerous! Before she could reply, however, there came the sound of voices in the hall, Philippa's and Fay's. There was that note of eager excitement in Fay's that Caroline always disliked. She had begun to take it for granted now that Philippa should bring out the worst in everyone she came in contact with, but she could never grow reconciled to the transformation of her grave, responsible little Fay into a giggling schoolgirl.

"How nice to hear Fay laugh like that!" said Richard.

She did not answer. Her mouth was a hard tight line. Richard, too. The very mention of her name had destroyed the understanding between them as if it had never been. The very sound of her voice had blurred his judgement, as it blurred everyone's. Nice to hear Fay laugh like that! A silly childish giggle that was utterly unworthy of her, that wasn't Fay at all . . . not the real Fay . . . *her* Fay. There came the sound of Fay's light footsteps running upstairs, and then Philippa entered smiling.

She was dressed in dark green and looked very beautiful, her pale cheeks slightly flushed, her dark eyes bright.

"I overtook Fay," she said, loosening her furs, "and so we came up together. How do you do, Richard?"

Richard. . . . She had called him by his Christian name at their very first meeting. It was disgraceful. No reticence, no real dignity, behind that delusive mask of breeding. She hadn't realised what a formidable enemy she'd set herself to fight. But she'd fight it. Surely Richard—or anyone else—would eventually see the difference between true metal, and false. If he didn't, he wasn't worthy of her.

"I'll ring for more tea," she said graciously.

"No, please don't," said Philippa. "I had a late lunch, and I don't really want any. Just give me a cup as it is. I don't mind it weak or stewed or anyhow. I'm terribly grubby. I ought to go straight up to wash."

Richard smiled at her radiant freshness.

"You look anything but grubby," he said.

Caroline poured out the tea.

"Well," she said as she handed her the cup, "did you visit your dressmaker and milliner and hairdresser?"

She meant to speak lightly, indulgently, as one might question a child about its toys and games, but something in her voice startled Philippa and made her glance at her keenly. What was the matter? Had she quarrelled with her handsome middle-aged suitor? But he looked untroubled enough.

"Oh yes," she said. "I wasted the entire morning on frivolities, then just had time to go to an agent about a flat before I came home."

"I hope he couldn't find you one," said Richard.

Caroline clutched the sides of her chair till her knuckles stood out like bare bones. How much longer could she endure to sit there and listen to Richard being cheaply flirtatious with this woman?

"I'm afraid he could find me literally hundreds," smiled Philippa, "but I hadn't time to start the hunt today. Marcia will be home next week, you know, and she wants me to go up and see her, so I'll combine business and pleasure and do some flat-hunting at the same time."

"You'd do far better to stay amongst us," said Richard. "We're dull but worthy. We have a Musical Contest of local talent in the winter, and in the summer there are Galas, Fêtes, and Fayres (we never stoop to anything as common as a Fair, of course). Moreover here, at any rate, your next-door neighbour will call on you."

"Is that an advantage?" smiled Philippa.

"A doubtful one, I grant you. It depends so much on the next-door neighbour."

"Exactly. One's duty to one's neighbour is one of life's most difficult problems. The Bible is explicit as far as it goes, but it doesn't go far enough. It must be so much easier to make practical arrangements for one's next-door neighbour when one finds him lying wounded on the road than it is to be pleasant when he comes round to borrow the garden shears for the fifth time in one week."

Caroline's heart was beating in hammer-strokes. "Dull but worthy." That Richard should sneer at their quiet, simple Bartenham life! The sneer might almost have been aimed at her personally. And—most cruel of all—they both seemed to have forgotten her existence. They were talking to each other as if she were not in the room. Designing. That was the word one used for women like that. And—to think it was her own mother!

She was relieved when Mrs. Beecham, the curate's mother, was announced. Mrs. Beecham was arranging the annual sale of work for the local hospital, at which Caroline usually had a stall. Conversation was general for a few minutes, then Mrs. Beecham began to discuss the arrangements for the sale with Caroline, while Richard and Philippa, on the opposite side of the hearth, continued their conversation. Caroline strained her ears to hear what they were saying, but could only catch a word here and there.

Richard was laughing a good deal more than he usually did, she noticed, and at nothing at all, as far as she could make out. Each time his laugh rang out, her heart contracted with a sharp physical pain.

"And you'll bring your usual band of young helpers, won't you?" said Mrs. Beecham. She was a large majestic woman with prominent features and a gushing manner. "You can do *anything* with young people. My Rosa always tells me how she used to love your lessons at St. Monica's. It's a wonderful gift, Miss Cunliffe, and I do congratulate you on it."

Caroline was silent for a moment, hoping that the other two had heard the little tribute, but Richard was laughing at something Philippa had just said, and it was clear that they had not heard.

"I've had a lot to do with young people," said Caroline clearly. "I understand them."

"I should think you do, Miss Cunliffe. We all know how *wonderfully* you understand them and what a wonderful mother you've been to your own young people."

Again Caroline was silent, but again it was obvious that the other two were not listening. They were discussing Philippa's visit to Town on Tuesday. Richard was suggesting that he should drive her up in his car. A sick hatred that she had never before known or even imagined filled Caroline's heart. Her breath came quickly, and a pulse seemed to beat so loudly in her ears that she could not hear what Mrs. Beecham was saying. By the time it stopped, Mrs. Beecham had left the subject of her hostess's perfections and was discussing the efforts that were being made in Bartenham to mitigate the lot of the unemployed.

"It's really pitiful, Miss Cunliffe. Some of them, of course, aren't on the dole at all. They can literally barely keep body and soul together."

"I know," said Caroline. "That's why I can't understand people spending money on expensive clothes when there's so much poverty and suffering in the world. It's nothing less than murder. It sounds fantastic to say that an extravagant woman's dress or hat may kill a child, but it's true. . . ."

Her voice rang through the room, high-pitched and unsteady, attracting the attention of the other two at last. A sudden silence fell as they turned to her, Philippa grave and concerned, Richard acutely embarrassed. Mrs. Beecham continued to look complacent and assured.

"I'm sure no one can accuse you of extravagance, Miss Cunliffe," she said.

"No, I inherited a strong social conscience from my father," said Caroline. "I think I can honestly say that I never spend a penny more than is absolutely necessary on myself. I went through a hard school, of course, in bringing up my young brother and sisters."

She had control of herself now and spoke quite steadily. The words were addressed to Mrs. Beecham, but really she was arraigning Philippa fiercely, passionately, at the bar of Richard's judgement.

"You don't look well, dear," said Mrs. Beecham solicitously.

"I feel quite well," said Caroline, "but—it's rather close today, isn't it?"

Mrs. Beecham rose, smiling.

"I think it's cold," she said, "but I always say no two people ever feel the same about the weather. It's all a matter of constitution. Well, I must really be going now, my dear."

She shook hands with the other two, and Caroline saw her to the front door. When she had gone, Caroline stood for a few moments in the hall, trying to recover her self-possession. She was still breathless and trembling. She had heard Fay come down to the dining-room. She must have had her tea now and be doing her home-work. She wondered whether to go in to her and wait there till she felt less agitated, but she didn't want the child to guess that anything was wrong. Even Mrs. Beecham had said that she didn't look well. She daren't let herself think of Philippa lest that hot breathless feeling of anger should surge over her again. She went slowly back to the drawing-room.

"I've just been telling Philippa about Mrs. Beecham," said Richard.

"What about her?" said Caroline.

Mrs. Beecham, with her gush and complacency and her habit of inaugurating innumerable pieces of social work and leaving them for someone else to carry on, was a local joke, and Richard and Caroline had often smiled together over her vagaries.

But now Mrs. Beecham seemed to Caroline part of the safe ordered world that was, she felt, being undermined by Philippa's baneful influence. So she fixed cold blue eyes on Richard and said:

"What about her?"

"In general and in particular. In particular of the time she met the Vicar of St. Mary's in the 'bus and said——"

"Please, Richard. Mrs. Beecham is a friend of mine."

"Sorry," said Richard. He looked at her, puzzled. "You *don't* look well, you know, Caroline."

"I'm perfectly well," said Caroline. She turned to Philippa. "Did you say that you overtook Fay?"

"Yes."

"You hadn't arranged to meet her?"

"Oh no. I'd no idea what train I'd be coming back by. That nice boy—what's his name?—Billy Dickson—came back with us, too, as far as the gate."

"How did that happen?"

Philippa smiled.

"How do I know, my dear? He just appeared."

At that smile of Philippa's—a smile that took it as a matter of course that Fay, Fay of all people, should indulge in the crude banality of a "boy friend"—the hot suffocating feeling of anger swept over her again.

"It was extremely impertinent of him," she said shortly. "I don't care for any of the Dicksons and neither does Fay."

"I thought that Sybil was her friend."

"They have to see a certain amount of each other at school, of course, as they're in the same form, but Fay doesn't care for either her or her brother."

"I suppose the piano's the attraction then?" said Philippa innocently.

Caroline stared at her in silence.

"The piano?" she said at last.

"Yes." Philippa was obviously puzzled by Caroline's tone. "The Dicksons' piano."

"What about the Dicksons' piano?"

"Well . . . I gathered that Fay sometimes calls there after school to play on it, that's all."

"Did Fay tell you so?"

"No. Billy was referring to it. I overtook the two of them. He generally walks up from school with her, doesn't he?"

Two red spots blazed in Caroline's pale cheeks.

"If anything like that had ever happened," she said, "Fay would have told me at once."

Philippa threw out her hands in a little deprecating gesture.

"But, Caroline, what does it matter? Fay's an attractive girl, and it's natural that she should enjoy a boy's admiration."

Suddenly Caroline's self-control broke down.

"I dare say it is to you," she flamed. "I can quite believe that your standards and mine on a subject like that would be as far apart as the poles."

"Caroline!" said Richard.

"It's all right, Richard," said Philippa. "I'm sorry, Caroline. I'm stupid and exceedingly tactless. I think I'll go up and wash now."

She went out of the room.

"You oughtn't to have said that to your mother, Caroline," said Richard as the door closed.

Caroline was very white.

"I think I'm the best judge of what I ought or ought not to say to anyone," she replied.

He shrugged.

"I'm sorry, anyway. I suppose I'd better go now. . . ." He held out his hand. "Goodbye, Caroline. Don't bother to come with me. I can let myself out."

"Goodbye."

He was gone. . . . She heard the closing of the front door. She stood where he had left her, staring in front of her, her lips tightly set. There were a lot of things to see to. She must speak to Fay, for one thing, though, of course, what Philippa had said was ridiculous on the face of it. Billy Dickson might have been with Fay today, but it had never happened before, or Fay would have told her at once. First of all, though, she must get back her serenity, that serenity on which she had always prided herself. It had been a trying afternoon. She had had to speak sharply to Philippa. She always disliked doing that, but sometimes, as this afternoon, it was necessary. There were times when one had to stand up for one's ideals without flinching, to speak out plainly and to the point, to rebuke what one disapproved of without compunction or compromise. That was what she had had to do this afternoon. It had been her clear duty, and she had not shrunk from it, even at the cost of offending both Philippa and Richard. Richard. . . . That, of course, was what hurt so intolerably. That Richard should fail her, should join the ranks of the disloyal. But, still, it was best that she should see him as he really was before it was too late, however much suffering it cost her. She thought of that bond of love and understanding that had seemed to unite them earlier in the afternoon, and her eyes swam suddenly with tears.

Perhaps that was the lesson she had to learn from life—the lesson of loneliness, the lesson of not lowering her high standards to conform with those of people around her. Alone upon the heights. ... She saw herself, a pathetic figure, alone, always alone, struggling along unaided, staggering under the weight of her too great burdens, but never sinking under them. It was, in a way, a gratifying picture, and, as she contemplated it, her serenity gradually returned. After all, whatever happened, she had one great comfort. She had done her duty. She had nothing, nothing whatever, to reproach herself with.

Chapter Twelve

FAY ran lightly downstairs to the dining-room, where her tea was laid on the big mahogany table. It had been lovely walking home with Philippa and Billy. When she was with them—both of them or either of them—she always felt happy and light-hearted, as if she needn't worry about the scholarship or how wicked she was, or any of the other things she generally worried about. She felt that she could just enjoy life instead of taking it seriously, as Caroline always wanted her to. But that brought her back to Caroline again, and at the thought of Caroline a heavy weight of guilt seemed to fasten itself upon her spirit. She hadn't told Caroline about coming home from school with Billy and calling at the Dicksons'. She'd done it every day for the past week, and she'd just let Caroline take for granted that she'd been kept late at school, which, with all her extra scholarship work, seemed natural enough. It was terribly deceitful not to have told Caroline about it. She could almost hear Caroline saying, "It's not like *my* Fay."

But then she wasn't Caroline's "my Fay," and the most dreadful part of it all was that right down at the bottom of her heart she didn't want to be. She was working hard at her scholarship subjects, but she didn't really want to win a scholarship or go to college or teach or influence other people for good or do any of the things that Caroline was so anxious for her to do. She wanted to take up music and enjoy life and have friends like Billy and Sybil and Philippa—who seemed so young though she was old—not like Freda Torrent. She'd thought that Caroline's reference to Doris Pemberton would have spoilt her friendship with Billy, but it hadn't done. She'd dreaded meeting him after it, but, as soon as she did meet him, everything was simple and natural and jolly again, and she could laugh at her secret fears, as she always could when she was with him. His uncritical friendliness gave her a lovely feeling of carefree happiness—so different was it from Caroline's anxious brooding affection. But still—her thoughts returned to it guiltily—she ought to have told Caroline about walking home with him and calling at the Dicksons'. She'd have to soon, of course. The weight of it on her conscience would suddenly become more than she could bear, and she'd go to Caroline and confess, and Caroline would be grieved and hurt but very, very sweet and would talk to her about how wrong it was and how she must fight very hard against her evil tendencies, and—she wouldn't be able to have anything more to do with Sybil or Billy.

One new and mysterious element in the situation was that sometimes now sudden gusts of hatred would come over her, hatred of Caroline whom really she loved so devotedly, so that she could hardly bear to look at her, so that even her touch made her want to scream. They took her by surprise, seeming to spring upon her from outside. She felt bitterly ashamed of them afterwards and would lie awake at night suffering agonies of remorse.

She pushed her plate away and poured out another cup of tea. She didn't feel hungry. She had a headache, but she often had headaches nowadays. She often had a curious ache in her throat too, as if she'd been crying for a long time, though really she hadn't been crying at all.

Richard and Philippa and Caroline were having tea in the drawing-room. Probably Richard would come in to speak to her on his way out. He generally did. She liked Richard. He was kind and understanding, and Caroline was always in a good temper when he'd been to tea. The front door-bell rang, and someone else was shown in. Fay listened. Mrs. Beecham. She made a little grimace to herself. How dreadful! The drawing-room door was shut again, and she could only hear a faint murmur of voices.

Her mind went back over the day. Sybil had discovered that it would be her birthday next month and wanted to give a party for her and invite some of their school friends and some of Billy's.

It had been so hard to explain that she and Caroline always spent her birthday together, and that she daren't even suggest doing anything else.

"But you've not fixed anything definite with her for this year, have you?" said Sybil.

"No, but I've always spent it at home with her. She'd be terribly hurt if I didn't."

"But you spend every blessed day at home with her. Surely for your birthday——"

"I can't, Sybil. It isn't any use."

She'd have to spend her birthday alone with Caroline as usual, and Caroline would buy a birthday cake and would be very sweet to her, and—oh, it was hateful of her to feel that she'd much rather be with Sybil and Billy and their friends.

The same thing had happened with Philippa this evening.

"When I get my flat in London," Philippa had said as the three of them walked up from the town, "and Fay's exam, is over, both of you—and Sybil, of course—must come up and have lunch with me, and we'll all go to a play."

"I say, how sporting of you!" Billy had said. "We'd simply love it."

But Fay had flushed and murmured:

"It's sweet of you, but——"

"But what, darling?"

"I don't think I could."

"Why not?"

And again she couldn't tell Philippa that Caroline would hate her to go up to Town with them, would consider it disloyal of her even to think of it. She couldn't explain why even to herself. It belonged to that dark world in which one groped one's way uncertainly, always in secret terror of hurting or offending Caroline, that world in which Caroline was the sun and moon and stars, and one must not even appear to be paying allegiance to anyone or anything else.

"We'll ask Caroline too," said Philippa, as if reading her thoughts.

"Oh no," said Fay unhappily. "I mean, I don't think Caroline likes theatres much."

It would be worse than not going at all to have Caroline there with them, to be on edge all the time lest one of them should say anything that Caroline wouldn't approve of. Sybil and Billy would be sure to make fun of something serious or laugh at a joke that Caroline wouldn't consider funny or be obviously bored by the things Caroline talked about. Caroline did occasionally take her up to Town on half-term holidays to the British Museum or St. Paul's or Westminster Abbey or some other "place of interest" as the *Guide to London* called them—but that wasn't the sort of going up to Town Philippa meant. Caroline taught her about architecture and history on those expeditions, and they took sandwiches with them and ate them in the park, or, if it was cold, in the waiting-room at the railway station. They were very earnest improving expeditions, and Caroline would playfully put her through a little examination the next day to see how much she remembered.

The drawing-room door opened. Mrs. Beecham was going. Caroline was seeing her off at the front door. The front door closed again. Caroline returned to the drawing-room. Probably she and Richard were telling Aunt Philippa about Mrs. Beecham now, how funny she was and how she loved to have her finger in every pie.

She went over to the writing-table and took some books out of her attaché-case. She'd do the French translation first. She opened her book at the place and read a paragraph without having recourse to the dictionary. Then she stopped and put her head in her hands. Jagged pains were playing about behind her eyes like small sharp knives. They nearly always did that now as soon as she began to work. She hadn't told Caroline. It wasn't long before the examination, and it seemed silly to start making a fuss about a thing like that just before the examination. If she told Caroline, of course, Caroline would be sweet to her, but she felt that she couldn't bear anyone to be sweet to her just now. If they were, she'd begin to cry and never be able to stop. It was hateful to feel that you might begin to cry at any moment for no reason, but she felt like that all the time nowadays. She'd nearly disgraced herself the other evening at the Dicksons'. She hadn't meant to play the piano, but Billy had asked her to, and somehow she'd found herself sitting there playing Chopin's Nocturne in E flat. And as she played all the tenseness of her spirit had relaxed, and she had forgotten everything else in the world—even Caroline and the scholarship. When she'd finished, Sybil and Billy had said "How jolly!" and begged her to play again, but they hadn't understood. All the rest of the evening the lump in her throat kept rising ... rising. She'd managed to control it till she went to bed, but there she had let it have its way with her and had lain sobbing convulsively, pulling the bedclothes over her head and burying her face in the pillow so that Caroline should not hear.

No, she mustn't let anyone persuade her to play again. Caroline was right. It unsettled her mind and took it off her work. Her work hadn't been good lately. She knew that the mistresses were disappointed, though they were very kind to her. She felt stupid and she kept forgetting things. A terrible certainty was forming in her mind that she couldn't possibly win the scholarship, and, of course, it would be better to die than to disappoint Caroline like that.

The drawing-room door opened, and there came the sound of Philippa's footsteps going upstairs. She was glad that Philippa was here. Something about even the thought of her made one feel less guilty, less frightened.

Someone was coming into the hall now ... opening the front door ... closing it. She glanced through the window. Richard was walking down the short drive. He hadn't come in to see her, after all. Perhaps Caroline had told him not to interrupt her at her home-work. And Caroline hadn't come to the door with him as she usually did. Perhaps she didn't want the sound of their talking to disturb her. Guiltily she returned to her French book, but again little knife-like pains began to stir behind her eyes. She turned sharply as the door opened. Caroline stood there. She looked very pale.

"How are you getting on, darling?"

"Oh ... I've only just begun."

"Well, bring it into the drawing-room, then I can give you a hand."

Rather reluctantly Fay gathered her books together and followed Caroline into the drawing-room. There she settled down at Caroline's writing-desk, and Caroline took her seat in the armchair by the fire. Suddenly she said:

"Fay, is it true that Sybil's brother walked home with you after school?"

Fay's heart began to beat unevenly.

"Billy? Yes. Philippa was there, too."

Caroline was on the point of saying, "Why didn't you tell me?" but stopped, realising that Fay had had no opportunity of telling her. Instead she said, "Has it ever happened before?"

"Yes."

"Sybil's brother has walked from school with you?"

"Yes."

"And you've called at their house before coming on here?"

"Yes."

"Why didn't you tell me?"

"I don't know."

"Fay," Caroline's voice was deep and vibrant with reproach, "this isn't like you."

Fay said nothing. She felt that a scene with Caroline just now would be more than she could endure. Caroline was moving her chair to make room for her on the hearthrug at her feet.

"Darling, come here. Let's talk this out. I don't understand. . . . It isn't like you."

Slowly, unwillingly, her heart still beating unevenly, Fay came across the room and sat down on the hearthrug at Caroline's feet.

"You know, darling," went on Caroline, "how I hate anything secretive. It isn't worthy of you. That's why it hurts me so. Why didn't you tell me?"

"I don't know," said Fay again in a tense breathless voice.

"I think it must have been because you thought I'd disapprove, because you knew that I think the Dicksons don't bring out the best in you. You know that yourself, if you'll be honest with yourself, don't you, darling? They make you silly and irresponsible—not *my* Fay."

Fay conquered a wild desire to cry out that Caroline's Fay did not exist, that Caroline had invented it, and Fay had tried to turn herself into it—tried till she was sick with trying—and hadn't been able to. "I'm myself," she wanted to cry, "I'm not anyone else's. Leave me alone, leave me alone, leave me alone."

Caroline's grave tender voice went on.

"Wasn't that why you didn't tell me, darling—because you knew that it would hurt and disappoint me to know that you were still on friendly terms with those Dicksons?"

"Yes."

"And don't you see how secretive, how disloyal it was?"

Disloyal. The word tore at Fay's heart, reminding her of all she owed to Caroline, of all Caroline had done for her, of Caroline's unfailing love and tenderness. Why, even now Caroline wasn't cross, only hurt and grieved and disappointed.

"Yes."

"Has Sybil's brother ever walked from school with you alone?"

"Yes."

"Fay, *darling*." The reproach was deeper, graver. "Don't you see how *cheap*, how *second-rate* it all is?"

The colour blazed crimson in Fay's cheeks. Her friendship with Billy was a pleasant natural boy-and-girl friendship, but Caroline seemed determined to spoil it, to dim its clarity, to invest it with some subtle quality of evil.

"But, Caroline," protested Fay, "if he's just passing when I come out of school—he comes out of school about the same time, you know—what can I do?"

"You must tell him that I disapprove of your walking home together."

There was a silence in which Fay tried to imagine herself telling Billy that Caroline disapproved of their walking home together.

"Oh, *Caroline*!" she protested unhappily.

"And, Fay," went on Caroline gravely, "I don't want to say anything against her because she's my own mother, but her standards aren't quite ours—yours and mine—and I don't want you to be on too intimate terms with her. You must be polite to her, of course, but I don't think there's any need for you to be more than that."

Again Fay was silent. Aunt Philippa, with her loveliness and charm, her radiant joy of life, and that hint of understanding tenderness that lay beneath all her dealings with one. . . . Sybil and Billy and Aunt Philippa. . . . She was to lose them all.

"But, Caroline," she said, "Aunt Philippa . . . she's—she's so nice. I mean . . ."

"Darling," said Caroline, "you must let me be judge in this case. I know her better than you." She put out an arm and drew Fay's slender figure against her knee. "Darling, you know what a lot you mean to me, and how terribly even the slightest disloyalty in you hurts me. You're my baby, you know, sweetheart. You're all I've got now Susan's gone. If ever you turned against me . . ."

"Caroline, don't," cried Fay in a strangled voice. "I *do* love you. . . . You know I do."

"I think you do . . . but love isn't just feeling, you know, dearest, it's *doing*. It's trying not to fail the one you love, to be worthy of their ideal of you, to be loyal to them in thought and word and deed, to . . ."

The hot sultry atmosphere of Caroline's love seemed to surround her on all sides, so that she couldn't breathe. And suddenly the tears that she had been fighting to keep back ever since Caroline began to speak to her came with a rush, in a sharp paroxysm of sobs. Caroline, smiling tenderly, gathered her into her arms.

"There, darling, don't . . . don't. . . . I know you're sorry. I . . ."

Fay flung off the encircling arms with a desperate gesture.

"Leave me alone . . . leave me *alone*," she sobbed, and rushed from the room.

Chapter Thirteen

CAROLINE was alone in the drawing-room when Philippa came down. Her face looked pale and worn in the half light.

"Fay's crying in her bedroom," said Philippa. "Is anything the matter?"

"No," said Caroline in a hard aloof voice. "She's a little overwrought, that's all."

Philippa was silent. After this afternoon's scene she felt that the only dignified course would be to suggest going up to London to stay in a hotel while she looked for a flat, but she didn't want to. This household of Caroline's was charged with electricity, and at any moment an explosion might occur. She felt inexplicably involved in it all. Fay, of course, was really no relation of hers, but there had been a feeling of kinship and understanding between them from the first moment of their meeting. The child was overworked and unhappy, on the edge of a bad nervous breakdown. For years her growing individuality had been denied every outlet by Caroline's possessiveness. At every turn it was hampered and thwarted by the sultry unhealthy emotion that Caroline called her "love." A less sensitive and fine-wrought character than Fay's would have found a solution in open defiance or a course of calculated deceit, but Fay struggled blindly, despairingly, to conform to Caroline's standards, and the struggle was obviously breaking down her health of both body and mind.

The very atmosphere of this house of Caroline's was so alien to her that that alone would have irked and oppressed her spirit. Fay was born for the sunshine, for gaiety and laughter and friendship. Caroline's heavy earnestness of purpose, her unrelieved drabness of outlook, were like clumsy fingers rubbing the bloom off a butterfly's wings. And Fay was an artist—an artist who was being mercilessly forced into a rigid academic mould. She had uttered no complaint to Philippa, nothing even that could be construed as a complaint, but Philippa guessed how integral a part of her being was her love of music. Her very fingers, which toiled so inkily at French and German exercises, were musician's fingers, slender, nervous, instinct with life. And there was Caroline, so pathetic in her self-righteousness, so ungrudging in her labours, so full of love—diseased, distorted, but still love—for the children to whom she had sacrificed her youth. One could only feel a heart-racking pity for her.

"She's not looked well lately," said Philippa tentatively. "Don't you think perhaps she's doing too much?"

"She's perfectly well," said Caroline shortly. "She's just a little tired, that's all."

"Those shadows under her eyes . . ."

"My dear Philippa, I understand Fay. I've looked after her since she was a baby. If she were ill, I should be the first person to see it. She's always had that look of delicacy, but it doesn't mean anything. She's quite strong. She's never had a serious illness in her life."

"I know. . . . I only meant that perhaps this scholarship work is a bit too much for her."

"That's quite impossible. I supervise her hours of work most carefully. . . . Of course, any competitive exam, is a certain strain, but I think Fay's standing it remarkably well. She has no other responsibilities. When I was working for my scholarship, I had to run the house at the same time and as often as not do the cooking."

"It was wonderful of you," said Philippa sincerely. It was useless to point out to Caroline the difference between her physique and Fay's, the fact that Caroline was a born student and that Fay was not. "Caroline . . ." she went on slowly, "would you like me to go and stay at a hotel in London till I've found my flat?"

Caroline looked at her with wide-open eyes.

"Why?"

"I thought you might prefer it."

"Of course not. . . . I told you that you were welcome here as long as you cared to stay, and I meant it."

"It will only be for a few weeks in any case."

This afternoon's little outburst, then, was to be ignored. That simplified the situation. Caroline had been jealous, of course, because Richard had appeared to be interested in her—a mild enough interest, it would have seemed to anyone less possessive than Caroline. Caroline would not marry him—Philippa had gathered so much—but she could not endure to see him making himself pleasant to any other woman. She allowed no rivals near the throne. . . . What would happen to her when her kingdom began to disintegrate? She would fight to the end for Fay, of course. . . .

Caroline's thoughts had gone again to Richard. Even now, probably, he was feeling acutely ashamed of his behaviour. She would be rather cold and distant to him next time she met him, then gradually, very gradually, she would reinstate him in his old position of confidence. Her love was out of the question—for the present, at any rate—but she would give him her confidence again. He was too clear-sighted to be deceived for long by a woman like Philippa. His remorse when he realised how nearly he had forfeited her friendship would be almost as bitter as Fay's had been. Her face softened to tenderness as she thought of Fay. Her penitence had been heartrendingly sincere. That tortured "Leave me alone," as if she were too much ashamed even to receive Caroline's forgiving kiss. . . . Poor little Fay! Caroline felt no real anxiety about her. She was always so quick to realise when she had been in the wrong. She was weak and impressionable, but her standards were firm enough, and she was innately fastidious. She only wanted a little help and guidance. There would be no more trapesing about the streets with that Dickson boy, no more wasting of her time by visits to the Dicksons' house. There would probably never have been any if it hadn't been for Philippa's influence. Well, she'd met and vanquished Philippa's influence there, and she would meet and vanquish it in any other form in which it showed itself. . . .

She went upstairs to Fay's room. Fay was just coming out of it.

Her eyes were red-rimmed, but she looked quite-composed again. Caroline slipped an arm round her.

"Darling," she said, "you do look a little tired. I think you'd better go to bed directly after dinner. I'll write a note asking them to excuse your homework. You can make it up at the week-end when you're feeling fresh again, can't you?"

"Yes ... thank you."

Fay was conscious of nothing but a sickening throbbing in her head and a longing for the comfort of Caroline's tenderness, the tenderness that had consoled her through all her childish troubles. That hateful "Leave me alone" was an unbearable weight on her conscience. How could she have said that to Caroline, to *Caroline*? . . .

"Caroline, I'm sorry ..." she whispered.

The clasp of Caroline's arm tightened around her, and she relaxed to it with a little sigh. One could always be so sure of Caroline's love and tenderness. It never failed one, however wicked one had been, however tired one felt.

"Sweetheart," Caroline was saying tenderly, "it's all right. I understand. Don't think of it again. . . . You're *my* Fay now, aren't you?"

"Yes."

Yes, she was Caroline's Fay now. If only the hammering in her head would stop! Every movement made it worse. And she was so tired. . . . She wished she were little again and could be gathered into Caroline's arms and rocked to sleep. She was Caroline's Fay now.

Fay went to bed immediately after dinner. Caroline helped her undress, gave her two aspirins, then sat on the bed, stroking the hot forehead with smooth cool fingers. . . .

"Caroline, *darling* ..." murmured Fay.

She was soothed and drowsy with sleep when Caroline left her and went downstairs. She had hardly taken her seat in the drawing-room when Susan burst in. It was plain even before she spoke that she was in a state of violent agitation. Caroline rose hastily to her feet.

"Darling, what is it? What's happened? . . . Tell me. . . . Is Kenneth . . . ?"

Suppose Kenneth were dead, she thought. An accident. A sudden illness. Such things did happen. Susan would come back here to live, would be able to take up her career again. It was providential that she'd just got the promise of that post at Merton Park for her. . . . Poor Susan! What a tragedy! But like all tragedies it would have its bright side. She and Kenneth weren't really suited to each other. Better this sharp sudden ending than a lifetime of disillusionment and regret.

Susan was fumbling with the clasp of her bag. At last she tore it open, took out a letter, and handed it to Caroline.

"I couldn't believe it . . . I couldn't believe it . . . but it's true. He says it's true. . . ."

Caroline read the letter in silence.

"Whom is this from?"

"A woman he lived with. I didn't *know* he was like that. I thought . . ." She burst into sobs. "I can't *believe* it. Oh, Caroline, what shall I *do*?"

Caroline drew a long deep breath. . . . There was no doubt where her duty lay. . . . There must be no compromise with immorality. Beneath the solemnity of that thought ran a fierce glad exultation. At last her enemy was delivered into her hand—this wretched boy who had dared to steal Susan from her, to change Susan, to blind her to all she had valued before. . . . It was her turn now, and she would not spare him. It was her duty not to spare him.

"How long have you known of this, Susan?"

"Only just now. . . . I found it. . . . He said he didn't know he'd kept it. He'd burnt all her other letters. . . . It happened before he met me, but . . . Oh, Caroline, I didn't *know* he was like that."

She sank down into a chair sobbing, and Caroline, sitting on the arm of it, gathered her tenderly into her arms.

"He'd told you nothing before?"

Susan raised her flushed face.

"No. . . . I took for granted that he—wasn't like that. I can't believe it even now. He said he'd never loved anyone in the world but me."

Caroline held her more tightly, laying her cheek against the soft brown hair.

"Don't, darling. Don't cry like that. . . . You'll come back to Caroline. Caroline will look after you now. . . . There, there! My baby, my sweetheart. . . . Listen, darling. Just tell me this. He knows you've found it, of course. What did he say?"

"He said it meant nothing."

"Meant nothing!" echoed Caroline contemptuously.

"That he gave her up as soon as he got to know me. . . . But—oh, Caroline, he must have been hateful to do it at all, mustn't he? It's wicked, isn't it? When I think that another woman—oh, I can't *bear* it. I just couldn't let him touch me. I—I feel I can never go back to him again."

"You mustn't go back to him," said Caroline quietly.

"But, Caroline"—Susan's tear-brimmed eyes were startled— "he—he *is* my husband. I married him."

"He's forfeited the right to be considered as your husband," said Caroline. Her lips were tight, her eyes blue and steely. "He should have told you before you were married. Then, of course, you wouldn't have married him. No decent girl would. He's tricked you into marrying him. You've a perfect right to refuse to go back to him."

Susan hid her face against Caroline's shoulder with a fresh tempest of sobs.

"I loved him so. . . . I *loved* him so."

"Darling, you loved the man you thought he was. . . . We must face this thing. He *wasn't* the sort of man you thought he was, was he?"

"N-no."

"Well, then . . . like so many other girls, precious, you were just in love with love. I wasn't happy about it right from the beginning. I was to blame in not having somehow managed to stop it. But—oh, I wanted you to be happy. Now I know the sort of man he is, I know that you could never be happy with him."

"But, Caroline," said Susan, sitting up and wiping her eyes, "he says that he's never—been like that since we were married, and he never will be. He says there was never anyone else besides—that woman—even before . . ."

"And you believed him?" said Caroline pityingly. "Susan, surely you realise that a man who's lived—that sort of life always lies about it. And a man who's once gone in for that sort of thing never gives it up. Oh, my darling, how I wish we'd known!"

"I was so fond of him," said Susan shakily, "and he seemed so fond of me. . . ." She turned to Philippa, who had sat silent throughout the interview, her eyes fixed gravely on Caroline. "What do you think about it, Philippa?"

"Shall I tell you?" said Philippa.

"Yes . . . please."

"I think that what happened before he met you isn't your business. I think that if he's been faithful to you since your marriage—that's all you've a right to ask."

Caroline's eyes were like blue ice.

"I don't agree with you at all," she said coldly, "but, even if we adopt your point of view, how is Susan to know that he has been faithful to her? A man who hadn't the honesty to tell her about the affair she's just discovered would hardly be likely to tell the truth about anything else."

"That's putting it rather strongly, Caroline."

"I feel strongly. There's no room for compromise in my ideals. And I'm not going to have this man or anyone else playing fast and loose with Susan's happiness. The marriage has been a failure from the beginning. It isn't only this. It's—everything. He's deliberately kept her short of money."

"Oh *no*, Caroline," put in Susan. "He couldn't help that. He——"

"Susan, darling, let me finish. I used to wonder how it was that there was so little money, when Melsham's used to be one of the best businesses in the town. This explains it, of course. A man who goes in for this sort of thing doesn't generally have much money left for his wife. . . ."

"Caroline, do you really think——?"

147

"I'm afraid so, darling. Much as I'd like to, I can't bring myself to think that the affair you've discovered is an isolated one. I'm afraid that you and all of us have been tragically deceived. I blame myself terribly. I never liked him. I ought to have guessed. . . ."

"Oh, Caroline, it's not your fault."

"Does he know you've come here, Susan?"

"Yes. He tried to stop me. He . . ."

She broke down again, sobbing helplessly.

"Come to bed, darling," murmured Caroline tenderly. "It won't take any time at all to get your old room ready for you."

"Oh no, Caroline, I must go back to him. I——"

"Darling, I know better than you in this case."

"But I can't leave him—I can't——"

"I don't say leave him, but you mustn't go back to him tonight. There must be a period of probation before you go back to him. Darling, you *can't* live with him again immediately after this."

Susan's face flamed crimson.

"I know . . . I felt like that. . . . I just had to go away at once . . . anywhere. . . . I couldn't bear it."

"Come to bed, dearest. You're tired out. Don't think about it any more. I'll help you get to bed and tuck you up and——"

"But suppose he comes. . . ."

"I'll deal with him."

Caroline's lips were grim.

"But, Caroline, don't let him think. . . . Tell him that it's just tonight. . . . He is my husband, but—oh, it's all so *horrible*."

"Darling, I understand. You can leave it all to me."

Susan's round tear-stained face looked like an unhappy child's.

"You always understand everything so wonderfully, Caroline. I don't know what I'd do without you."

"That's what I'm here for—to help you all," smiled Caroline. "Now come along, darling."

"Goodnight, Philippa."

"Goodnight, dear."

Caroline drew her from the room, and the door closed behind them.

Philippa sat gazing into space, her brows drawn into a frown. The fact that she was Caroline's guest made her position a difficult one. She liked both Susan and the young husband, and it wasn't easy to sit by and watch Caroline deliberately spoiling their chance of happiness. She was still wondering how far she would be justified in going to Susan and forcibly putting his point of view before her, when the door opened and Kenneth entered.

He entered breathlessly as if he had been running. His face was white and strained. He looked round the room, then stopped short.

"Where is she?" he said.

"Susan? She's upstairs with Caroline."

"She told you?"

"Yes."

"I know it's—beastly. I tried to tell her before we were married. I did, honestly. Over and over again. And I couldn't. I thought it would—spoil things. I meant to—make up for it. I never loved the girl. I loathed the very thought of her once I'd met Susan. But I ought to have told her. I knew all along that I ought to have told her. Then this beastly thing wouldn't have happened."

"There hasn't been anyone since you married Susan, has there?" said Philippa.

"Of course not."

There was a silence, then he said, "You believe me, don't you?"

"Yes . . . but Caroline's been trying to make out that there must have been others."

A look of bitterness came into his face, stripping it of its youth.

"She would," he said with a short hard laugh. "She'll be as pleased as Punch over it. She's been working for it all along. She's never given us a chance right from the beginning. I always knew when she'd been to see Susan, even when Susan didn't tell me. She made her—different. She tried hard to stop her marrying me, of course, but that wasn't any good. I used to think that it would be all right once we were married, that she'd leave us alone then, but she didn't. It was the same with Robert and Effie. She had no peace till she'd come between them. Effie was a jolly little thing once, but Caroline made Robert see her as a fool, and that turned her into a fool. It does, you know. And Susan. ... She made her see things as grievances that would have just been part of the fun if she'd left us alone. I was keeping her short of money ... I was turning her into a drudge. ... She had the impudence to suggest her getting a job. She'll never let Susan forget this all the rest of her life."

"I suppose that Susan's—rather weak?" said Philippa.

"It isn't that Susan's weak. It's that Caroline's strong. She's like iron. She never gives in. I always disliked her, but I used to think she was negligible. I'm finding out that she isn't. Just as Effie found it out. ... And, like Effie, finding it out too late. You're her mother, and I oughtn't to say all this to you, but—you've been here long enough to see how things are, haven't you?"

"The difficulty is," said Philippa slowly, "that Caroline really loves them."

"Love!" he echoed contemptuously. "She loves them so much that she hates everyone else who comes near them. She'd really rather kill Susan than share her with anyone, just as she is killing Fay. I suppose you've noticed that she's killing Fay? But Fay's not my business. If I can get Susan from her sane, that's all I care about. God, how I hate her! I've lain awake whole nights *sick* with hatred of her. And now—this! What a crazy fool I've been!" He looked at her for a moment in silence. "You'll help me, won't you? You must. You see——"

The door opened and Caroline entered. When she saw Kenneth she drew herself up to her full height. Her eyes were blazing.

"How *dare* you come here after what Susan has told me?" she said.

His face went white with anger.

"I've come for Susan."

"She's not going with you."

"I won't take that from you. Where's Susan?"

"She told me to tell you that she's not going home."

"May I see her, please?"

"No."

"Why not?"

"She doesn't want to see you. I don't know how you have the effrontery to come here at all."

"Is it effrontery to want to see my own wife?"

"Certainly, after the way you've treated her. I wonder you aren't ashamed to look me—or any decent woman—in the face."

"I won't discuss that with you. That's a matter solely between Susan and me."

"What concerns Susan concerns me. I'm responsible for Susan's happiness. I've stood by long enough and watched you making her unhappy."

"Stood by!" he burst out. "My God! I like that. . . . Stood by indeed! It's your damned interference that made her unhappy, not me. You don't care how unhappy she is as long as you can keep your devil's claws in her."

She shrugged disdainfully.

"Your insolence doesn't affect me in the least. If you've only come here to make a scene, you'd——"

"I haven't. I've come to fetch my wife home."

"Susan is staying here."

"Where is she? I'm going to her."

"She's gone to bed, and she particularly said that she did not want to see you. You've forfeited all claim on her by your behaviour."

He made an obvious effort to control himself.

"You're using this deliberately to get back your hold on Susan," he said slowly and unsteadily, "but you know as well as I do that a wife is justified in overlooking a solitary affair that took place before marriage."

"And what proof have we," said Caroline, "that it is a solitary affair? If you've deceived her over this, I've no doubt that you've deceived and are still deceiving her over many other similar affairs. She only found this out by accident, you remember."

His mouth took on an ugly line.

"That's what you've told her, I suppose."

"Of course. It was my duty to tell her. . . . The tragedy is that her discovery is so belated. If she'd known the sort of man you are she would certainly never have married you. I think you'd better go now."

He was trembling uncontrollably.

"All right, I'll go," he said in a choking voice. "I'll go to the devil as you're so anxious for it. And I hope to God that one day Susan will know what you've done to her."

He flung himself from the room and a moment later they heard the slamming of the front door.

"A most unpleasant interview," said Caroline, with an expression of fastidious disgust, "but it had to come and I'm glad to get it over." She seemed quite unaffected by the boy's passionate outburst. "One can't undo the marriage, of course, unless——" She was silent for a moment and her eyes grew thoughtful. Then she went on briskly. "Well—meantime we can make the best of a bad job. It's lucky that I'd just got that post at Merton Park for Susan. . . . She can take it up at once. Fay will be going to college next year, and it will be nice to have Susan here." She glanced round the room, speaking more to herself than Philippa. "She can have her desk in that window just as she used to have. I can help her with her work if she finds she's got out of the swing of it. . . ."

"Caroline," said Philippa slowly, "are you seriously considering Susan's staying here indefinitely?"

Caroline's eyes hardened as she looked at her.

"If Susan's marriage has turned out unhappily, it's only natural that she should wish to return to her old home."

"It's hardly a question of that," said Philippa dryly. "Caroline, she *can't* leave him just for one lapse and that before they were even engaged."

" 'One lapse', as you call it, Philippa, proves the type of man he is. Personally I feel very sceptical about its being 'one lapse'. It's the only 'lapse' that poor Susan has discovered, I admit, but, as I said to her, once a man takes to that sort of thing. . . ."

"Caroline, do listen to me. He's *not* that type of man. He's a thoroughly clean-living, decent boy. You can see that by just looking at him. I've had more experience of the world than you——"

Caroline interrupted, speaking in her most suave tones.

"I don't deny your experience of the world, Philippa, nor do I envy you it. As I told you this afternoon, your ideas and mine on certain subjects are necessarily as wide apart as the poles."

Philippa shrugged.

"There's nothing more to be said, then?"

"Nothing."

"I'm sorry. . . . Goodnight, my dear."

"Goodnight."

Philippa went to her bedroom. She heard Caroline come upstairs and enter Susan's bedroom, heard Susan's eager, tearful, "What did he say, Caroline?", heard Caroline's low voice, then the closing of the bedroom door.

After some minutes it opened again.

"And now get to bed, darling. I'll come back in half an hour or so and tuck you up."

There followed the closing of Caroline's bedroom door . . . then the furtive opening of Susan's and a small soft tap at Philippa's.

"Come in," whispered Philippa.

Susan entered. She looked more than ever like an unhappy child, her face swollen with crying, her eyes bloodshot. She was still dressed and held a sodden ball of a handkerchief in her hand.

"What am I to do, Philippa?" she said in a tear-choked voice.

Philippa looked at her gravely.

"No one but yourself can decide that, Susan," she said.

Susan sat down on the bed.

"Caroline says . . ." she began, then her voice broke on a sob. She made an effort to control herself and went on shakily, "I owe everything to Caroline, you see . . . and she knows so much more of the world than I do. . . . She says it would be *fatal* to go back to him now at once . . . that it would make him think that I didn't really mind, and that then he'd go on doing it."

She began to sob again. Philippa watched her dispassionately.

"Do you love him?" she said at last.

"Yes . . . terribly . . . that's why I care so. . . ."

"If you really loved him you'd forgive him."

Susan raised brimming eyes.

"Would *you?*"

"Yes."

"Caroline says——"

"Never mind what Caroline says," said Philippa shortly. "This isn't Caroline's business. It's yours."

"Would you—go back to him?"

"Yes."

"Now? . . . Tonight?"

"Yes. At once."

"But Caroline . . ."

"Don't tell her you're going. Just go. As quietly as you can."

Susan looked at her. Hope seemed to shine suddenly through her, misery.

"Oh . . . I'd love to do that."

"Do it, then. And hurry. And don't make a sound."

"You'll—explain to Caroline?"

Philippa smiled wryly.

"I'll do my best."

"Oh, thank you," said Susan, throwing her arms about her and pressing a hot damp cheek against hers. Then she broke away and went back to her room. A moment later Philippa heard her cautiously descending the stairs, then the quiet, almost inaudible, closing of the front door.

It was about half an hour after that that she heard Caroline go to Susan's room.

Then came a quick tap at her bedroom door.

"Come in," said Philippa.

Caroline entered.

"Susan's not in her room."

"I know."

"You know? Where has she gone?"

"She's gone back to her husband."

"Why?"

Philippa was silent.

"Did you advise her to?"

"She asked what I'd do in her place, and I told her."

Caroline drew a deep breath.

"You—*dared*," she whispered.

In the silence that followed they heard the sound of fumbling at the front door.

"She's come back," said Caroline. There was a terrible note of exultation in her voice.

She left Philippa's room abruptly and went down the stairs to the front door. Soon she came up again, her arm round Susan. Susan's face was white and drawn. They both looked at Philippa standing at the top of the stairs.

"He was drunk," said Susan in a dull, far-away voice. "It was—horrible. . . . Horrible. . . . He—laughed. . . . He said—beastly things about Caroline. I can't go back now. I didn't know . . . Oh, *Caroline* . . ."

"Come to bed, darling," said Caroline tenderly.

She turned to Philippa, her blue eyes narrowed till they were mere slits.

"Perhaps you'd be good enough not to interfere in my affairs again," she said icily.

Chapter Fourteen

PHILIPPA lay back in her chair in Marcia's flat and glanced round her approvingly.

"It's charming," she said. "I can't find anything half as nice."

"It's partly Neil," said Marcia. "He has an eye for the right thing in the right place. Besides, I've spent all day dolling it up for you—and secretly feeling terribly nervous. I thought it would be so embarrassing meeting one's mother for the first time, as it were. But somehow when it happened it wasn't a bit, was it?"

"Not a bit," agreed Philippa with a smile.

"Tell me. . . . I suppose you just remember me. I was about two, wasn't I? Have I changed much?"

"Very little," said Philippa. "I remember you as a mischievous little girl with dimples and an attractive smile. You're bigger, of course, but otherwise not much different."

"Splendid!" laughed Marcia. "While as for you——" She considered Philippa with her head on one side. "Now I've met you, of course, I realise that you'd have been something of an asset as a family background. Father and Nina and Caroline were all distinct liabilities. For the first time since you went I feel rather annoyed with you for deserting me like that without a qualm."

"It wasn't quite without a qualm, my dear. I never worried about Caroline, because even at four Caroline was eminently capable of looking after herself, but for years, just about your bedtime, I used to imagine someone else tucking you up and saying goodnight to you, and it gave me quite a nasty little pain inside."

"It was probably indigestion. I'd like to pretend that I cried myself to sleep for you every night after you'd gone and said, 'Have the angels taken Mummy back to Heaven, Daddy?' but the truth is that I didn't miss you at all. I didn't even realise you weren't there. Even at that age as long as I got my meals regularly I never worried about anything else. I remember that later when I went to school I rather enjoyed having no mother. It made me feel important and pathetic. I sometimes posed to myself as an orphan or tried to think of Nina as a cruel stepmother. Poor little Nina! Anyone less like a cruel stepmother could hardly be imagined. She couldn't manage me at all, but she was so terrified of father's finding it out that she used to hide all my sins from him and bribe me to be good when he was there. I'd be *very* good a whole evening for twopence and moderately good for a penny. She was scared to death of father. And of Caroline. I believe she was completely under Caroline's thumb before Caroline was ten. Even father was, to a certain extent. I was the only person in the house who refused to be. Caroline and I fought like cats till I got married. She likes to absorb everyone around her, and I refused to be absorbed. She's very determined, and she's clever, too, in her own way, and at times I found it quite hard not to be absorbed, but my natural perversity saved me." She laughed, then grew serious. "Caroline's a joke in a way, isn't she? But in another way she's not a joke at all. . . . How are things going on? I never go to Bartenham now. I daren't. Right down at the bottom I'm frightened of her."

Richard and Philippa and Fay had come up to London for the day in Richard's car. The original arrangement had been the one proposed by Richard on the afternoon when Mrs. Beecham called—that he should drive Philippa to London for a day's flat-hunting. Fay's joining them had been arranged later and much against Caroline's will. Fay's form mistress had noticed that Fay's eyes seemed to be troubling her, and had written to Caroline suggesting that she should be taken to an oculist. Caroline had been tenderly concerned.

"But, darling, why didn't you tell me? How silly of you not to say anything! There's so little time left before your exam., and, of course, you must get glasses before then. We must have it seen to at once."

Caroline would have taken her up to Town herself, but all her time was occupied by her coaching engagements. Besides—there was Susan, pale and wan and silent, setting off every morning to Merton Park School, returning tired and dejected at tea-time, listlessly preparing her work for the next day, then going to bed to sob herself to sleep. Caroline was very affectionate and patient, helping her with her corrections, encouraging and reassuring her.

"Darling, you're getting on beautifully. Of course, it's not easy to pick up the threads again. Periods of transition are always a little trying, but you're managing splendidly. It will get easier and easier till soon you'll find that you're enjoying it all just as much as you used to in the old days. And, sweetheart, you've got the comfort of knowing that you're doing the right thing, that you're being true to yourself and to your ideals, that you're breaking away from a life that could bring you nothing but unhappiness and degradation."

And Susan agreed, trying to fight down the longing for Kenneth that kept her awake, sick and heartsore, night after night. . . .

There had been another scene with him. Dishevelled and distraught, he had forced his way into the drawing-room when Caroline and Susan were alone together and had pleaded with Susan to return to him. Caroline had curtly ordered him out of the house, and he had turned on her with a stream of angry accusations that had roused Susan to a tearful defence. The scene had then resolved itself into a bitter quarrel between husband and wife to which Caroline listened with a quiet smile.

"All right," Kenneth had said at last. "I'm through with it. If you're as anxious as all this to be rid of me, you shall be. I've been faithful to you so far, but I'm damned if I will be any longer. You can have your evidence for a divorce whenever you want it."

With that he flung out of the house. He had played into Caroline's hands, of course. She could now take for granted, on his own admission, that he was living a life of such flagrant immorality as precluded even the possibility of Susan's returning to him.

"Darling, I think it proves that what I said all along is true. He never has been faithful to you, but now——! If he doesn't send us evidence for the divorce, of course, I'll ask Richard to get it for us."

"Oh, *Caroline*."

"I know, my darling. . . . I know how you loved him. But he's never been worthy of your love. He's never really loved you at all. . . . Do you want to share him with other women?"

"No . . . *no!*"

"That's what it would mean. He's said so himself. . . . I know how it hurts you, darling. It's like having a festering limb cut off. However painful it is, it's the only thing to do."

Susan agreed and went languidly about her work, trying unsuccessfully enough to take an interest in her pupils and their progress, terrified by the black emptiness that life had suddenly become to her, grateful to Caroline for her constant care and affection. Caroline, after all, was the only person in the world whom one could really trust, the only person who really loved one. . . .

And so Caroline didn't want to take Fay up to the oculist's, even though she might have arranged to do so. It meant that Susan would have had to come home after her day's teaching to an empty house instead of to Caroline's tender ministrations. Caroline was very particular about that. Susan, tired after her day's work, must be fussed over and petted, must be put into her favourite chair, with cushions at her back and Caroline to pour out her tea, wait on her, and beguile her with cheerful conversation. No . . . Susan was going through a hard time, and Caroline couldn't desert her. Moreover—poor little Susan was not really strong. Bereft of Caroline's guidance, even for an afternoon, she might do something foolish and irrevocable, might even jeopardise her whole future happiness by making overtures of reconciliation to the brute who was her husband. Therefore, somewhat reluctantly, she had allowed Fay to go up to Town with Philippa and Richard.

Fay, for her part, was glad to get away from the house. There had been a nightmarish quality over everything since Susan came back. It had begun the night she came—the night when Fay had lain awake, her heart hammering in her breast, listening to Susan's hysterical sobs in the next room, to Kenneth's angry voice downstairs, to Caroline's voice, icy and contemptuous, to the constant coming and going . . . Susan creeping into Philippa's room . . . creeping down the stairs and out of the front door . . . Caroline going to Philippa's room . . . Susan coming back up the stairs . . . more talking. . . . She wanted to go out and ask what it was all about, but she was afraid. It was something horrible . . . so horrible that she couldn't face it. Then it had all died away into silence except for Susan's sobs in the next room—muffled convulsive sobs that went on and on throughout the night.

Caroline had, of course, explained things to her the next day. Susan had had to leave Kenneth because she'd found out that he wasn't a good man. Fay knew what she meant. She meant—*that*. The thing one wasn't supposed to talk about, or even think about. Kenneth was *that* sort of a man. . . . Caroline said that if Fay met him in the street she wasn't to look at him or speak to him. The dreadful thing was that she couldn't feel as Caroline wanted her to feel about him. He'd always been so kind and jolly. She couldn't think of him as wicked, however hard she tried.

And now Susan was living at home again and setting off each morning to teach, as she had done before she was married. There was a sense of strain between the three of them. Susan and Fay had never been very friendly with each other. Each had been devoted to Caroline, but not to the other. Fay had always had an odd unreasonable sense of guilt towards Caroline whenever she was on friendlier terms than usual with Susan. They had never had very much to do with each other, even when Susan lived at home. It was partly the differences in their ages, of course, and partly that Caroline generally made a third when they went out, and each was conscious of Caroline, not of the other.

Although Caroline's attentiveness had often irked Fay when the two of them lived alone, she found that she was jealous now that it was transferred to Susan. She often felt sulky and neglected when Caroline was fussing so affectionately over Susan. And sometimes she suspected that Caroline knew that she felt like that and was pleased by it. Caroline didn't seem at all worried by the tragedy of Susan's marriage. She seemed, in fact, happier than she had seemed for a long time.

But, despite Caroline's cheerfulness, there was a curiously oppressive atmosphere about the house, so that at times Fay felt that she could hardly breathe in it. She missed Billy, too. Billy would have made it all less horrible, but she hadn't seen or spoken to him since her talk with Caroline. She now did some of her home-work in the dinner hour and left school earlier. That meant that she got home before Billy was out of school and so could not walk home with him. She refused all Sybil's invitations to tea on the score of work. Sybil smiled and said, "I'm not going to take offence. I'm far too fond of you for that. I'll just go on asking you till you do come."

The expedition to Town with Philippa and Richard in Richard's car came just when she felt she couldn't bear things any longer. It was a glorious respite. As soon as she heard of it her depression fell away, and a bubbling well of happiness seemed to spring up inside her. Even her headache felt better. Instinctively she tried to hide her excitement from Caroline, lest even at the last minute she might decide to join the party. But she didn't. She just stood at the door, smiling gravely till the car was out of sight. . . . Then a heavenly sense of relief seized Fay. It was all right. It was really happening. Nothing could stop it now.

During the journey Philippa and Richard teased her and made jokes that Caroline would have considered unworthy, and they all laughed a great deal, and Fay felt so happy that she wished it could go on for ever. It was over at last, however—far too quickly—and Richard took them to the oculist's, then went to garage the car.

The oculist was a tall thin man with a kindly manner that put Fay at her ease at once and seemed a natural part of the wonderful holiday. He examined her eyes carefully and said that there was nothing wrong with them and that the pain was neuralgia.

"Oh, I'm so glad," laughed Fay. "I was dreading having spectacles. I know I should be always losing them."

He gave Fay some illustrated papers to look at and took Philippa into another room.

"She ought to be thoroughly overhauled by a doctor," he said. "I should say that her nerves are in a pretty bad state. Has she been subject to any severe nervous strain lately?"

"She's working hard for a scholarship examination," said Philippa.

"That must be it. She's obviously not got the stamina for that sort of thing. Anyway, see what the doctor says. I know what I'd say in his place."

They met Richard for lunch, and it was Richard who suggested taking Fay to hear Moiseiwitch at the Queen's Hall while Philippa looked at flats. Fay's face flushed and paled with excitement at the suggestion.

"But . . . Oh, how lovely!" she stammered, then made them laugh by saying quite seriously, "I feel I don't mind how soon I die after this."

They arranged to meet at Marcia's for tea. Philippa spent the afternoon looking at several of the new blocks of flats that had recently appeared in London. They were all furnished in impeccable taste, but she found something depressing in the thought of the seven or eight hundred of them under the same roof, all furnished in exactly the same way.

"I suppose I'm old-fashioned," she said to Marcia, "but this modern craze for uniformity does depress me so. I think I'll come up again next week and look at unfurnished flats, and then I'll start haunting sales and buy some second-hand furniture. It will be far more exciting. One couldn't ever make companions of furniture that had been chosen by somebody else, and I like to make companions of my things."

The meeting between her and Marcia had been unexpectedly easy. They had taken to each other at once. They were sitting now by the tea-table, waiting for Richard and Fay to come from the concert.

Marcia shrugged faintly when she heard about Susan.

"I'm not surprised, of course. Susan's a dear little thing, but she hasn't much character, and she's always looked on Caroline as a sort of god. I often wondered whether, when it came to the point, Ken would be able to hold his own against Caroline."

"It's Fay I'm worried about," said Philippa, "not Susan."

"Yes . . . Fay's a different proposition. Fay has character, though so far Caroline's managed to dominate her completely."

"It reacts on her health."

"Yes, I can see that. She looks worn-out. She gets it, of course, in a concentrated form. She's the baby, the ewe lamb. I wonder Caroline let her come with you."

"She wouldn't have done but for Susan. . . . The tragedy is that she's really fond of them and that they're really fond of her."

"I know. . . . I never got on with Caroline, but in a way I've always admired her. She was wonderful when they were children. Really wonderful. She did give up her whole life to them. She was utterly devoted. When Robert had pneumonia she didn't go to bed for a week. And it wasn't only what she did. It was what she was. She really was sweet to them. I have to hand it to her, though I dislike her. She was always so patient and kind. She loved them so terribly. Terribly's the word. They were her children, and she was their entire world. She made a lovely home for them. She was always arranging games and amusements for them. They didn't need any outside interests or friends. She saw to that. And she couldn't bear it when they grew older and developed individualities of their own and wanted to try their wings. She fought like a demon—literally like a demon—to keep them as dependent on her as they'd been when they were babies. She never let them see what she was trying to do, of course—she's too clever for that—and they adore her, all three of them—even Fay, though she's eighteen, and is treated as if she were still in the nursery. If it weren't so horrible, it would be funny."

"They're not particularly fond of each other, are they?"

"Oh no. Caroline saw to that, too. *Divide et impera*—that's her motto. She was very clever at planting little seeds of division and distrust among the three of them. Of course, the difference in their ages helped. . . . What do you think of Richard?"

"I like him. . . . He and Caroline are great friends, aren't they?"

"Yes. She's never told me so, but I believe he's proposed more than once. He's a dear old thing, though a little slow-witted. He's taken her at her face value. The perfect example of womanly self-sacrifice. The elder sister who's given up her whole life to her little brother and sisters. And, of course, it's true. She *is* ... she *has* ... I think it would do her good to marry Richard and have half-a-dozen children of her own. It would work the poison out of her system."

"I gather that you and she don't see much of each other."

"No.... Neil and I used to go to stay with her, but—even though I understood her so well, I always began to have a feeling of grievance against Neil when I was staying there. I don't know how she did it. She knew I'd never belong to her, but she couldn't bear to see me belonging to Neil. Her possessiveness is a sort of disease. I shouldn't be surprised to hear any day that she'd gone off her head."

"You and Neil are happy, aren't you? I've only to look at you to see that."

"Yes. We get on very well on the whole. As well as two people can get on who have to live on the top of each other in a modern flat. It's an acid test, isn't it? I wonder so many people survive it. My feelings for Neil have always gone round in a sort of circle. I suppose that most people's for most people do. He begins to get on my nerves, and gets on them more and more and more till I wonder how much longer I can bear him, and then quite suddenly he seems terribly nice again, and I think I'm lucky to have him. I believe his feelings for me go round and round like that, too, but it was only when we stayed with Caroline that we were on each others' nerves at the same time—and so badly that we could hardly speak to each other. That's why we stopped going, though we never said so to each other. I just said that I thought it was too much for Caroline and he agreed. ... Fay's the real problem, of course. It's tragic how Caroline's made her give up her music just because it took her into a world where she couldn't go with her. She has real talent, you know, but that meant nothing to Caroline. Caroline saw it only as something that would separate them. If she just goes to college and then takes a teaching job—in Bartenham, probably—Caroline can continue to order her life for her indefinitely as she did Susan's, which is all she cares about."

"I want to have Fay to stay with me when I get my flat."

Marcia laughed.

"You won't, my dear. I've often tried. Caroline always has some perfectly good reason why she can't come. Poor little Fay! It's hardest on her. She's much more sensitive than either of the other two. And she—needs her own life in a way that Susan never did. That's the artist in her. Robert, of course, being a boy, Caroline never tried to possess in the same way in which she's possessed Susan and Fay. Still—he adores her. Effie was sick of the sound of her name long before they were married. Her mistake was the same as Ken's—in thinking that it would be all right once they were married. If she'd only pretended to think Caroline as marvellous as Robert thought her it would have been all right. Caroline has no personal vanity, but she's got a sort of diseased appetite for affection. It's pathetic in a way. And she must possess wholly. Don't you adore the way she talks about 'loyalty' and 'disloyalty'? Anyone who likes her is 'loyal' and anyone who doesn't is 'disloyal.' She's just a little stupid, too, with all her cleverness. It would be quite easy to pretend to adore her even if you didn't. Evelyn's proved that. I believe that, at the bottom, Evelyn hates her more than anyone, but she knows which side her bread's buttered. It would have been better for Effie if she'd realised that. Oh well . . . I'm far enough away from it all, I'm glad to say. I'd get out of it, too, if I were you, as soon as I could. . . . Oh, here they are!"

Richard and Fay entered. Fay was flushed and starry-eyed.

"It's been lovely," she said in a dreamy voice. "I shall remember it all my life."

"It evidently quite came up to her expectations," smiled Richard, "but she's decided not to die immediately, after all."

"I can't *tell* you what it was like," said Fay.

She was aglow, with a soft radiant happiness. None of them had ever seen her like that before. The shy uncertainty, the faint unhappiness, that hung about her normally had gone. It was as if she had been swept away from them into another world.

"Well, how did the flat-hunting go on?" said Richard, sitting down by Philippa.

Marcia poured out tea while Philippa described the various flats she had inspected. Fay sat wrapped in her dreams, her cheeks still flushed, her eyes bright. She ate little and heard nothing that was said around her.

Neil came in when they were half-way through tea. He was a big, red-haired man, with a rough-hewn face and humorous expression, to whom Philippa at once took a liking.

"Here's a mother-in-law for you," said Marcia. "I'm afraid she won't run to type, but you must just do the best you can." She smiled at Philippa. "Neil's always missed a mother-in-law. He says that he likes to sample all the experiences that life has to offer, and that that is one of the most poignant."

Neil smiled at her as he shook hands.

"No, she doesn't look really typical," he said. "Not poignant enough. What does one call her? Philippa? Good!"

"He was always so glad that you weren't on hand to show him snapshots of me in my childhood," said Marcia. "He does so hate snapshots of people in their childhood."

He laughed and tweaked Fay's ear as he went to his seat. She gave him her sweet dreamy smile.

"And Marcia's just been telling me how much she enjoyed being motherless," said Philippa. "I appear to have been, despite myself, the perfect parent."

They talked in a desultory fashion as they had tea. There was a happy sense of intimacy about them, of absence from strain. It formed a pleasant background to Fay's dreams.

"How's Caroline?" said Neil suddenly to Philippa.

Something of Richard's serenity dropped from him at the question. He had been thinking a good deal about Caroline lately. When he proposed to her, the week before Philippa arrived, he meant it to be for the last time. If she refused him, he would not propose again. He would put her out of his mind as an impossible dream. Though he still did not mean to propose again he was worried—not by the thought of her refusal, but by a growing feeling of relief at her refusal. In these last few weeks Caroline seemed to have changed. Or rather he had a suspicion that Caroline was the same, but that he was looking at her, as it were, from a different angle. He felt as if he had walked round to the back of an imposing statue and found it hollow. Or as if the imposing statue had suddenly begun to dwindle before his gaze till it had reached pigmy size. He didn't know how it had happened or indeed exactly what had happened. It was since Philippa had come, of course, but that hadn't anything to do with it. Or had it? Was it something large and generous in Philippa that had revealed Caroline's smallness to him? Had Philippa's keen sense of humour shown him that Caroline was quite devoid of any sense of humour at all? Had Philippa's quick amused interest in everything around her shown Caroline as rather pompous, rather limited, rather self-sufficient?

Then there was Susan. ... Everyone in Bartenham knew that Susan and Kenneth Melsham had quarrelled and that Susan had come back to live with Caroline. There were a dozen different accounts of the affair going about the town. But it wasn't the fact that Susan had left her husband that worried Richard. It was the fact that Caroline seemed to be making no effort to bring the young people together. When he—very tentatively—questioned her on the subject, she hinted darkly that young Melsham was living a grossly immoral life and that she had only just rescued Susan from him in time, which was absurd, on the face of it, for young Melsham, though a little headstrong and quick-tempered, perhaps even a little weak, was as decent a boy as one could hope to meet anywhere. It wasn't like Caroline. She'd been so different in the case of Robert and Effie. He didn't know Robert very well—Effie he knew hardly at all—but Caroline had often told him about them, and, reading between the lines, he knew how hard she had worked to make that marriage a success, how patient she had been with harum-scarum little Effie, straightening the tangles of her inefficient housekeeping, doing her accounts for her, engaging her maids, taking over her domestic responsibilities, ready always to go to the rescue cheerfully and without reproach, however tired or busy she was. She'd saved the marriage from shipwreck a dozen times. He could tell that even from her own account, and Caroline always tried to minimise the good she did. And then, finally, by a stroke of good luck or genius, she'd engaged Evelyn Marston, who appeared to be almost as capable and tactful as Caroline herself. Effie was certainly lucky in having Caroline for a sister-in-law. Or was she? The question was a monstrous one, but it lodged itself suddenly and immovably in his mind, as he sat stirring his tea and listening to Marcia's chatter. Suppose he knew Effie and Robert and Evelyn intimately and hadn't only Caroline's story to go on, would Effie seem as fortunate as Caroline's story made her out to be? What did Effie think of Caroline? He felt, for the first time, very curious about that. He glanced at Marcia. She was laughing at something that Philippa had just said, and an elusive likeness between the two women struck him. It didn't lie in any particular feature. It was rather some quality—something keen and humorous and generous that was lacking in Caroline. What did Marcia think of Caroline? He had never seen much of Marcia, and Caroline had generally met any reference to her with, "I'm very fond of Marcia, of course, but we haven't really very much in common." His infatuation for Caroline had made that equivalent to an unqualified condemnation of Marcia. Moreover, he'd secretly resented the way in which Marcia had left Caroline to bear the burden of their father's young family alone and unaided. Now suddenly he felt curious to know what Marcia's account of the situation would have been, what Marcia thought of Caroline. . . . And Philippa. . . . What did Philippa think of Caroline? He'd give a good deal to know that, too. He'd ask her one day when he knew her better, though he felt that he knew her extraordinarily well already. What a delightful companion she'd been on the drive and during lunch, so quick and amusing and responsive and understanding! He mustn't lose touch with her when she left Bartenham. He would drive her to Town again on her next flat-hunting expedition, and when she was settled in London he would come up for an occasional evening, and they would have dinner together and go to a show. . . . He was conscious of a feeling of relief that Caroline had so definitely and finally refused him. . . . His gaze travelled on to Fay. There was still that dreamy, rapturous haze about her. Her soft eyes were fixed on the distance. She saw nothing, heard nothing, of what was going on around her. Had it been anyone but Fay you would have said that she was in love. But Fay was living again every moment of this afternoon. . . . And yet another doubt of Caroline arose in his mind. It was as if seeds had been sown on a vacant plot of ground without the owner's knowledge, and suddenly all began to spring up simultaneously, to his surprise and dismay. Caroline had seemed so wise in her decision that Fay must give up all interests that might interfere with her career. But—surely music itself should have been her career. . . . In the interval of the concert she had talked to him with an enthusiasm that had amazed him. She was transfigured—a Fay he had never seen before. Then he had said something about her going to college, and it had brought her abruptly to earth. All the glow had faded. She had become listless, dejected, as if he had reminded her of something distasteful. He had at once taken her back to the subject of music, and the glow had returned. Had Caroline been as wise in this matter as he had thought? She could not realise, of course, that she was depriving the child of what was part of her very being, but—oughtn't she to have realised? Could one tell her? No, he remembered that Caroline never took kindly to advice given her by other people. She liked to give advice but not to receive it. Again he pulled himself up with a sort of horror. It was dreadful to be criticising Caroline like this, Caroline who had always seemed to him the ideal of womanhood. Disloyal . . . that was it. He remembered her saying that Marcia was 'disloyal.' . . . Watching Fay, he became aware of a feeling of uneasiness. Despite her radiance, there was a look of strain about her, a suggestion of something fine worn almost to breaking point.

Philippa was gathering her things together.

"Time we were starting back, Richard, I'm afraid. What about the infant? She's had nothing to eat at all."

"I had a huge lunch," smiled Fay. "I just don't feel hungry now. . . . It's been such a lovely day."

"Glad you haven't got to wear goggles," said Neil, helping her into her coat, "though you'd have looked a nice little owl in them. . . . When is Caroline going to let you come and stay with us? We keep asking, you know."

The glow faded again.

"I—don't know. I'm—terribly busy working for my exam, now."

"Always some excuse!" said Neil.

"Don't tease her, Neil," said Marcia. "We'll wait till Philippa's living in town, too, then we'll make a grand concerted effort."

"That sounds lovely," laughed Fay, but she knew that, however much of a grand concerted effort they made, Caroline would never let her go and stay with them. "Darling, I just couldn't *spare* you. I do so miss my baby when she's away from me. . . . I know Marcia's kind and means well, but—darling, I couldn't trust her to look after you properly. . . . I tell you what, sweetheart, we'll have a day in Town together next week, just you and I—shall we?—for a treat. We'll go to the National Gallery. We've never been there yet. I'll show you the Italian Primitives, and we can eat our sandwiches in Trafalgar Square. Won't that be fun?"

She followed the others slowly out to the car. It was almost ended—the lovely, lovely day. Soon it would be only a memory, the sort of memory you go over and over again every night in bed, the sort of memory you cling to when everything seems so hateful that you can hardly bear it. . . . It wasn't only the concert, though the concert had been heaven. It was—everything. The happy care-free atmosphere, the absence of strain and effort (she tried hard not to think "the absence of Caroline"), the affectionate teasing of Neil and Richard, the underlying kindliness and understanding of them all. . . . It had gone so terribly quickly, but—never mind, she reassured herself, you'll have it to think about and to remember always. . . .

Neil and Marcia stood at the door waving as they set off.

"Don't forget," Neil called to her. "You're coming to stay with us soon."

She curled up on the back seat, and her mind floated off over the roseate memories of the day. The sound of Philippa's and Richard's voices was wafted back to her, blending happily with her dreams.

Chapter Fifteen

CAROLINE was alone in the drawing-room when they reached home.

They told her of the day's doings, and Philippa gave her the oculist's report.

Caroline laughed.

"I rather thought there was nothing in that scare," she said. "Some of these young mistresses are intolerably officious."

"But he said that she ought to see a doctor," Philippa reminded her gently.

Caroline smiled at Fay, who was still flushed and bright-eyed with excitement.

"She *looks* as if she needed to see a doctor, doesn't she?" she said, slipping an arm round her affectionately. "But, of course, I'll make an appointment. The jacks-in-office shall be satisfied at every point, shan't they, darling? Well, did you enjoy it?"

"Yes ... awfully," said Fay, but she spoke constrainedly. She couldn't tell Caroline how much she'd enjoyed it. For one thing, she wouldn't have understood; for another, she hated you to enjoy anything without her, and you were such a coward that you nearly always pretended that you hadn't enjoyed things much if she'd not been with you. And—the reaction was setting in now. All the glory of the day was fading, leaving a heavy depression. Her head had begun to ache, and she felt so miserable that it was all she could do to keep the tears back.

"There's some supper for you in the dining-room," went on Caroline briskly, "so you'd better have it quickly and go to bed. It's the French test-paper tomorrow, isn't it? I want you to be fresh for that. Come along, darling. I'll just see that you've got all you want."

When she returned a few moments later Philippa was sitting in the armchair by the fire, and Richard was standing on the hearthrug, smiling down at her. The suggestion of friendliness, of intimacy almost, between them struck her like a blow in the face. She frowned and tightened her lips. Surely she wasn't jealous, she told herself. Jealous of her own mother. And Richard. It was absurd. Yet, as they turned to her, she had again the sensation that they were united in a bond of alliance against her. The smile—intimate, understanding—faded from their faces. They looked wary, on their guard. Allied against her. The pain in her heart sharpened, deepened, till it was almost intolerable. She spoke in her quiet, unmodulated voice.

"I think you made a mistake in taking Fay to the concert, Richard. That sort of thing only unsettles her. If I'd known you had any idea of it I'd have asked you not to. I suppose that she didn't like to refuse, but I've just been telling her that it would have been more—well, more honest not to have gone. She decided herself to give up music because it was taking up too much of her time and thoughts, and she ought to have kept to her decision in the spirit as well as the letter. It's no use putting one's hand to the plough and looking back."

"But, Caroline," protested Philippa, "she needs some recreation."

Caroline looked at her with blue eyes narrowed.

"I understand Fay, Philippa, thank you." She turned to Richard. "Richard knows I do, don't you, Richard? I've made a study of her from babyhood."

Richard would support her there, at any rate—Richard, who knew that she had been more than a mother to Fay; Richard, who had often resented her devotion to the child. But Richard was looking self-conscious and embarrassed.

"Well, I don't really know, Caroline," he said, avoiding her eyes. "I think music means more to her than you quite realise."

She drew in her breath sharply. That Richard—*Richard*—should suggest there was anything about Fay that she didn't understand, that the child wasn't an open book to her, wasn't, in a way, her own handiwork! She'd moulded her character, formed her tastes, from babyhood. And *Richard* dared to say, "I think music means more to her than you realise." The colour faded from her cheeks. She seemed to feel the foundations of her kingdom shake beneath her. It wasn't the first time. She'd felt it once before when Richard had said "You shouldn't have spoken to your mother like that." Your mother ... yes, it was Philippa's coming that had assailed the security of her kingdom. It had been as firm as a rock before. And now Richard—oh, but he had spent the day with Philippa. He'd had tea with Marcia and Philippa. She thought of that little tea-party round Marcia's fireside as a monarch might think of a meeting of disaffected subjects. Marcia had been disloyal from the beginning, and that sort of thing spread like rot, like canker, through a group. Richard, weak, perhaps, but never disloyal till now. .... Richard, affected by the taint. And Fay. .... No, Fay was still loyal, thank God! What a fool she'd been to let Fay go with them! She would be more careful in future. Again she tried to think that she was fortunate in having discovered Richard's true character before it was too late, but all she was conscious of was the fact that he had deserted her and the pain of it was like physical torment. Why had she let this woman come into her life, wrecking her happiness, poisoning the minds of everyone around her? She gave a short unsteady laugh.

"My dear Richard," she said, "you really can't teach me anything about Fay."

"I wasn't trying to," he said with a smile. "Well, goodbye, Caroline ... goodbye, Philippa." Again the special intimate smile for Philippa that tore at Caroline's heart. "Give Fay my love. I won't disturb her at supper. No, don't see me out. Goodbye."

He was gone, leaving Caroline to wrestle with this new anguish that seemed to rack soul and body. Absurd and impossible that she should have come really to love him just now when he had proved himself so unworthy of her ... and yet the memory of the love that he had offered and that she had so casually rejected filled her suddenly with a blind sick longing she had never known before.

She pulled herself up sharply. She must fight this thing, she mustn't yield to it even in her thoughts. She must stand alone, as she had always done, strong in the knowledge of her own rectitude. She should not have expected sympathy or even understanding from anyone. She had given, given, given, all her life. She must go on giving, without stint, without hope of reward. She was strong enough for that. She tried to ignore the pain that still tore at her heart.

"Is Susan in bed?" Philippa was saying.

"No. . . . She's gone to Dr. Bennett's."

"Why? Isn't she well?"

Caroline shrugged.

"She's been a bit nervy lately, and I thought she'd better get a tonic. She suggested going to Dr. Bennett's herself, as a matter of fact. He had to attend a consultation this afternoon, that's why he gave her such a late appointment. She ought to be back any minute."

Fay came in to say goodnight. She said it docilely, like a little girl, kissing first Caroline, then Philippa. She looked very pale, and there were dark shadows beneath her eyes.

"The whole day's been too much for her," said Caroline, as soon as she had gone out of the room. "I shall take care that it doesn't happen again."

She tried to speak calmly but was aware that her voice sounded quite unlike her usual voice, unsteady, almost shrill.

There was a sudden tension in the room. The sound of the opening of the front door came as a relief to both women. Then Susan entered, slowly and draggingly. Her eyes were dilated in her white face, and there was a strange dreamlike air about her, as if she were walking in her sleep. She sat down, fixing her eyes on Caroline, but as if she were focussing something a long way off, and spoke in a low toneless voice.

"Caroline . . . I'm going to have a baby."

Caroline drew in her breath.

"Oh, my dear! When did you know?"

"Not till tonight. Dr. Bennett told me. I wasn't sure, I mean. I'd begun to suspect last week."

"Darling," said Caroline, "why didn't you tell me?"

"I ought to go back to Ken—now."

A cold steel-like glint came into Caroline's eyes, but her voice was deep with tenderness.

"Darling—not now. You can't now. You've—the child to think of now as well as yourself. You can't give your child a drunkard and a libertine for a father."

"He wanted a child. He'd have been so glad."

"I wonder if he would. He'd probably have grudged every penny he had to spend on it, just as he grudged every penny he had to spend on you."

"He often said he wanted a child."

Caroline shrugged.

"That sentimental sort of talk came easy to him. It meant no more than the breath he used to say it with. Do you remember how, when you were engaged, he said he'd rather die than cause you a minute's unhappiness, and now——"

"*Don't!*" cried Susan sharply.

"Oh, my dear, I understand. I do honestly, sweetheart. I suffer for you in this almost as much as you're suffering yourself . . . but we've got to be practical. We've got to face facts. Don't you see, darling? I keep on telling you it's no use thinking of an idealised Kenneth who never really existed except in your imagination. The real Kenneth is very very different. You've no right to give your child a father like that. Its life is in your hands to make or mar. Before this you could have gone back to him."

"Why didn't you let me, then?" said Susan. "Why didn't you let me?"

Caroline's eyes hardened again. Another tremor in the foundations of her kingdom.

"Did I ever stop you?" she said. "Didn't you go back and find him—drunk? Hasn't he told you since then that he doesn't want you back? Wasn't it he himself who suggested a divorce? Can you go crawling back to him after that—and with a child? What sort of a life would you be condemning your child to—not to speak of yourself? Come, Susan . . . this isn't my brave girl. You've been so plucky up to now."

Susan eyes, dark and heavy with despair, moved from Caroline to Philippa, then from Philippa back to Caroline. Her face looked wan and drawn. Her figure sagged despondently.

"But, Caroline"—she threw out her hands helplessly—"what can I do? I can't—cadge on you? And how can I go on teaching if I have the child?"

Red patches burnt in Caroline's cheeks. A feeling of exultation possessed her. A child of Susan's . . . *her* child, really . . . to care for and guide and train. Oh, she would spend herself gladly for it. Another life given into her charge, another character to mould with loving care from babyhood as she had moulded Fay's. Perhaps a girl . . . like Fay . . . sweet and loving and malleable. Or a boy . . . like Robert . . . staunchly loyal and dependable. How reverently and lovingly she would undertake this new task!

"Ken must help, anyway," Susan was saying wearily. "With money, I mean."

Again that hard glint came into Caroline's eyes.

"I don't want Kenneth to help," she said. "I can manage perfectly well. I don't want Kenneth to have any claim on the child at all. He's forfeited his rights."

Yes, she'd manage. The child should not suffer in any way. She'd manage. It would mean taking on more work. She couldn't afford to relax now that this fresh responsibility was laid on her shoulders. Oh well, she'd been giving, giving, giving, all her life. She'd go on giving, more unremittingly, more generously. It was her nature to sacrifice herself for others. Only so could she find her true fulfilment.

Susan dropped her head into her hands with a little sob.

"Oh, it would have been so different if——"

Caroline put her arms around her.

"I know, darling, but listen. Caroline won't fail you. She'll stand by you. . . ."

"You're so *good*, Caroline."

"Nonsense! You can go on teaching for a few months yet, can't you? When is it to be?"

"In May."

"That leaves us plenty of time to make our plans. You'd better go into a nursing home for it. I think that would be best. We'll get a good nurse for the child, of course, because we shall both be working, and—we'll all be so happy together, sweetheart. We'll give our baby a real home. She—let's pretend it's going to be a girl, shall we?—will have everything she can possibly need. There's the old nursery—the one you and Fay and Robert had. We'll start getting it ready, at once, shall we?"

Her cheeks still flushed, her eyes bright and dreamy, she went on planning, scheming, making arrangements. To do so dulled the pain of Richard's defection, the pain that nagged so unceasingly at her heart. (Yes, no use thinking of Richard. There would be no room for Richard in her life now.)

Susan's eyes were shut, her lips a tight bitter line.

Chapter Sixteen

MAGGIE fussed happily about the drawing-room, shaking up the cushions and altering the positions of the ornaments on the mantelpiece.

It was the last day of Philippa's visit, but she didn't feel unhappy about it, because the visit had been so lovely, and Philippa had said that she would come again soon.

It had been Maggie's idea to invite Philippa over for a week-end. She had missed Philippa very much since she went to live in London. When she was living with Caroline she would often call to see Maggie, bringing flowers or the sugared almonds that Maggie loved, and she would always ask to see Maggie's garden and hear Sweetie sing.

Caroline, of course, was too clever to care about things like that, and when Maggie mentioned them used to frown in a way that brought the familiar quiver of fear and dismay over Maggie and made her hair come down. Philippa never frowned. She laughed instead, and Maggie had to laugh, too, though often she didn't know what they were laughing at. Maggie enjoyed laughing, and there hadn't been very much of it in her life on the whole. When she woke up in the morning there was something exciting in the thought that she might meet Philippa in the town, or that Philippa might call with a bunch of flowers or a bag of sugared almonds and ask to hear Sweetie sing and say how nice Maggie looked in her necklaces and give her that happy feeling inside that only Philippa could give her.

And so when Philippa left Bartenham altogether and went to live at her flat in London, Maggie felt lost and forlorn. It was so dull going into the town and knowing that by no possible chance could she meet Philippa there. It was so dull waking up in the morning and knowing that by no possible chance could Philippa pop in with a bag of sugared almonds and ask to hear Sweetie sing. And then came the idea of inviting Philippa to stay with them for a week-end. Charles was at first taken aback by her suggestion (they'd never had anyone to stay with them before), but finally he became almost as much excited by it as Maggie.

After all, why not? He liked Philippa, and there wasn't any nonsense about her. She played his game of discreet-admiration-with-a-tinge-of-regret to perfection, giving it just the right touch of reality, never more, never less. Even when she seemed to be laughing at him, her laughter was so kindly that he was rather flattered than offended. Nana, too, welcomed the idea of the invitation. She approved of Philippa and, touched by her kindness to her charge, had relaxed her grimness in her case.

Caroline was the only one who didn't seem pleased. In fact Maggie, setting out in eager excitement to tell her about it, returned in a state of inexplicable panic, with her hair in wild confusion down her back. She didn't know what had upset her. Caroline had been quite nice about it, but, as soon as she told her, Maggie got the feeling of being in disgrace—a feeling that, since the days of her childhood, had reduced her to stark terror. Of course, she assured herself when she reached home, it must have been her imagination. Caroline just hadn't been very much interested and that was natural, because poor Caroline had a lot of things to worry her at present.

For one thing Susan had left her husband and gone back to live at home. Maggie was rather vague about what had happened, except that Kenneth Melsham had turned out to be a Bad Man, which was a pity, as Maggie had always liked him.

Then there was Fay. The oculist had said that she ought to see a doctor, and the doctor had said at first that she oughtn't to sit for her scholarship examination, and that, of course, would have been terrible after all the trouble Caroline had taken over it. So in the end he had said that she could sit for the examination, but that she must not be "pushed." He'd given her a sleeping draught and a tonic, and, according to Caroline, she was very much better already. Caroline said that nerves were chiefly a matter of self-control, and that Fay must get a firm grip on herself. She said that she, Caroline, had never had "nerves" in her life. She couldn't afford to have them. So Fay was trying hard to be self-controlled and to get a firm grip on herself. But, of course, it was all very worrying for Caroline, and, Maggie assured herself again, one simply couldn't expect her to show any interest in such a little thing as Philippa's visit. Maggie herself was so much excited that she couldn't eat or sleep. She bustled about making preparations, getting out innumerable clean sheets and towels from the linen cupboard, which Nana patiently put back, making endless lists of things to be seen to and losing them all as soon as she'd made them. When the spare room was at last ready for Philippa, she stood in the middle of it, glowing with happiness and excitement and thinking how well she had arranged everything. As a finishing touch, she fetched Sweetie's cage and put it on Philippa's chest of drawers, so that Philippa could wind it up herself whenever she wanted to. Charles, too, made his simple preparations for the visit. His hair went a richer shade of chestnut in the course of a night, and he sent all his suits to the local tailor's to be pressed, though they had been pressed only a week ago.

The visit had come up to Maggie's highest expectations. It had been lovely from the moment Philippa arrived, with a large bag of sugared almonds and a little clockwork figure of a harlequin that pirouetted round and round for several minutes after it had been wound up. Maggie was wildly excited by the clockwork harlequin and watched it all evening, munching sugared almonds. Nana had to come in three times before she'd go to bed. On the Saturday morning they had coffee and cream buns in the town, and a lot of people who'd met Philippa when she was staying with Caroline came up and spoke to her, and Maggie felt proud to be sitting with her, because she was so smart and pretty and popular.

In the afternoon the three of them went for a walk, and Philippa described the other people in the flats where she lived, and made them laugh by telling them about the woman in the flat just above, whose Peke had its place laid at table with her and ate all the same meals. In the evening Maggie and Philippa played draughts, and Maggie won every game.

And now it was Sunday, the last day of the visit, and Philippa was going to tea to Robert's and then straight from Robert's to the station to catch her train to London. She hadn't been to Caroline's. Caroline had said that of course she must come the next time she was over, but just now Susan was so busy setting exam papers and Fay so busy working for her scholarship that they weren't having any visitors at all.

"Ours is the sort of household in which work must come first," Caroline had said in that bright brisk way that people always thought so "splendid."

She would be at Robert's, however, this afternoon and would meet Philippa there. Maggie and Charles had been included in the invitation, but Maggie had said that she had all her household lists to make out and was afraid she wouldn't have time. Philippa's visit had been so lovely that she didn't want it to end in having tea with Caroline. Caroline would be sure to make her feel that Philippa hadn't enjoyed it and that it had been silly of her to ask her.

And, of course, it was quite true. She *had* her list of things to make out for the week, and it always took her most of Sunday afternoon to do it.

Charles, too, said that he didn't think he'd be able to go. He said that he had a lot of letters to write, and that also was true, because Charles had quite a large circle of correspondents— middle-aged ladies, for the most part, whom he had met at hotels when he went for his holidays, and with whom he kept up a regular correspondence for years without ever meeting them again. As a matter of fact, Charles preferred not to meet them again. With the lapse of time the memories took on a glamour that a second meeting would have ruthlessly dispelled. The real reason why Charles didn't want to go to Robert's, however, was known only to himself.

When first Evelyn was put in charge of Robert's household, Charles had been much interested in her and had formed with her one of those friendships he was so fond of forming with attractive women past their first youth. He had given her flowers and invited her to have coffee with him on several occasions in the town. Then—he had taken fright. He didn't quite know what had frightened him. Certainly she never by word or act overstepped the bounds he set to his very discreet flirtations. But Charles suddenly became aware that he was being hunted and that he must escape while there was yet time. He escaped with such precipitancy that it was now several months since he had seen or spoken to her.

Philippa entered the room, followed by Charles, who was going to carry her suitcase as far as Robert's.

"Goodbye, Maggie," said Philippa, kissing her. "Thank you so much. I've had a simply lovely time. You must both come and see me in London as soon as I get really straight."

"Rather!" agreed Charles.

He had enjoyed Philippa's visit almost as much as Maggie. It had made him feel young and debonair. There was something arch, almost roguish, in the letters he wrote to his lady friends that afternoon.

Caroline and Evelyn were sitting in the window recess when Philippa was announced.

Evelyn, as usual, received her as the mistress of the house.

"Effie's playing with the children upstairs," she said. "You'll see them all at tea-time."

Robert gave her his slow, pleasant smile.

"How's Aunt Maggie?" he said. "I suppose you've had a marvellous week-end playing draughts."

"I'm sure visitors are too much for her," said Caroline. "She's always worse after any excitement."

They asked her about her flat, but their interest was obviously perfunctory. She in her turn asked anxiously after Fay and Susan, but Caroline replied shortly and non-committally, almost as if the question were an impertinence.

Then the tea-bell rang.

Effie came down with the children and greeted Philippa absently.

Philippa thought that she looked pale and overwrought. Everyone was rather quiet at tea. Once Evelyn spoke sharply to Carrie for some breach of table manners, and Carrie nestled for comfort against Effie, who was sitting next her. Effie slipped an arm round her, and Evelyn said, "Now, Effie . . ." in mild expostulation.

After tea Effie stayed in the dining-room to play with the children again, and the other four went into the drawing-room. They heard laughter and the sound of running, as if some game were in progress. Once, when the dining-room door opened and the children ran laughing into the hall, Evelyn went out, and they heard her say:

"I won't have romping in the hall. Go back into the dining-room at once. Effie, please keep this door shut.

"Sunday's really supposed to be my afternoon out," she went on as she came back into the room. "That's why Effie's looking after the children. I hardly ever *do* go out, as a matter of fact. I'm like a cat and hate leaving my own fireside."

Caroline turned to Philippa with a smile.

"The last time Evelyn went away for a night Effie left the electric iron on, and the house was nearly burnt down. And, of course, it would be too cruel to condemn Robert to do his crossword puzzles alone. So Evelyn nearly always spends her afternoon out in, and I pop round to help with the easier clues."

"Well, don't let me keep you from it," said Philippa. "I'm no good at crossword puzzles, but I can listen and learn."

"You can be looking at the snapshot album," suggested Caroline. "I don't think you've seen it. There are some nice ones of the children."

Evelyn fetched her the book, and Philippa sat, turning over the pages idly and glancing at the snapshots. Effie as a young bride—pretty, alert, with an air of gamin impudence. Effie with her first baby, proud and important and radiantly happy.

The other three were already deep in the crossword puzzle.

"Could it be 'Fugger'?" said Evelyn. "They did write memoirs."

Caroline took a volume of *Encyclopaedia Britannica* from the bookshelves and turned over the leaves.

They heard Bubbles go upstairs with Effie, then Bobby and Carrie came in to say goodnight, while Effie stood at the door.

"Don't let them dawdle and play about, Effie," said Evelyn, "and be sure they brush their teeth. Now off you go, children."

Philippa noticed again the overwrought look on Effie's face, and an unaccountable feeling of apprehension surged over her.

Effie took the children up to bed. Evelyn, Robert, and Caroline went on with the crossword puzzle. Robert was like an absorbed child. He had no thought for anything else. He had kissed the children, saying "Good, Evelyn! That's splendid. It finishes that corner," as he did so.

Philippa returned to the snapshot album. There was a charming one of Fay as a child of twelve, holding the three-month-old Bobbie on her knee, smiling shyly, proudly. Even then there had been something exquisite about her. Exquisite and subtly withdrawn. She had never yielded the essential part of her to anyone—not even to Caroline. Philippa's heart ached with tenderness as she looked at it. She was terribly disappointed not to have seen Fay on this visit, but Caroline had evidently made up her mind that she should not. She could, of course, have called to see her, but in the face of Caroline's obvious disapproval it would only have made trouble for the child.

"Could it possibly be 'parenthetical'?" said Evelyn.

"Of *course*," said Caroline. "Evelyn, you're a marvel."

Evelyn was clearly the most quick-witted of the three. She would be, thought Philippa grimly.

She turned over another page. Susan and Kenneth arm in arm. It must have been taken before their marriage, as Susan was ostentatiously displaying a solitary ring on the third finger of her left hand. Her eyes shone with love and confidence. Kenneth was smiling down at her. Both looked poignantly young and defenceless. The snapshot was slipped loosely into the page. Philippa felt sure that Caroline did not know it was there. She would have made some excuse to remove it, had she known.

Effie came in. She had taken off her nursery apron and tidied her hair. Her face still wore a look of strain, as she sat on the sofa near Robert, ignoring Philippa. The other three took no notice of her.

"Robert," she said in a strange breathless voice.

"Yes, dear," said Robert absently, then, without waiting for an answer, "Is there such a word as 'ceresin', Evelyn?"

"Robert," said Effie again unsteadily.

"Yes, dear," said Robert again and began to look out "ceresin" in the dictionary. "Yes, there is. . . . Here it is."

With a sudden movement Effie laid her head on her arm on the sofa-end.

"If you're as tired as all that, Effie," said Evelyn, without turning round, "why don't you go to bed?"

Neither of the other two took any notice.

Effie rose abruptly and went out of the room. They continued animatedly to wrestle with the crossword puzzle. They had solved the second corner now. . . . Philippa closed the snapshot album and, slipping quietly from the room, made her way upstairs. Effie was just coming out of her bedroom. She wore her hat and coat. Her lips were set, her eyes hard and bright. Philippa put a hand on her arm.

"Where are you going, Effie?" she said.

"Leave me alone," said Effie unsteadily.

"Where are you going?"

"I don't know. I'm going. I can't stand it any longer."

"What are you going to do?"

"I don't know. Only I'm not coming back. You can tell them if you like. I'll fight my way out if they try to stop me now. But they won't. They want me to go. *She* can have him now. I've tried to keep him, but it's no use. I can't stay and—watch it any longer."

Philippa put her arm round the small taut figure.

"Just come back a moment, Effie."

"You can't stop me going."

"I won't try to. But they'll hear us if we talk here."

Effie allowed herself to be drawn back to the bedroom. There she sat down on the bed and stared at Philippa defiantly.

"What do you want?" she said.

"I only want to understand," said Philippa.

"Don't you understand? You've seen us this afternoon—and before. Well, it's all over. She can have him. She wants him, and he wants her. . . ."

"He doesn't, Effie."

"Oh yes, he does. I love him, and I ought to know. I wouldn't mind if I didn't love him. I've tried to stop, but I can't. And—he doesn't even know whether I'm in the room or not. You saw that just now. He thinks of no one but her. He cares for no one but her. They can have each other now. I'm clearing out. I've stood it as long as I can—seeing her treated as mistress of the house by everyone, being snubbed by her, watching her bullying the children, and smarming up to him. I stayed while I thought there was a chance, but there isn't now. She's won. . . ."

"But, Effie, the children. They need you if no one else does. Think of Carrie. . . ."

"No, my being here makes things worse for them. Carrie knows we're fighting over her, and that's what's making her so nervy. She feels it in the air. It *is* in the air. Don't you feel it? My hatred of her and her hatred of me? It's like poison—all over the house. I can't breathe in it. And the children feel it. They don't understand it, but they feel it, and it's bad for them. They'd be better if I weren't here. I make things worse for them, you see. She tries to punish me through them. She's jealous because she hasn't really taken them from me. She's taken Robert but not them. Well, she can have them all now. She can have everything. I'm through with it."

"Effie, you can't," pleaded Philippa." You can't run away from things like this. Give Robert a chance. Tell him that if he doesn't get rid of her you'll go."

Effie's lips twisted with an ironic smile.

"You're forgetting Caroline," she said. "Even if he did send her away Caroline would get someone else as bad. You see . . . I didn't understand. I thought of her as a silly old maid. I made fun of her. I was rude to her when she tried to interfere in what was my business. I didn't understand. If I'd had any sense I'd have buttered her up as Evelyn does. She hates me. She's never forgiven me for the things I said to her then, and she never will. From the beginning she's never given me a chance. And she's won. Oh, what's the good of *talking*? I gave myself today as a sort of test. I said, 'If it's better today I'll try again,' and—you saw what it was like today."

"What are you going to do?"

Effie's eyes met hers defiantly.

"I'm going down to the railway to put my head under a train."

"Oh no, you're not," said Philippa.

"I can't stay here. I *can't*."

"All right, my dear, you shan't. You shall come with me."

"Where?"

"To my flat in London. You're going to stay there and look after me, and I'll look after you. We're both rather lonely people."

Effie stared at her for a moment in silence, then shrugged wearily.

"Oh, well. I dare say I couldn't have done the other thing when it came to the point. I'm an awful coward really."

"Let's pack quickly, then," said Philippa. "This is your suitcase, isn't it? Bring me your things. . . . Hurry, child."

"It's awfully good of you," said Effie sulkily, bringing her things to Philippa, who packed them deftly into the small case. "It's been driving me mad. I don't care where I go as long as I get away from it. I stayed awake all last night wondering whether to kill myself or Caroline. No, honestly, I did." As Philippa smiled. "It sounds funny now"—reluctantly she smiled, too—"but it didn't then."

"Come along," said Philippa, fastening the clasp of the case, "let's go and drop the bombshell."

They went downstairs together, Philippa carrying the case. In the hall she put it down and drew Effie into the drawing-room with her. The other three turned as they entered.

"I want to take Effie back with me, Robert," said Philippa. "Do you mind?"

They stared at her in amazement.

"I think she needs a change," went on Philippa in her light pleasant voice. "She's tired and rundown. And I'm lonely. I was going to ask her to stay with me later, but it would do us both good if she came now. If Robert doesn't mind, that is."

Effie's eyes were fixed on Robert. Her face was white and set. He was still looking at her in blank surprise.

"But, Effie," he began, then turned to Evelyn, as if for explanation and advice. The amazement was fading from Evelyn's face. There was a faint smile on her lips.

"You have seemed a little tired lately, darling," she said affectionately. "I was going to suggest your taking a holiday. It's an excellent idea. Don't you think so, Caroline?"

Caroline had been looking as perplexed as Robert.

"Why, yes, I suppose so," she said uncertainly. There was the ghost of compunction in her eyes as they rested on Effie. "I'm sorry you've not been feeling well, Effie."

"But, Effie," broke in Robert, "I'd no idea ... I—hadn't you better see a doctor, dear, if you aren't well?"

"Now, Robert, don't fuss the child," smiled Evelyn. There was an air of furtive excitement about her. "All she needs is a change. Change of air and change of interest. She'll come back a different little woman, won't you, darling?"

Effie's eyes remained fixed on Robert.

"Do you want to go, Effie?" he said slowly.

"Yes."

"Come along, then," said Philippa. "We must start at once if we're going to catch the train."

Robert rose, with the air of one abandoning a problem too intricate for solution.

"I'll come and see you off," he said.

"Don't come to the station," said Philippa. "Just see us on the 'bus."

He took up the suitcase and went with them to the gate. The 'bus was approaching as they reached it.

"Goodbye, Effie," he said. "You'll write, won't you?"

He bent towards her, and she offered him her cheek.

"Goodbye," she said in a dull toneless voice.

He gave the case to the conductor, and the two of them mounted the step.

"Goodbye, Effie," he said again.

She gazed at him intently for a moment, then followed Philippa into the 'bus. Evelyn came out and stood by Robert, smiling. The 'bus jerked off. Robert and Evelyn watched it out of sight, then turned and went back to the house.

Chapter Seventeen

ROBERT opened the door with his latch-key and entered the hall. The atmosphere of method and orderliness that Evelyn had imparted to the whole house seemed to meet him on the threshold like something tangible. Not a speck of dust anywhere. The furniture polished till it gleamed like crystal. A bowl of chrysanthemums sharply reflected in the surface of the small mahogany table by the door. No personal belongings to mar the general effect. Hats and coats neatly stowed away in the wardrobe whose purchase had been one of Evelyn's first suggestions.

He remembered the time when he would come home to find the hall littered with Effie's belongings—coat, hat, gloves, scarf. She never could learn to put things in their places. The children's toys, too, would be all over the floor—Bobbie's engine, Carrie's dolls. He remembered how it used to irritate him, and at the memory his heart contracted oddly. He seemed to see a small harassed Effie picking them up hastily, nervously. "I'm terribly sorry, Robert. I'd meant to get it all cleared up before you came home, but somehow I've been so rushed."

He hung his hat and coat in the wardrobe, then stood looking about him. It occurred to him suddenly that the hall was exactly like the hall of a "show-house" at some exhibition. The umbrellas in the umbrella-stand had been deliberately put there in order to lend a clever touch of verisimilitude to the scene.

The drawing-room door opened, and Evelyn came out. Her face wore a smile of welcome.

"Oh, there you are, Robert. I thought I heard you. Dinner's almost ready."

"I'll just go and have a wash. . . . Children all right?"

"Oh yes. Splendid. . . . Carrie's running a temperature again—the little monkey!—but it's nothing to worry about."

Carrie was fretting for Effie, but Evelyn was convinced that she was doing it out of a perverse desire to put herself into the limelight.

"It's the heroine complex," she said. "Effie encouraged it by taking notice of all her fads and fancies. What the child really needs is a little wholesome neglect. I just laugh at her—kindly, of course—and she's growing more sensible already."

Robert agreed, but he didn't feel quite happy about it. The child looked peaky and sullen. She'd been a bundle of mischief before Evelyn came. Her high spirits had, in fact, got on his nerves so much that he had welcomed Evelyn's regime with heartfelt relief, but now he wasn't sure. Was it quite natural for children to play as quietly as Carrie and Bobby did? And those nightmares from which Carrie awoke screaming night after night. . . . She'd never had them in the old days. Was Evelyn's regime, kindly enough—he knew she was never unkind to the children—too repressive? Effie used to romp with them, but since Effie had gone they had grown quieter than ever. Evelyn discouraged all "noisiness" and "roughness". Perhaps—oh well, he didn't know. It was the women's business. Caroline approved, and, if Caroline approved, it must be all right.

His thoughts went idly back again to the early days of his marriage. Effie, singing and laughing and forgetting things and leaving things about, playing absurd tricks on him, preparing absurd "surprises". . . . It had delighted him throughout the honeymoon, but when ordinary life began he felt that method and dignity should take its place. But Effie had remained harum-scarum and flighty. Her attempts at housekeeping had been ludicrous, and, what was worse, she had not seemed to realise the seriousness of it all. She laughed at her mistakes, made jokes of her ignorance. Caroline had tried to help her, but—even now the memory brought back something of the old resentment—she had behaved atrociously to Caroline, refusing her offers of help with almost incredible rudeness. Despite that, Caroline had continued to stand by, showing no resentment, unfailingly kind and patient. Few other women would have done it. But then Caroline wasn't like other women. She was herself, unique—the only woman Robert had ever known in whom it was impossible to find any fault.

He came out of the bathroom and stood for a moment at the door of the night nursery. He would have liked to go in and see the children, but he remembered that that was one of the things Evelyn had been most emphatic about when she took over the reins of the household. Goodnight visits to the children after they were in bed unsettled them and made them wakeful. Even Effie was not supposed to go in to see them if she came back from shopping or a tea-party after they were in bed. It was quite right, of course. Caroline had supported Evelyn, and that alone proved that it was right. It was strange how, since Effie had gone, his thoughts kept turning to the days of their early married life—to the elfin harum-scarum Effie who'd had such an endless store of little intimate jokes with him, jokes that seemed very silly now but that he'd enjoyed quite as much as Effie in those early days, before he realised the importance of settling down to a dignified family life in a well-ordered house. It was the expression on Caroline's face, he remembered, that had first roused him to the importance of that—Caroline, who, too kind to hurt Effie's feelings by any criticism, still could not hide her conviction that it was time Effie's silliness came to an end, and that she applied herself seriously to mastering the business of housekeeping. It would all have been so simple if Effie had responded to Caroline's kindly offers of help.

He went slowly downstairs to the hall and looked again at the letter-rack on the wall by the door, in which his letters were always put. A few circulars ... nothing from Effie. He had had only one letter from her since she went to Philippa's—a short impersonal letter, giving him a bald account of all she and Philippa had done since they left Bartenham (they seemed to be going about a good deal), but with no mention of her return. It might have been written by the merest acquaintance.

"What sort of a day have you had?" said Evelyn.

She was sitting by the fire, working at a green smock for Carrie.

"Not too bad," he said.

"Well, come and sit down till the gong goes. I'm sure you're tired."

He felt a sudden irritation at being invited to sit down in his own house, as if she were the mistress of it and he a guest. He had thought her perfect while Effie was still here, but since Effie had gone all sorts of unimportant little things about her had been getting on his nerves.

She looked up again, smiling, from her work.

"I hope you've been energetic and started the crossword puzzle," she said. "I simply haven't had a minute since morning."

"I'm afraid I haven't. . . ."

Another strange thing was that since Effie had gone all the zest seemed to have vanished from the interests that he and Evelyn had in common. Effie had taken no part in them, but she had been there in the background. He missed her poignantly from the background, more, in fact, than he had ever dreamed he would. The savour seemed to have gone out of everything. He felt restless and depressed.

"Lazybones!" she teased, with a smile that increased his vague irritation against her.

The dinner-gong sounded in the hall, and Evelyn rose, folded up her needlework, and preceded him into the dining-room. Yes, it was all too tidy, too cleared up, he decided as he went through the hall. He hated untidiness, but there ought to be something of someone's lying about somewhere . . . the sort of thing that made a difference between a home and a display of "specimen rooms" in a furnishing establishment. He felt a bit nervy tonight. . . . He missed Effie. And he had a little nagging sensation of remorse that he wouldn't face but that yet depressed him. Perhaps he hadn't taken as much notice of her lately as he ought to have done. He'd been tired and just wanted peace when he came home in the evening. As long as she was there he hadn't worried about her or even—he had to confess it—thought about her. She had been rather quiet lately, he remembered. Perhaps she hadn't been well. Philippa had noticed it, and Evelyn had noticed it. Evelyn ought to have mentioned it to him, he told himself resentfully. He couldn't be expected to—yes, he *could* be expected to notice it, he *ought* to have noticed it. . . .

Evelyn took her place at the foot of the table opposite him. She had been sitting at the foot of the table for some time now. It was easier for her to keep an eye on the children when they were there, and it hardly seemed worth while to change places with Effie for the only meal the children did not have with them. He had never resented Evelyn's sitting opposite him when Effie sat between them, but now, illogically, he did. He resented, too, the mistress-of-the-house air that hung about her as she sat there, handsome, well dressed, smiling at him across the table. And he was ashamed of his resentment, remembering her unflagging zeal in his service, her careful training of the children, her methodical ordering of the house. He ought to be grateful to her. Well, hang it all, he *was* grateful to her, but—he missed Effie. And he was worried about Effie. Suppose she were really ill and they were hiding it from him. Women did hide things from one. Even Caroline, from sheer affection and a desire not to worry him, might keep a thing like that from him. Suppose Effie had gone to London to have an operation. He saw her lying in a hospital bed, white and still. He saw himself hurrying to her side . . . perhaps too late. Even the letter she had written to him might have been a blind. She might have written it from hospital just to lull his suspicions. Women were capable of such things. . . .

He interrupted Evelyn's account of the conversation she had had with Bobby's headmaster's wife, whom she had met in the town, to say, "Do you know if Caroline's heard from Effie, Evelyn?"

A slight expression of annoyance crossed Evelyn's face.

"I really don't know," she said. "She hadn't when I last saw her. I expect Effie's far too busy enjoying herself to write."

That reassured him but left an after-sting. He didn't altogether relish the thought of Effie's being too busy enjoying herself to write. Surely she could enjoy herself at home. But could she? Again that nagging little feeling of compunction stirred at his heart. It was a long time since he'd taken her anywhere. Of course, there weren't many places in Bartenham where he could take her, but in the old days they used to go up to London for a night occasionally and see a show or go to a dance. .... They'd stopped doing it when the children came, but there wasn't any reason why they shouldn't do it again now that Evelyn was in charge. Caroline hadn't approved of their doing it, he'd forgotten exactly why. But, anyway, it was his business, not Caroline's. .... That thought startled him, and he felt almost guilty at having admitted it into his mind. He was for ejecting it immediately and pretending that he had never admitted it, but suddenly he decided not to. It *wasn't* Caroline's business. Caroline was wonderful in every way, but, after all, a man's relations with his wife were no one's business but his own. Perhaps Caroline had never quite understood Effie. Perhaps . . . no, better not pursue that line of thought. It was too thorny, too fraught with mental discomfort. Effie was a dear little thing who'd been somewhat flighty at first, but now, thanks to Caroline's help and guidance, had settled down nicely and was very happy and comfortable in the home that Evelyn had made so happy and comfortable for them all. Effie, indeed, was remarkably lucky. Not many wives and mothers had as few responsibilities and were looked after as well as Effie.

Evelyn was telling him those little bits of local gossip that she always managed to collect and that generally he found so interesting, but, like everything else, they seemed to have lost their savour since Effie went. Perhaps he was a little run down himself. Pity Effie had rushed off like that on the spur of the moment. They might have taken a holiday together, leaving Evelyn in charge of the children. He could have arranged it if he'd had a week's notice. It was years since he and Effie had gone away together without the children. .... The dinner was excellently cooked and excellently served, as were all the meals since Evelyn's arrival, but somehow he didn't feel hungry. That little nagging feeling of anxiety and compunction about Effie worried at the pit of his stomach all the time, taking away his appetite.

When they went back to the drawing-room Evelyn poured out coffee, and he lit her cigarette for her in silence. There was a small secret smile on her face. She looked like a woman who is sure of herself, who can afford to bide her time. When he had put aside his coffee cup she handed him the paper.

"There!" she said. "See what you can do. There are some of your specialities for you. You know I can never do anagrams."

He took the paper and sat for some moments, looking at it unseeingly. His uneasiness was gradually yielding to the sense of well-being induced by the cosy firelit room, the cigarette, the coffee, and a feeling of pleasant end-of-the-day weariness. It was silly of him to worry about Effie. Philippa had asked her to go and stay with her, and Effie had naturally jumped at it. Effie had always enjoyed going up to Town, even for a day, and it was a long time since she'd had the chance of going. And what was more natural than that she should go with Philippa then and there? Philippa evidently wanted company, and they were both rather impulsive. He wasn't sure that he altogether approved of the arrangement. Effie was impressionable, and, although Caroline was loyalty itself, he couldn't help knowing that she'd not had too easy a time with Philippa. She had not said a word against her, but he had gathered that she'd found her irresponsible and frivolous—as, of course, one would expect a woman of her history to be. He knew that Caroline had been glad for Fay's sake when Philippa left Bartenham. He glanced across at Evelyn, sitting on the other side of the fireplace, her head bent over the little green smock, her firm white hand drawing the silk in and out with gentle rhythmic movement. He felt ashamed of his feeling of irritation with her. Thinking of Philippa had made him realise her merits again. She was wonderful—more like Caroline, in fact, than any woman he had ever known. And how kind she always was to Effie, how motherly and tender and patient! Just like Caroline. . . . Yes, they were lucky to have her. Women like Caroline and Evelyn were the salt of the earth. One was apt to take them for granted till one came across women like Philippa, who had frittered away their lives in self-indulgence and lived only for pleasure, who in their old age were almost as silly and flighty as they had been when they were young. Caroline had hinted that Philippa had even tried to attract Richard, but Richard, of course, had too much sense for that sort of thing. Oh well, there was nothing really to worry about. Effie had just gone away for a short holiday. Meanwhile he was very happy and comfortable here with Evelyn. . . .

He made a slight movement with his head as if dismissing a problem that was now completely solved, and turned his attention to the crossword puzzle.

Evelyn went on with her needlework in silence, that small secret smile still on her lips. She understood his state of mind as well as if she could actually read his thoughts. He was restless and uneasy without Effie, but that would soon pass. He was not introspective or analytical. He accepted things at their face value. He liked peace and quiet and his creature comforts—and those she could give him. Already he depended on her more than he realised. Effie had gone, and not for a moment did Evelyn think that Effie would ever come back. She didn't quite know why she was so confident on that point, but she was. She knew that Effie would never come back. Not while she was there, at any rate, so what she had to do was to consolidate her position, and ensure that she would be there. After all, only she was aware by what ceaseless pinpricks, administered under a cover of affection, even of tenderness, she had made Effie's position in the house intolerable. She hated Effie—had hated her from the beginning, even before she had realised the possibilities of the situation. She hated her for her inefficiency and vagueness and weakness, for her appealing, blue-eyed prettiness. . . .

The smile faded from her lips, and something hard and bitter took its place. Her mind went back over her life. . . .

Her father had been well off, and, as his only child, she had spent her girlhood in an atmosphere of luxury, petted and made much of by everyone around her. In those days she had never even contemplated the possibility of having to work for her living. Her father's death had coincided with the failure of his business, and she had been left penniless.

She had taken a post as companion to a wealthy old lady, looking upon it merely as a temporary expedient. She had decided to restore her fortunes by a "good match," and she thought that her employer's *milieu* would provide the necessary husband, who was, of course, to be a man of wealth, breeding, and personal attractions. But somehow her ideal failed to materialise, and, tiring of the old lady's querulousness, she left her and took another post. She had never stayed long anywhere, and the years had slipped by till she realised that she was on the verge of middle age. Men had fallen in love with her (she had had several very discreet "adventures"), but never the right sort of men. Either they didn't want to marry her, or, if they did, they were not rich enough to make it worth her while. The right sort of men had somehow—she didn't know why—fought shy of her. And the years had slipped by. . . . She had hoped that in Bartenham she might find someone suitable. Her demands were no longer extravagant. They had, in fact, come down considerably in the last ten years. Wealth, breeding, and good looks were no longer essential. She would be content with quite a small establishment and a very ordinary husband as the condition of her freedom. But Bartenham seemed singularly devoid of middle-aged bachelors of independent means. She had even been driven once to consider Robert's uncle—a dreadful old man with dyed hair and a pinched waist—but she didn't think she would ever have considered him seriously even if the old fool hadn't suddenly seemed to take fright. (He'd been as ridiculous in his terror of her—starting off like a timid gazelle at the very sight of her in the distance—as he'd been in his earlier admiration.) The half-witted sister would, of course, have complicated the situation too much. It might have been difficult to get him to agree to put the old horror away into a home—where she ought to have been years ago—though, once married to him, she'd have given him no peace till he did. But—the situation here was interesting. That little fool Effie had gone and wouldn't come back. There were always plenty of men ready to snap up a juicy little morsel like Effie. She had been near the end of her tether when she went, and she would take readily enough to "consolation." She must realise—just as Robert himself must eventually realise—that their marriage had been a failure. Evelyn felt that she didn't know Philippa very well—she thought of her as the "dark horse"—but she had gathered from Caroline that Philippa had lived an immoral life and that Caroline was anxious about her influence over Fay. She had even, Evelyn had gathered, tried to vamp the respectable Richard, much to his disgust. Men always flocked round a woman of that type, however old she was. There would be plenty of them for Effie to choose from—Effie like a child out of school, sick of her life in Bartenham, full of secret bitterness and resentment against Robert. Oh, Effie would never come back. And Robert? Robert was fortunately neither subtle nor perceptive. He would soon get used to Effie's absence. He would soon become so dependent upon her, Evelyn, that he would not be able to contemplate life without her. Like all men he hated having to arrange domestic details. He was intensely conservative and disliked changes of any sort. And—like all men—he was very dependent on his comforts. Yes, Robert would soon find out that he couldn't do without her. She looked forward a year ahead, seeing Effie's divorce safely over and herself Robert's wife and mistress of this house. . . . She'd get on quite well with Robert. He was very easy to manage. Her chief feeling for him was, in fact, contempt because he was so easy to manage. And—the secret smile curved her lips again—she'd enjoy coming out into the open against Caroline after truckling down to her all this time. Oh yes, she had a good many grudges saved up against Caroline, and Caroline was going to pay for every one of them. She'd go about it in a very different way from the way that little fool Effie had done. . . .

Robert looked up from the paper.

"I've done all but two," he said. He handed the paper across to her. "See what you can make of them."

Chapter Eighteen

Susan lay back in the easy-chair by Philippa's hearth and threw a slightly resentful glance round the room.

Philippa had finally taken a "converted flat" in an old house in Hampstead and had spent an enjoyable month furnishing it. The result was, as Philippa said, unashamedly old-fashioned. The high spacious rooms made an admirable background for the Chippendale and Sheraton that she had picked up in sale-rooms with Richard's help. There were cream-coloured walls, with curtains and chair-covers of glazed chintz. The carpet was deep blue, and on the Adams mantelpiece were some pieces of Dresden china that had belonged to Philippa's grandmother.

"It's awfully restful," said Susan. "I don't know whether it's you or the room."

"It's the room," smiled Philippa. "It's old enough to have learnt not to fuss. New rooms fuss all the time. This one is, I suppose, about a hundred years old. It's learnt to take things quietly."

"I wish it would teach me," said Susan.

Philippa looked at her quickly. Her lips were tight and bitter. Her eyes still wandered restlessly about the room.

"You'd better not have Fay here," she went on. "She'd go mad if she saw your piano. She can't bear even to see one nowadays. Caroline was right, of course," she added. "The kid used to waste hours over it. You can't work for a scholarship and waste three hours a day over the piano as well."

It was strange, thought Philippa, how little friendship or understanding there seemed to be between the two sisters.

"But if she was so fond of it," she suggested tentatively, "why couldn't she have taken it up professionally?"

Susan shrugged.

"I dunno. I expect Caroline went into all that. There isn't much money in it, you know. A music mistress doesn't get as much as a modern language mistress. They're not eligible for posts of special responsibility for one thing. And anything else—concert work, I mean—is too precarious."

"Still—Fay loves it. It's been a terrible sacrifice for her to have to give it up."

Susan's face hardened.

"Well, why shouldn't she make some sacrifice? The rest of us have to. . . . I'm sorry——" she went on. "I sound a beast. I am a beast. I think I hate everyone and everything in the world."

"I don't think you do," said Philippa quietly.

Susan had arrived unexpectedly. She'd come up to town to see about some books that she needed for her teaching and had finished her business earlier than she'd expected. She hadn't wanted to go home and was too sick with misery to think of doing anything else. So when she saw a Hampstead 'bus, she got into it on an impulse and found her way to Philippa's flat. She'd never been there before, and she had a feeling of guilt for having come now. It seemed disloyal to Caroline, who had been so good to her, to whom she owed everything. But—she'd felt better ever since she entered the room. There was something about Philippa—Susan didn't know quite what it was. She was probably—she was certainly, Susan corrected herself hastily—all the things that Caroline thought she was, and yet she made one feel better somehow.

"I suppose Effie's still here," said Susan suddenly.

"Yes. She'll be in to tea. She's just gone out to do some shopping."

"How long is she staying?"

"I don't know."

"She's left Evelyn cock-of-the-walk, hasn't she?"

"Has she?"

"Oh yes. I called in with a message from Caroline the other evening. A tableaux of domestic bliss. Evelyn sewing and Robert reading bits of the evening paper aloud to her. Made one wonder where Effie ever had come in the picture." She threw another restless glance about the room. "I like your curtains," she added suddenly.

"I think I'd have had dark ones," said Philippa, "if I hadn't remembered how charming the light curtains looked in your drawing-room."

Susan's mouth tightened, but she said nothing.

"It was a darling little house," went on Philippa. "What's happened to it now?"

"Nothing, as far as I know," said Susan shortly. She got up and went over to the open window, standing there with her back to the room. "Are those plane trees in your garden?"

"Yes ... but it's not my garden. That's the worst of a flat, of course. One doesn't have a garden. I loved your little garden. There were two old apple trees in it, weren't there?"

"Yes," said Susan stonily. "It had been an orchard before they built on it."

"There was something so—home-like about it all," said Philippa dreamily. "I suppose that was partly because you were the first people to live in it. You'd made it, right from the beginning. These old houses have learnt not to fuss, as I said, but they're detached and impersonal. They don't care what happens to you. Your little house did care. It was part of you. You'd given it its life. It was interested in everything you did. Didn't you feel it? Didn't you feel it holding its breath when you tried a new recipe out of your cookery book? Didn't you feel it waiting for Ken to come home in the evening and hoping he'd had a good day, wondering if——"

Susan wheeled round. Her cheeks were flaming, her eyes bright with tears.

"Can't you leave me *alone*?" she burst out. "I wish I'd never come here. I——" She stopped. There was the sound of the opening of the front door of the flat, and almost immediately Effie entered, smiling, her arms full of flowers.

Susan noticed at once that she was different. It might have been the new coat and hat she wore, but she seemed more poised, more sure of herself. She had lost her old air of a nervous sulky child.

She looked better, too, physically. She held herself more erect. She had even grown a little fatter. The smile died from her face as she saw Susan.

"Hello, Effie."

They greeted each other with that faint hostility that, Philippa had noticed, every member of Caroline's circle seemed to show to every other member.

"I didn't know you were coming," said Effie.

"Neither did I," replied Susan ungraciously.

Effie handed her flowers to Philippa.

"I just couldn't resist them," she said.

"Darling, how sweet of you! I'll go and get some water."

She went out, leaving the two girls together. Effie stood by the fire, drawing off her gloves. Susan still stood by the window. Her eyes were dry and hard again now. There was a short silence, then Susan said:

"Well, I suppose you want all the latest news of Bartenham?"

"Not particularly," said Effie.

Their eyes met in a long slow challenge. The new serenity that hung over Effie seemed to deepen the pain at Susan's heart.

"You're making quite a long visit here, aren't you?" she said.

"Yes."

"When are you coming back?"

"I don't know."

"There's nothing to hurry back for, of course. Robert and Evelyn are getting on quite well without you."

She was striking out viciously in a blind desire to hurt, as though by so doing she could dull something of her own misery.

"So I gather," said Effie quietly.

Philippa came back, carrying the flowers in a tall jar.

"Aren't they lovely?" She touched the bell. "Now let's have tea."

"I've just been asking Effie when she's coming back," said Susan.

Effie turned to her.

"If you really want to know," she said, "I'm coming back when Evelyn's gone."

Susan gave a short dry laugh.

"You'll have to wait till doomsday for that."

"Very well," said Effie. "I'll wait till doomsday, then."

"Have you told Robert?"

"No. He hasn't asked me yet."

The maid brought in tea, and the conversation drifted off to trivialities. Susan gathered that Richard was a fairly frequent visitor at the flat. It occurred to her that they had not seen him lately at Caroline's. Oh well, Caroline wouldn't mind. Caroline had always found him rather a nuisance.

Caroline. ... At the thought of her return tonight her heart sickened again into despair. How could she go on with it, day after day, day after day ... teaching, correcting exercises, preparing lessons? She *couldn't* tell Caroline how much she hated it all—Caroline, who was so sweet and tender and helpful, so eager and excited about the child. Caroline thought that she had forgotten Ken, that she was happy. She tried, for Caroline's sake, to pretend she was, tried to pretend that she was glad about the child, while really the thought of it was like a nightmare. Her lips twisted bitterly when she remembered how she had once longed and prayed for a child. Oh, it would all have been so different if. ... But Caroline was right. No woman with any self-respect could go crawling back to him after the way he'd treated her, the things he'd said to her. She hadn't seen him since that horrible time when he had forced his way into the house and insulted her and Caroline. She'd had one letter from him, but, on Caroline's advice, she'd sent it back unopened. She glanced at Philippa and, finding Philippa's eyes fixed on her with a grave compassionate expression in their depths, looked away quickly with flaming cheeks. Did Philippa guess about the child? They hadn't told anyone about it, except, of course, Fay, who had to know. Her figure showed no signs of it yet, but perhaps, even so, a woman as experienced as Philippa would know. She felt a desperate longing to confide in her, to tell her everything—about the child, about her unhappiness, about the secret tormenting love for Kenneth that she couldn't tear out of her heart however hard she tried—but the old loyalty to Caroline restrained her. It was bad enough to have come here at all. She would never dare to confess to Caroline that she'd been.

"I'd better go now," she said, rising abruptly to her feet.

She collected her things, took an ungracious leave of Effie, and went with Philippa into the little hall.

"Isn't it tiny?" smiled Philippa. "It's a quarter of one of the original rooms. They made the cloakroom and kitchen out of the rest. I rather like a small hall myself. It's so much more welcoming than a large one. Yours was a darling, wasn't it? I loved that yellow crinkly sort of wallpaper you had there. Ken used to say that it looked as if someone had thrown custard at it, didn't he?"

Susan had a sudden vision of Ken hanging up his coat in the little hall, then turning to take her in his arms. She closed her eyes and dug her teeth into her lip. She couldn't bear it. She hated Philippa. She was cruel. She only said things like that because she knew how much they hurt. Caroline had been right. She was a wicked woman. Oh, why had she come here? Wasn't there anywhere in the whole world where she could find peace?

It was dinner-time when she reached home. Caroline came into the hall to greet her as soon as she arrived.

"Oh, my dear, how tired you look! You oughtn't to have gone up to Town. It's a good thing you've not much work tonight. I've corrected your French exercises for you."

"Thanks so much. But I'm not a bit tired, Caroline."

"Did you get on all right?"

"Yes, thanks."

She noticed suddenly that Caroline herself looked tired and worried.

"Is Fay all right?" she said.

"Yes. She had one of her crying fits after tea so I sent her to bed early. She needs rest, that's all."

"What was she crying about?"

"Nothing. She didn't know."

Little fool, thought Susan savagely. What on earth has she to cry about? A child like that doesn't know the meaning of trouble. Caroline has thoroughly spoilt her.

"It's nerves," Caroline went on. "It does seem too absurd. This generation goes in for them to a most ridiculous extent. It's a sort of fashion, I suppose. We never had them. It's all a matter of self-control. I'll speak to Fay really seriously about it when her exam.'s over. I can't risk bringing on another attack before."

"I suppose she's working pretty hard?"

"She is, in a way. But she takes no real interest in her work. It's very disappointing. I was as keen as mustard when I was her age."

Susan gathered that the day had not gone too smoothly at home.

"Oh well . . . I'd better go up and wash," she said listlessly.

Caroline went into the drawing-room and stood by the fireplace, gazing into the fire with a frown. She'd had an exhausting day. She tried to be patient with Fay, but she couldn't help feeling that with a little effort she ought to be able to master those nerve attacks. It was so absurd to cry for no reason at all, and very ungrateful, considering that everything was being done to give her a good chance in life. But something else was worrying her more than that. She'd been to see Evelyn in the afternoon, and there had been something in Evelyn's manner that had never been there before. Thinking it over afterwards, she had come to the conclusion that it must have been her imagination, but still she could not quite rid herself of the uncomfortable feeling that the visit had left with her. There was nothing that she could actually point to as having been in any way different from usual, but the difference had been there. Evelyn had welcomed her effusively, had asked her advice, as she always did, on various household matters, had been as affectionate as ever, and yet behind it all there had been an elusive hint—though really the very thought was incredible—of mockery. The old sense of sympathy and understanding, the old happy confidence in Evelyn's loyalty, had gone. And the monstrous thought struck her, making her heart beat unevenly—had it ever really existed? At that suspicion, the foundations of her kingdom seemed to rock beneath her again. The foundations seemed always to be rocking now, the foundations that had seemed so firm in the old days. Marcia's disloyalty, Effie's,

Philippa's, she took for granted. It did not trouble her. But Evelyn's. No, she couldn't believe it. . . . She couldn't believe it. As if she hadn't enough to bear just now with Fay and Susan! Fay with her "nerves," her new strange sulkiness, her stormy fits of tears. Adolescence, of course . . . but to call it adolescence didn't make it any less difficult to deal with. And Susan, with her listlessness, her lack of interest in things. . . . Oh well, she must just go on being kind and patient with them, as she'd always been, go on bearing her burden alone, as she'd always borne it. What would happen, she wondered with a wry smile, if she allowed herself the luxury of nerves and listlessness? What would happen to any of them without her? They relied on her for help at every turn, and—she squared her shoulders, drawing her slender figure erect—she wouldn't fail them. They were her children. They belonged to her. She wouldn't fail them. Beneath her weariness and depression surged again that deep, almost sensual, joy that the knowledge of their dependence on her always brought with it. Her thoughts returned to Evelyn, and she tried again to remember what exactly had given that impression of mockery, of covert hostility, almost of challenge. Words and tone had been as affectionate as ever, but—it had been there. Now that her confidence in Evelyn was shaken, she was feeling anxious on Robert's behalf. The situation was unconventional, to say the least of it. She had hinted as much to Evelyn, only to be told by Evelyn, with that new mocking light in her eyes, that it was quite usual for the mother's help to stay at home to look after the children when the mother went away for a holiday, that it was, in fact, her obvious duty to do so. Yes, the more she thought of it, the more certain she was that there *had* been a veiled hostility in Evelyn's manner. Surely Philippa couldn't have tampered with her loyalty—Philippa who, from a sheer perverse delight in interfering with other people's business, had carried Effie off to London with her, Philippa whose disloyalty was spreading like a disease through the family. Her influence had stormed and taken citadels that she would have sworn were impregnable. How long was it since Richard had been to see her? No, she wouldn't think of Richard. She couldn't. It hurt too much.

Susan came downstairs. She had washed and changed, but she still looked pale and exhausted.

"I oughtn't to have let you go, darling," said Caroline solicitously. "I always feel a rag myself after a day in London. It's the atmosphere, I suppose. Come along in to dinner. You've had some tea, I suppose?"

"Yes," said Susan guiltily. She'd have to lie now if Caroline asked where she'd had it. It would seem so strange not to have mentioned it at first. But all Caroline said was, "Oh, those tea-shop teas aren't meals at all. You must be starving," and, slipping her arm through hers, led her gently into the dining-room. During the meal Caroline gave her a cheerful account of her day's doings, and Susan made mechanical comments and rejoinders, her eyes fixed on her plate, her heart aching with misery. If only she hadn't been to Philippa's! If only Philippa hadn't talked about the little house! She'd been trying so hard to forget it—the sun streaming in through the brightly coloured cretonne curtains . . . the crinkly paper in the little hall . . . Ken turning from the hat-stand to take her in his arms . . . Ken putting on her apron to wash up . . . doing a skirt dance in it while she held her sides with laughter . . . Ken waking her with kisses in the morning. Ken . . . Ken . . . Ken . . . She couldn't bear it. There was nothing left to live for. Perhaps she'd die when the child was born. She hoped she would.

"And I saw Aunt Maggie in the town," Caroline was saying brightly. "She looked really terrible. Her very worst."

"How ghastly!" said Susan, but she wasn't thinking of Aunt Maggie. She was thinking of the little house, thinking of it as Eve might have thought of her lost paradise. She wondered what had happened to it. She had heard that Ken was now living in rooms at the other end of the town. Perhaps he had sold it. She hadn't been near the neighbourhood since she left it.

"Let's go and have coffee," said Caroline, rising.

They went into the drawing-room.

"I told you I'd done your corrections, didn't I?" went on Caroline cheerfully. "You've not much else to do tonight, have you? What about the test paper?"

"I don't get that in till tomorrow."

Caroline put down her coffee cup and, going to her bureau, took from a drawer a small parcel, wrapped in tissue-paper.

"Look, darling. I got it this afternoon."

Susan unwrapped it.

It was a tiny white woollen matinee-jacket. "How sweet of you!" she said in a choking voice.

Then she rose abruptly.

"Caroline . . . I've got such a headache. I think I'll go for a little walk. I won't be long."

Caroline looked at her in tender surprise, but Susan went quickly from the room. A few minutes later she set off down the darkening street. In her bag was the key of the little house, which she had had with her ever since she left it. The longing just to see it, just to stand outside and look at it, had become uncontrollable. It was Philippa who had made her feel like that, of course, Philippa who with careless cruelty had brought agonisingly to life the memories she had been trying so hard to kill. She knew that her abrupt departure had hurt Caroline, that Caroline was longing to talk to her of the child, to plan its upbringing, as she loved to do—but she didn't care. She had to go back to the little house, had just to stand outside and look at it once more. Her heart beats quickened as she entered the rough uneven road that led to the "estate." It was like finding again in real life the scene of some far-off glamorous dream. There it was—silent, empty, forlorn, its dark windows conspicuous among its brightly lit neighbours, its silence emphasised by the sounds of laughter that came from the next house. Its air of desolation sent a sharp pang through her heart. The gay cretonne curtains seemed to hang in weary folds behind the dusty panes. A handful of dead flowers drooped disconsolately in a vase on the window-sill.

She went up the little path through the front garden. Like the house, it wore a forsaken, dejected air. Both house and garden, she thought bitterly, were symbolic of the love that had flourished there—once glowingly alive, now cold and dead.

She took the key from her bag, opened the front door, and stood on the threshold, looking about her. Dust everywhere. An old raincoat of Ken's still hanging on the hat-stand. A large cobweb over the electric light shade. . . . She went into the drawing-room and dining-room, switching on the lights. Over everything that thick film of dust, that damp airless atmosphere. On an impulse she fetched an apron and some dusters from the kitchen and set to work to dust and polish. She couldn't bear to see the rooms where she had once been so happy sunk into dinginess and neglect. She worked till the downstairs rooms wore a semblance of cleanliness, then went slowly upstairs. Outside the bedroom door she stood for some moments, her lips tightly set, her heart beating tumultuously before she entered . . . then, glancing almost fearfully about the room, began to dust the table by the bed with quick unsteady movements. Suddenly she stopped, the duster fell from her hand, and, dropping upon the bed, she lay there sobbing. . . . The sound of the opening of the front door roused her. She started up and stood motionless, hardly breathing, staring at the door. Footsteps were coming upstairs. The door opened and Kenneth entered.

"Ken!"

"Susie!"

She didn't know whether she was comforting him or he was comforting her, but, once they were in each other's arms, all the things that had seemed to matter so terribly didn't matter at all. Nothing mattered but their love for each other.

"Ken . . . how did you happen to come here tonight?" she said at last, gently disengaging herself from his arm.

"Philippa rang me up. You'd been there today, hadn't you?"

"Yes."

"I've been to see her once or twice lately. I'd told her that I was absolutely sure you hated me so much that it wasn't any use even asking you to come back . . . and tonight she rang me up and said that I was wrong, that she knew you loved me. She told me to go round to your house and insist on seeing you alone, even if I had to gag Caroline and lock her up in the cellar to do it. So I went round, and you were just coming out of the gate. You didn't see me, so I followed you."

"Ken . . . did Philippa tell you . . .?"

"Yes. At least she said she was almost sure. I'm terribly glad, darling."

"I am, too, now. Ken, I ought to have told you. I feel so ashamed of not doing. Caroline . . ."

"I know, dear. I understand."

"I've been wrong all the time."

"No, it was all my fault."

"I was so silly and proud, and Caroline said . . ."

"I know."

"She said that you'd been going with other women. . . ."

"I haven't. You know I haven't."

"Ken, I can't bear to think of what a beast I've been. But it'll be all right now. I've been so wretched. I shall never leave you again whatever happens."

"It's been hell," he said slowly. "I used to lie awake at night, longing for you and hating Caroline. . . ."

"Don't hate her, Ken."

"No, I won't—now. She'll never come between us again—not now we both know what it's like."

He held her tightly in his arms. Her head was on his shoulder, her eyes gazed dreamily into the distance.

"Poor Caroline!" she said.

Chapter Nineteen

"AND when are you coming back?" said Robert, trying to keep the question on the casual note that Effie had so determinedly set for the whole conversation.

He had passed through several stages of feeling with regard to Effie since she left home. At first he had felt merely uneasy without her. Then his uneasiness had gradually changed to resentment. She was perfectly well. She must be perfectly well. She seemed to be going to concerts and theatres and dances continually, accompanied by Philippa and her innumerable friends. It wasn't right, he told himself indignantly. She'd no business to be gadding about like that. At her age, too. The mother of a family. She should be at home, ordering the house and looking after the children. He even found it slightly exasperating that the house and children were as well looked after as when she had been at home. He wanted to feel neglected and pathetic—he *did* feel neglected and pathetic—and it was annoying that his surroundings should not look as neglected and pathetic as he felt. Carrie was still fretting for her, and the others kept asking about her, and he'd been tempted more than once to tell her that in his letters, but hers never mentioned the children, and his pride prevented his doing so.

Then, as time went on, his resentment had faded, and he had been conscious only of a longing for Effie's warm familiar presence, for the unquestioning devotion that had once formed the background of his life. Evelyn, of course, was a wonderful companion. She was much cleverer and more amusing than Effie, but she was the least bit of a strain. She took so much living up to. One had to try always to be clever and amusing, too, which, when one was tired after a day's work, was difficult. Funny that he'd never felt that when Effie was there. It was as if the tired part of him had then taken comfort and refreshment from her presence without knowing that it was doing so. Now he missed it poignantly. He had begun to look on Philippa as the villainess of the piece. Effie and he had been perfectly happy together till she came along and lured Effie away from him. He'd been a fool to let her go so meekly, but he'd been taken by surprise and she'd gone before he realised what was happening. Caroline's tacit warnings should have put him on his guard against her. She was a dangerous woman. She'd made a mess of her own life, and she took a malicious pleasure in making a mess of other people's. She couldn't bear to see him and Effie happy together, and she'd known no peace till she'd managed to unsettle Effie and take her away. He had made up his mind quite suddenly this morning to come down to see Effie today.

His tenderness had flowed out to her as the train brought him nearer, and beneath the tenderness stirred again that faint feeling of self-reproach. Effie was weak. He should have looked after her better, not have left her exposed to such an influence as Philippa's. He was to blame almost as much as Philippa herself. He felt a glow of generosity as he made this admission. He sat forward in the seat of the taxi that took him from the station to Philippa's flat, as if to propel the vehicle more swiftly by his own efforts. Soon Effie would be in his arms, clinging to him, sobbing out her contrition for having left him, protesting her love and devotion. And he'd take her back with him tonight. As for Philippa, he'd just ignore her. She'd soon find out that her influence weighed for nothing against his love.

Effie was alone in the flat when he reached it. She explained that Philippa had gone out to tea with some friends. He gathered that Effie had been going, too, and had only stayed in because of his telephone message. He was glad, on the whole, that Philippa was out. It cleared the stage for the scene of reconciliation. He stepped forward to take Effie in his arms, and then, to his amazement, the embrace he'd been looking forward to so eagerly was over. Or rather it hadn't taken place at all. Effie had offered him her cheek, a cool smooth cheek, and then had quickly disengaged herself. She certainly wasn't sobbing out her love and contrition on his shoulder as he'd meant her to. Far from it. She was considering him with a faint smile from the opposite side of the fireplace.

"Sit down, Robert," she was saying. "How nice of you to come up! Philippa's so sorry not to be here. Would you like tea now?"

"How nice of you to come up!" As if he were the most casual of acquaintances. He looked at her resentfully, critically. Yes, she was—different. She looked absurdly young and smart for one thing. Her hair was arranged in a more fashionable way. Ear-rings dangled from her small white ears. Her dress was different, too. It wasn't just that it was a dress he hadn't seen before. It was a different sort of dress. Even her figure seemed to have changed, to have become *svelte* and elegant. A feeling of desolation swept over him. Where was his Effie, his loving, untidy little Effie, with her soft warm curves and dumpy frilly dresses?

"Don't you want to know about the children, Effie?" he said reproachfully.

"I know," she said calmly. "I've heard from Janet every day."

Janet, the quiet little maid whom Evelyn had trained so efficiently.

"Janet?" he said. "You mean Evelyn, don't you?"

"No, I mean Janet. I asked Janet to write. Oh, Evelyn's written, too, of course, but I think that Janet's accounts are more reliable. Well, what's happening down at Bartenham?"

She lit a cigarette as she spoke. That was another shock. She'd smoked in the old days, but not like this, not with this air of sophistication.

He began to tell her the news of Bartenham, speaking sulkily, warily, as if not quite sure whether she were making fun of him. She, in her turn, told him of her own doings—pleasantly, but still as if he were a stranger. He gathered that Philippa had a large circle of friends—old friends and friends she had made abroad.

"I think I've met more people in the last month," said Effie, "than I've ever met in my life before."

As she talked he began to have an uncomfortable feeling that she was looking at him from a new angle. The old unquestioning love had gone. She'd got away from him and could see him in perspective, as it were, could criticise him, could compare him with Philippa's friends, whom he saw suddenly as a host of charming, cultured, impeccably dressed, impossibly handsome males. His desolation changed to a seething jealousy.

"Do you and Evelyn still do crossword puzzles in the evenings?" Effie was saying.

She spoke unconcernedly, as one might speak of something so far off that it can have no possible connection with oneself.

Evelyn . . . it was partly because of Evelyn that he'd come up today. It had happened last night. He'd glanced up suddenly from his newspaper and found Evelyn's eyes fixed on him with a curious look in their depths. She had made some casual remark and returned at once to her needlework, but over Robert had come a strange sensation of panic. He felt as if he were some small animal being pursued by Evelyn, fleeing from her but aware that she was gaining on him . . . gaining . . . gaining. The thing had invaded his dreams—Evelyn, large, sleek, feline, pursuing him through an interminable forest, in which he knew that, despite all his efforts, he had no chance of escape. And, waking from the nightmare in a sweat of terror, he had decided to come down to see Effie today.

"Generally," he said rather sulkily.

He wanted to tell her that everything—even crossword puzzles, acrostics, and anagrams—had lost its savour since she had gone away, but somehow he couldn't. He felt that he could have told the old warm loving Effie, but not this assured stranger. Of course, there would have been no need to tell the old Effie. The old Effie would never have gone away. Suddenly he blurted it out.

"When are you coming back, Effie?"

She looked at him for a moment in silence, then answered:

"I told Susan. Didn't she tell you?"

"No. I haven't seen her. She and Ken have gone up North, you know."

"I know. They came here to say goodbye." She smiled at him with faint malice. "How pleased Caroline must be!"

He didn't rise indignantly to Caroline's defence as he would once have done. He didn't feel that Caroline had been absolutely right in this affair of Susan's. She couldn't help Susan's and Kenneth's quarrelling, of course, and she couldn't help Susan's coming home to her when they had quarrelled, but he didn't feel satisfied that she had done all she could to reconcile them. He felt rather strongly just now on the subject of wives who leave their husbands. Kenneth wasn't a bad sort, but Caroline seemed to have a down on him for some reason or other. All he'd been able to get out of her as justifying her disapproval of him was that he'd been drunk once since his marriage and had had a woman before it. She kept saying that Susan was unhappy with him, but Susan had looked a good deal unhappier since she'd left him. No, he still loved Caroline, but his old complete confidence in her judgement was shaken. He felt that she hadn't acted altogether wisely in the case of Susan and Kenneth. Kenneth, by the way, was lucky to have sold his business to Fox & Glazonby and to have got a job as manager of one of their biggest branches in Liverpool. Melsham's had been doing very badly lately and he was on his beam-ends when Fox & Glazonby made their offer. Caroline would miss Susan, of course. Poor Caroline! She'd looked dreadfully old and worn the last time he saw her. But—the more he thought about it, the more convinced he was that Caroline hadn't acted wisely. He must take care that she never made mischief between him and Effie, as, however unconsciously, she'd made it between Susan and Kenneth.

"When are you coming home?" he said again.

"I'm coming home when Evelyn's gone—not before," she replied calmly.

He was silent from sheer surprise. Evelyn ... who'd relieved Effie of all the worry and responsibility of housekeeping, who was always so patient and affectionate to her. He'd taken for granted that Effie was, at the bottom, deeply attached to her, that she would have refused even to contemplate a return to the old muddling, haphazard, Evelyn-less life. She had been moody and ungracious to Evelyn, but she was like that to everyone occasionally, even to Caroline, even to him. That was just "nerves," of course. The idea that she could even think of getting rid of Evelyn came as a shock to him and—he discovered with some surprise—a relief. He realised suddenly that he was tired of Evelyn's brightness and briskness and unfailing efficiency. He was tired of her, and—though he wouldn't have admitted it to himself—afraid of her. He was, in fact, a frightened little boy who had run to Effie for comfort and protection. He had tried to forget last night's nightmare and the large sleek feline Evelyn who had pursued him, but he hadn't quite succeeded.

Effie was watching him with that new detached smile.

"Perhaps you'd better consult Caroline before you give me a definite answer," she said.

"Of course I won't," he replied indignantly.

As if he'd ever let Caroline, dearly as he loved her, interfere in any detail of his dealings with Effie!

"Because I can save you the trouble of doing that," went on Effie. "I can tell you just what she'll say. She'll say that you mustn't give in to my childish whims and fancies, that if once you begin doing that there'll be no end to it. She'll say that it's far kinder to me in the long run to make a firm stand over the question, and that for the sake of the children, and incidentally yourself, it's your duty to insist on Evelyn's staying."

"Nonsense!" he said.

"That's what she'd say if you asked her."

"I'm not going to ask her."

"You mean—you'll get rid of Evelyn?"

"Yes."

She looked at him and the smile died out of her eyes.

"Listen, Robert. You remember what things were like before Evelyn came, don't you?"

"Yes."

"Well, I can't promise that they'll be any better. I think they will, but I can't promise. The point is that you've got to put up with me as I am, or let me go altogether. I won't be treated again as if I were a child by either you or Caroline."

"But, Effie . . ."

"No, listen. Don't interrupt. I mean just that. I'm to be the mistress of the house, and if I manage it badly then I manage it badly, and you'll have to put up with it. I won't submit again to having someone set over me."

"Set over you?" he repeated in pained expostulation. He could hardly believe that he had actually heard the words aright.

"Yes. Set over me. You don't see it that way, but that's what it was. Evelyn was set over me by Caroline. I won't put up with anything of that sort again. I won't have Caroline interfering in my affairs again in any way at all."

"Caroline never has interfered in your affairs, Effie."

"Oh yes, she has. She's interfered right from the beginning. She couldn't bear to let you go, just as she couldn't bear to let Susan go, just as she can't bear to let Fay go. . . . Oh, never mind," as she noticed the look of utter bewilderment on his face. "It doesn't really matter whether you see it or not. I think I like you better for not seeing it. The point is that it's got to stop. It's what I say that must go in future, not what Caroline says. Will you promise that?"

"Of course. I hadn't realised . . . Effie, if I ever have let Caroline interfere, I'm terribly sorry. I didn't mean to. You see, she was so awfully good to me when I was a child. I can't forget that."

"I don't want you to forget that, Robert."

"But, of course . . . she doesn't quite understand. I realise that. Poor old Caroline!"

Effie drew a deep breath.

"It's worth a lot to me to hear you say that, Robert."

"Say what?"

"'Poor old Caroline.' But—you do understand, don't you, Robert? If you have me back, you must just accept me as I am with all my faults. I won't be reformed or altered by anyone. I'll try to reform and alter myself, of course, but that's different."

"Effie, I don't want you altered in any way."

She smiled at him—the old warm smile.

"I expect we'll muddle along somehow. We'll start fresh anyway."

"Then—when will you come, Effie?"

"I told you. I'll come as soon as Evelyn's gone."

"I'll send her off tomorrow."

"Poor Robert! You'll hate doing it, won't you?"

"No," he said slowly. "No, I don't think I shall."

"Won't you? I used to think you liked her so much better than you liked me."

"Effie!"

"When I went I had the feeling of nobly giving you up to her, because she'd make you far happier than I ever could."

"Effie!"

"It was silly, of course, because I knew at the bottom that she was hateful. I was insane, I think, Philippa's made me sane again."

He looked at her, and again that vague jealousy swept over him. Again he saw innumerable males of irreproachable good looks, impeccable manners, and untold wealth, surrounding her on all sides. Suppose she were only coming back to him from a sense of duty. . . .

"Effie," he said hoarsely, "there isn't—anyone else, is there?"

She turned to him with a sudden movement, and he caught her in his arms. It was the old Effie, warm, loving, who clung to him.

Chapter Twenty

It had been arranged that Maggie should hold her birthday party at Philippa's flat. Maggie was always childishly excited about her birthday and generally gave a party, consisting of Charles, Susan, Robert, Effie, Caroline, and Fay, to celebrate it. Nana would make a large iced cake for the occasion, and Maggie would cover it with candles. She liked the entire cake to be covered with candles. Their number never had any connection with her age.

Since Philippa went to live in London, Maggie had been a frequent visitor at her flat. She would go up in the morning, have lunch with Philippa, go to the pictures (Maggie adored the pictures) in the afternoon, then return to Philippa's flat for tea. She was so delighted by these expeditions that, when the time for her birthday party came round, she could not consider its taking place anywhere but at Philippa's. They must all go up to London, she said, go to the pictures, and then have the birthday tea at Philippa's flat.

The guests were to be unusually few in number this year. Susan and Kenneth had gone to Liverpool and were living in rooms while they looked for a house. Susan's letters radiated a deep quiet happiness. Ken liked the work, and they were making a lot of new friends.

Robert and Effie were away, too. Effie had engaged a nurse to look after the children, and she and Robert had gone to the Lakes for a holiday together. They were staying at the same hotel where they had spent their honeymoon. So that only left Caroline and Fay. Maggie had, however, invited Richard as well. She had met Richard several times at Philippa's, and had taken a fancy to him. She'd known him, of course, for many years in Bartenham, but she'd always been afraid of him in Bartenham, just as she was afraid of almost everyone there. Somehow one couldn't be afraid of people at Philippa's. . . .

Caroline had been at first inclined to refuse the invitation, giving Fay's work as the excuse, for Fay's scholarship exam took place next week and every minute was precious. Then it occurred to her that a day's holiday might be good for Fay. Fay had been making a great effort to control herself. There had been no more tears or nerve storms, but there was a look of strain about the child that made Caroline uneasy. She must certainly take a long holiday once this exam was over. . . . All Caroline's anxious love was now concentrated on Fay. Susan had deserted her, deserted and betrayed her with a callousness the memory of which still tore at her heart. Susan had spurned her love, thrown back her sacrifices in her face, taken from her, not only herself, but that new life on which Caroline had been building such high hopes, for which she was prepared to pour out all the riches of her tenderness and devotion. She had chosen, instead of Caroline's tried and tested love, the fickle passion of a selfish youth, who had known her only for a few short months and had already failed her at every turn. She would never all her life forget that moment when Susan had rushed in from the night, radiant, starry-eyed: "Caroline . . . I'm going back to Ken . . ." and had run upstairs to pack her bag, deaf to all Caroline's expostulations and entreaties. "I can't stop. . . . He's at the gate . . . he's waiting for me. . . . Darling, it's all right. . . . I'm so happy I can hardly bear it. . . . You don't understand. . . . Oh, you don't understand. . . . I love him so terribly. . . . We've both been so silly. . . . I'm going now. Goodbye. No, I don't know where we're going. I've no idea. Oh, I'm so happy. . . ." And had rushed downstairs with her erratically packed suitcase, cutting off Caroline in the middle of a sentence.

Caroline connected Susan's desertion with Philippa. It was Philippa who was the centre of disaffection, Philippa whose disloyalty had spread slowly but surely throughout the group. Even Robert was different, though Robert had had so few dealings with Philippa. It wasn't that Robert wasn't kind. He was, indeed, kinder than he had ever been, but there was a touch of gentleness, of forbearance, almost of pity, in his kindness that made it intolerable to her. The old deference, the old unquestioning acceptance of her every opinion, had gone. He had not even asked her advice about dismissing Evelyn. She couldn't understand that. She'd hardly been able to believe it when he told her that he'd dismissed Evelyn, given her a month's wages, and asked her to go the next day. Caroline wasn't quite as indignant about the actual dismissal as she would have been a few months earlier. She hadn't liked Evelyn's manner lately, and had begun to think that perhaps she'd been mistaken in her. Effie, of course, never had known how to manage her employees, and in Evelyn's case had let her get far too familiar. And then it had been a mistake to leave her for so long mistress of the house. That, again, was Philippa's fault. . . . Philippa, who had lured Effie away from her obvious duties and probably completely unsettled her. And that brought her back to the difference in Robert. He had even allowed Effie to engage a nurse for the children, though everyone knew that Effie had simply no idea of how to engage maids, and had always made a mess of it in the days when they'd let her do it, and had been almost short in his manner to Caroline when she offered to do it instead, or at any rate to be there to help Effie when she interviewed the applicants. And Effie . . . Effie had been very pleasant and polite and distant, quite sure of herself and of Robert. Caroline felt bewildered by it. That Effie, of all people, should be polite and assured. . . . And it was absurd of her to want another holiday after her long stay in London. But that, Effie told her suavely when she remonstrated, was Robert's suggestion.

Robert, apart from his sentimental idea of a second honeymoon, was glad to get away from the house for a short time. It seemed full of Evelyn's devastating rage. The memory of the interview in which he had dismissed her still set his heart beating unevenly.

"And may I ask the reason?" she had said slowly when he told her of his decision.

"My wife wishes to take over the management of the house herself," he said, trying to speak with dignity, but feeling a little pompous and ridiculous and, beneath it all, more than a little frightened. And then she had laughed, and there had been something so offensive in her laugh that he had lost all his fear of her and felt only dislike.

"I'll pay you your month's salary," he said, "and I'd be glad if you could see your way to going tomorrow."

"Oh yes. .... I'll even see my way to going today," she had said insolently.

He felt that he ought to thank her for all she had done for them—for she had certainly done a lot—and was trying to find appropriate words to do so, when she began to speak in a quiet voice, covering both Effie and him with abuse, ridiculing his little mannerisms and domestic habits, imitating his way of speaking, with a concentrated venom that brought the blood flaming to his cheeks. And then she'd gone at once, packing her trunks and sending for a taxi without another word. He had rung up Effie and Effie had arrived the next morning. It had been heaven to get her back.
. . .

And now they had gone to the Lakes for a month. They had come to say goodbye to Caroline the night before they set off.

"I'll keep an eye on the children for you," said Caroline, deciding not to bear malice against them to the extent of withholding her co-operation.

"That's quite all right, thank you," Effie had said, with the new dignified friendliness that was so disconcerting. "Nurse is really awfully good with them, and I think it's better for her to be left in complete charge while we're away."

And Robert had agreed with her. It was ridiculous the way Robert had begun to defer to and agree with Effie. It seemed to renounce and reject all Caroline had done for them both in the past. It hurt her inexpressibly.

And so they, too, had gone, and Caroline was left alone, shaken and bewildered by the crashing of the walls of her kingdom about her ears. There was no one left her but Fay, not even—no, she daren't let herself think of him. He had been to see her a week ago, but his visit had been worse than his long neglect. It was so obviously a duty visit. The atmosphere had been strained, the conversation unnatural. And he could not hide from her—did not attempt to hide from her—his growing friendship with her mother.

She was glad when he went. ... She wouldn't admit her love for him even to herself. It was undignified, it was shameful, to love a man who did not even make a pretence of loving her in return. ... Her heart sickened as she remembered that afternoon, shortly before Philippa's arrival, when he had pleaded with her to marry him and she had refused him. If only time could be set back again! If only she had known then how she would be deserted and betrayed by those for whom she had sacrificed so much!

Her lips took on a bitter curve as she thought of it. That bitterness was invading her every thought now. It marred the serenity of her lips, the quiet austerity of her expression. But—Fay was still left her, her baby, her darling. And at that thought all the bitterness faded. She would be on her guard with Fay. She would fight to the last to save Fay from the influence that had stolen the others from her. With Fay she was warned in time. And Fay was docile, malleable, sensitively responsive to her love. Just now she seemed quiet and listless, but that, of course, was because she was working so hard.

And so her first impulse was to refuse the invitation to Aunt Maggie's tea party. Fay made no objection, but her look of disappointment when she heard Caroline's decision—a disappointment poignantly resigned and unchildlike—sent a pang of compunction through Caroline's heart. The child needed a little relaxation, and it couldn't possibly do any harm. It would not be like allowing her to visit Philippa alone. She would be there and Aunt Maggie and Uncle Charles and—no, she wouldn't admit to herself that the fact that Richard would be there influenced her decision in any way. If she'd let herself admit that, she couldn't have gone, of course.

Fay's face had lightened when she told her that they were going to Philippa's, after all. Yes, thought Caroline, watching her, she *did* look tired. There were dark shadows beneath her eyes. ... These competitive exams, were very trying. Perhaps they might go abroad after it for a real change ... to France or Germany, where Fay could keep up her languages and yet have a holiday at the same time. She told Maggie that, though she and Fay could not come to the pictures with her, they would be very much pleased to come to tea at Philippa's. Instead of going to the pictures she took Fay to the Victoria and Albert Museum.

Maggie, Charles, and Richard were in the flat when Caroline and Fay arrived. Philippa noticed with secret anxiety the suggestion of tension that lay over the sisters. Caroline looked worn and Haggard. About Fay was the glancing tremulous brightness, the suggestion of hysteria, that marks intense nervous strain. ... She had looked pale when she entered the room, but now her cheeks were flushed and her eyes bright. There was an unsteady note in the laughter with which she received Richard's friendly teasing. Philippa greeted Caroline with grave tenderness, but there was no mistaking the cold hostility of Caroline's response.

Maggie, who was by now completely dishevelled and in a state of great excitement, at once began to tell Fay the plot of the film she had just seen. She had already told it twice to Philippa, although Philippa had been with her when she saw it. Charles began to talk to Caroline about the state of the London streets and how much more difficult it was to get about now than it had been when he was a young man, while Philippa and Richard busied themselves with the cake and preparations for tea. Fay sat by Maggie, making mechanical little interjections of interest, but not listening to anything she said. She was holding herself in tightly. She'd been holding herself in tightly for weeks. She felt that, as long as she could do that, it would be all right, but that, if ever she let go, something dreadful would happen. She didn't know what it would be, but it would be something dreadful. At times she felt as if she were clinging on to a narrow ledge with both hands, and that if she let go she would fall down, down, down into some endless abyss. ... It was somehow frightening living alone in the house with Caroline now that Susan had gone. Susan's coming had been terrible, but her going had been more terrible still, bringing that hard tight look to Caroline's face, so that, though her tenderness to Fay had increased, Fay felt an odd fear of her that she couldn't overcome. A fear and a shrinking repugnance that made her feel desperately ashamed. She dreaded Caroline's speaking to her. She felt that, if ever Caroline tried to have one of the old affectionate intimate talks with her, she wouldn't be able to hold on to herself any longer. She'd let go, and that dreadful thing—whatever it was—would happen. Fortunately, Caroline hadn't attempted an intimate talk. ... Fay was aware of her brooding sultry tenderness surrounding her on all sides, aware that Caroline watched her furtively, could hardly bear her out of her sight, but that yet Caroline herself was a long way off, in some dark region of torment where no one could follow her. Fay pretended to be absorbed in her work. She hurried from the house to school, from school back to her homework. Sometimes, when Caroline came into the room where she was working and hesitated there as if she were about to say something confidential, Fay's heart would begin to beat in loud hammer-strokes. When in passing Caroline laid her hand affectionately on Fay's shoulder, a shudder of revulsion would run through her, and she would have to stiffen every nerve in her body to hide her shrinking. And yet she loved Caroline . . . she *did* love Caroline. She couldn't understand it. The only explanation was that she herself was wicked, utterly wicked, so wicked as to be beyond all hope of forgiveness. Her headaches were more frequent and more severe now, but when Caroline asked her if her head ached she always said "no." She felt that she wouldn't be able to bear Caroline's sympathy and tenderness if she admitted it. One just went on . . . a minute at a time . . . a minute at a time . . . one daren't look forward or backward. She wasn't worrying about the exam. now. Not getting the scholarship seemed an ordinary everyday sort of trouble compared with the vague unformulated terrors that haunted her even in her sleep. She felt like someone stumbling blindly along a dark road at the edge of a precipice. . . .

She saw very little of the Dicksons. Sybil had tired at last of giving invitations, only to have them refused. "I like you, Fay," she had said, "and I'm always here if you want me, but—" she shrugged and left the sentence unfinished. With Billy she had definitely quarrelled. Waylaying her, in an attempt to "have it out," he had said things about Caroline that had infuriated her. She had turned on her heel and walked away, telling him never to speak to her again, and she hadn't seen him after that till yesterday, when she had found him waiting for her at the end of the road on her way home.

"Fay," he had said humbly, "I'm terribly sorry."

"It was my fault, Billy," she began unsteadily, then, as she met his eyes, felt, to her horror, the uprising of tears and the shaking of the wall she had built around herself, the wall that could never be built up again once it had fallen. She turned from him abruptly and ran home through the gathering dusk. . . .

Aunt Philippa was lighting the candles now, and Uncle Charles was drawing the curtains. Aunt Maggie was so much excited that she couldn't keep still but danced about in her seat, all her necklaces jingling. . . . Richard was making a speech, very solemnly but with twinkling eyes, congratulating Aunt Maggie and wishing her many more birthdays and inviting himself to all her birthday parties till she was a hundred and two. Caroline sat back in her chair, gazing into the distance, as if the whole thing were too childish for her notice. Her mouth was set in that new tight line of suffering.

Then Uncle Charles went out to do some shopping, saying that he would call back for Aunt Maggie in about an hour's time. The maid cleared away the tea things, and a silence fell, broken only by Maggie's excited twitterings. Suddenly she stopped, as if struck by a new idea, and looked from Fay to the piano that stood in the corner of the room.

"You can play here, dear," she said. "There's a piano. . . . Do play. . . . You play so nicely."

"No, Aunt Maggie, the child's tired," said Caroline sharply, but Fay was already crossing the room slowly, dreamily, as if walking in her sleep. She sat down at the piano and began to play . . . fumblingly at first, then gradually with more sureness. They listened to her in silence, aware of some new tension in the atmosphere that they did not understand. She stopped playing abruptly, with a little gasp. It had happened. ... While she was playing she had forgotten everything else in the world and—she had let go. The dreadful thing was going to happen. It was too late to stop it. Even now she didn't quite know what it was, but—whatever it was—it was going to happen. Her eyes, Unnaturally brilliant, were fixed on Caroline. She spoke in a voice that seemed to come from a long way off.

"Caroline," she said, "I'm not coming back to Bartenham with you. ... I'm not going to take the exam."

There was a sudden silence. Everyone looked at Caroline. She had gone very white.

"What on *earth* do you mean, Fay?" she said.

"Just that," said Fay. "I can't—go on with it. It's all over."

"What's all over?"

"Everything," said Fay unsteadily. "Oh, don't you understand? I can't go back there. I can't go on living there. I know I'm wicked, but I can't help it. I can't go on. ... I've tried, but I can't. ...."

"Fay," said Caroline sternly, "you don't know what you're saying."

"I do know. I mean it," cried Fay hysterically. "I can't go on. Oh, I wish I could *die*."

"You're overwrought. We should have put off your exam, till next year, after all."

"It's not that. Oh"—wildly—"you've got to let me *go*. ... *I don't* care where I go, but I've got to *go*. I shall die if I don't. You've made me hate you. ... I feel I never want to see you again. I can't help it. I've tried not to. I've tried not to. ... I won't go to college or go on living with you or teach. I won't, I tell you." She was sobbing restrainedly now. "Music was all I cared about, and you took it from me."

From among the ruins of her kingdom Caroline spoke in a hard angry voice.

"That was your own choice."

"You *made* me choose it, you know you did," sobbed Fay. "Nothing in all my life's ever been my own choice. I can't bear it any longer. Oh, it isn't just that. It's—everything. Even Sybil ... even Billy." Caroline pursed her lips disapprovingly. "It wasn't what you think. It was only a friendship. Billy didn't want anything else and neither did I. But you spoilt it. You've spoilt everything all my life ... everything. ..."

Suddenly Maggie said soothingly: "You should live with Philippa, dear. That will be the best. She'll look after you. She understands. It was just the same with her and Gordon. She had to go. I understand now. She wasn't wicked. She felt just like you. ... And there's a piano here, which is so nice. I always thought it was a pity that Caroline got rid of the piano."

"Oh, let me, Aunt Philippa," sobbed Fay wildly. "Let me live with you. ..."

"Fay, are you *mad*?" said Caroline.

Philippa went up to the piano and put her arm around the slender sobbing figure.

"Come, darling ... come and lie down for a moment."

She drew her out of the room and closed the door!

Caroline rose to her feet, but there was a thick mist before her eyes, and her knees felt too unsteady to walk. She sat down again, staring at the door through which Philippa and Fay had gone.

"You see, there's a piano here," said Maggie again. "That makes it all so simple. And Philippa's so kind. ..."

The sound of the sobs across the passage gradually died away, and soon Philippa returned alone, closing the door behind her.

"She's lying down," she said. "I've given her a bromide, and she's going to try to sleep. She's on the edge of a very bad breakdown," She looked at Caroline for a moment, then said, "Will you let her stay here, Caroline?"

"I suppose so—just for tonight," said Caroline in a hard stony voice. "She's hardly in a fit state to go home."

"I don't mean just for tonight," said Philippa slowly. "I mean—will you let her stay here and study music at the Academy? I'll be responsible for the financial side, if you'll allow me to be. I'd love it. ..."

Caroline's face was ashen.

"How *dare* you suggest that?" she said. "Haven't you done me enough harm without—this?"

"What harm have I done you, Caroline?"

Caroline gave a short unsteady laugh.

"You ask me that?"

"Come, Caroline, it's Fay we have to think of now. Her whole future's at stake."

Caroline made an obvious effort to control herself.

"My dear Philippa," she said, trying without success to recapture something of her normal manner, "I know Fay better than you, and I've had more experience of schoolgirls than you. If you think I'm going to take a child's hysterical vapourings seriously . . ."

"Caroline, this isn't a child's hysterical vapourings and you know it."

Caroline turned to her and spoke in a low tone of concentrated fury.

"You've taken them all from me . . . one by one. Couldn't you have left me just Fay? It wasn't much to ask of you."

Philippa threw out her arms in a little helpless gesture.

"Oh, Caroline, if only you'd understand. I've taken none of them from you—none. You've sent them away yourself. . . ."

"Robert . . . Susan . . . and now Fay," said Caroline. "I wish to God you'd never come back. You ruined my father's life, and now you're ruining mine. I think you're a devil. You've bewitched them. You've no *right* to take them from me. I worked for them and slaved for them, I denied myself everything for them, while you were living in luxury without a thought of them, and now—you come back, and all I've done for them goes for nothing."

"Caroline, it's not me," said Philippa gently. "It would have happened just the same if I hadn't come. . . . You can't make people—belong to you, as you've tried to. They *must* belong to themselves."

Caroline dropped her head onto her hands.

"It's the ingratitude that hurts me so. Fay . . . after all I've done for her. . . ."

"What have you done for her?" said Philippa.

"What have I done for her?" repeated Caroline, raising her head and staring at Philippa in slow amazement. "I've loved her as if she were my own child——"

"No, you haven't," said Philippa, speaking with sudden passion. "You haven't loved any of them. You've loved yourself in them. You've loved your power over them, their dependence on you. You've hated their real selves, their individualities. . . . You've thwarted them at every turn. You've been jealous of Effie, of Kenneth, of every friend and interest of Fay's that lay apart from you and your interests. You didn't care how unhappy you made Robert, provided you took him away from Effie. You didn't care how unhappy you made Susan, provided you took her away from Ken. It was jealousy . . . it wasn't love. And Fay . . . you've just seen what you've done to Fay. Why didn't you let her take up music? Why did you force her to take up a subject that you knew in your heart she hated? Because you were jealous of her having any interests that you couldn't share with her, because you wanted to possess her. Caroline, one human soul *can't* possess another. It's the unforgivable sin. It kills them both. . . . Oh, don't you *see* it?"

She stopped, her voice trembling with emotion, her cheeks flushed. It was the first time any of them had seen her other than calm and poised.

"You *must* see it, Caroline. . . . It's a sort of poison. It's killing you. . . ."

There was a silence. The two women had quite forgotten the others. Maggie looked at them with an expression of bewilderment. Richard stood on the hearth-rug, gazing into the fire with a frown.

Suddenly Caroline laid her head on her hands along the arm of her chair and began to sob, slow difficult sobs that seemed to tear her thin frame.

"I'm not like that . . . I'm not. . . . It's you . . . you've made me seem like that. . . . Even to myself. . . . I've seemed like that since you came. . . . I've tried not to see it . . . but—I wasn't like that before you came. . . . I wasn't . . . I wasn't. . . . I'm not like that now. . . . It's you. . . . You've made me seem like that. . . . Even to myself . . . I hate you. . . ."

Richard turned and looked at her. He had loved her for her

perfection, her freedom from every human frailty, then that love had slowly died. Now that he saw her sobbing there in misery and abasement, his love woke suddenly to life again, not the old distant reverence, the humble devotion of the worshipper, but a new protective tenderness, a deep yearning pity that wrung his heart. He longed to take her in his arms and comfort her. He longed to charm away her unhappiness, to give her back the youth she had spent so ungrudgingly, to make life sweet and gay and easy for her. She had faltered in the high task of lonely duty she had set herself, but what other woman would ever have set herself such a task? Her sacrifice, her self-denial, her untiring effort, had been real enough. Her failure made her human—human and infinitely dear. He felt a faint resentment against Philippa. Need she have been quite so brutal?

Caroline raised her head. "I'm going in to see Fay," she said in a strangled voice. "I shall ask her to choose, and, if she chooses to stay here, I'll let her. I shan't ask her again."

She went from the room, and they heard her open the door into Philippa's bedroom.

"I don't understand," said Maggie. "Is Fay going to stay here?"

"I don't know."

"She ought, you know, because of the piano. She plays so nicely."

Then Charles returned. There was a subdued excitement in his manner. He had been to see his hairdresser, and his hairdresser had given him a new specific that, he said, was guaranteed to make the hair grow again (and not only grow again but grow again luxuriantly) on bald patches on the temples. He said that the first application made a noticeable difference, and Charles was longing to go home and make the first application.

"We've only just time to catch the train, Maggie," he said. "Is Caroline coming?"

"No, she's catching a later one," said Philippa.

"It's all about the piano," said Maggie mysteriously. "You see, there *is* one here, and Fay plays so nicely."

Charles hurried her down to the waiting taxi.

"I've had a simply lovely birthday," she said, as she went.

As the door closed behind them, Philippa turned to Richard.

"Richard," she said, "you loved Caroline before I came, didn't you? Have I spoilt it?"

He shook his head.

"No one knows as well as you how splendid she's been," she went on. "She's right in saying she sacrificed everything. She did. If her motive wasn't quite the one she thought it was—well, God knows the motives of pretty few of us will stand close examination."

"I know. . . . I was thinking that just now."

The door opened and Caroline came in. Her face looked ravaged but quite composed. She held her head erect, and there was about her an air of dauntless courage.

"Fay wants to stay here," she said quietly. "She'd like to take up music at the Academy as you suggested. We can arrange the business part of it later, can't we? I've said goodbye to Fay." Her lips trembled for a moment, then she mastered her emotion and went on in a low steady voice: "Go to her, will you, Philippa? She's terribly upset by all this, of course. And impress upon her that I'm not angry or disappointed, that I'm—glad she chose it. I think she's made the right choice."

Richard's heart ached with love and pity as he looked at her.

She held out her hand to Philippa.

"Goodbye, Philippa," she said. "I'm sorry I made such a fool of myself just now." She turned to Richard. "Goodbye, Richard."

He looked at her for a moment in silence.

"I'm coming back with you, Caroline," he said.